THE FIRST MOUNTAIN MAN
PREACHER'S RAGE

THE FIRST MOUNTAIN MAN
PREACHER'S RAGE

WILLIAM W. JOHNSTONE
with J. A. Johnstone

PINNACLE BOOKS
Kensington Publishing Corp.
www.kensingtonbooks.com

PINNACLE BOOKS are published by

Kensington Publishing Corp.
119 West 40th Street
New York, NY 10018

PUBLISHER'S NOTE
Following the death of William W. Johnstone, the Johnstone family is working with a carefully selected writer to organize and complete Mr. Johnstone's outlines and many unfinished manuscripts to create additional novels in all of his series like The Last Gunfighter, Mountain Man, and Eagles, among others. This novel was inspired by Mr. Johnstone's superb storytelling.

All Kensington titles, imprints, and distributed lines are available at special quantity discounts for bulk purchases for sales promotions, premiums, fund-raising, educational, or institutional use. Special book excerpts or customized printings can also be created to fit specific needs. For details, write or phone the office of the Kensington sales manager: Kensington Publishing Corp., 119 West 40th Street, New York, NY 10018, attn: Sales Department; phone 1-800-221-2647.

PINNACLE BOOKS, the Pinnacle logo, and the WWJ steer head logo are Reg. U.S. Pat. & TM Off.

ISBN-13: 978-0-7860-4392-7
ISBN-10: 0-7860-4392-X

First printing: January 2019

10 9 8 7 6 5 4 3 2 1

Printed in the United States of America

Electronic edition: January 2019

ISBN-13: 978-0-7860-4393-4
ISBN-10: 0-7860-4393-8

The Jensen Family
First Family of the American Frontier

Smoke Jensen—*The Mountain Man*
The youngest of three children and orphaned as a young boy, Smoke Jensen is considered one of the fastest draws in the West. His quest to tame the lawless West has become the stuff of legend. Smoke owns the Sugarloaf Ranch in Colorado. Married to Sally Jensen, father to Denise ("Denny") and Louis.

Preacher—*The First Mountain Man*
Though not a blood relative, grizzled frontiersman Preacher became a father figure to the young Smoke Jensen, teaching him how to survive in the brutal, often deadly Rocky Mountains. Fought the battles that forged his destiny. Armed with a long gun, Preacher is as fierce as the land itself.

Matt Jensen—*The Last Mountain Man*
Orphaned but taken in by Smoke Jensen, Matt Jensen has become like a younger brother to Smoke and even took the Jensen name. And like Smoke, Matt has carved out his destiny on the American frontier. He lives by the gun and surrenders to no man.

Luke Jensen—*Bounty Hunter*
Mountain Man Smoke Jensen's long-lost brother Luke Jensen is scarred by war and a dead shot—the right

qualities to be a bounty hunter. And he's cunning, and fierce enough, to bring down the deadliest outlaws of his day.

Ace Jensen and Chance Jensen—*Those Jensen Boys!*
Smoke Jensen's long-lost nephews, Ace and Chance, are a pair of young-gun twins as reckless and wild as the frontier itself . . . Their father is Luke Jensen, thought killed in the Civil War. Their uncle Smoke Jensen is one of the fiercest gunfighters the West has ever known. It's no surprise that the inseparable Ace and Chance Jensen have a knack for taking risks— even if they have to blast their way out of them.

CHAPTER 1

Preacher dropped to one knee, cocked the two flintlock pistols as he raised them, and then pulled the triggers.

The weapons bucked in his hands as they went off with a deafening double boom. Preacher always loaded plenty of powder and two heavy lead balls in each pistol. The powerful recoil would have broken the wrists of some fellas, but not the rangy, beard-stubbled mountain man. His muscles were more than a match for it.

Four attackers charged toward Preacher. In most fights, four-against-one odds would have been over-whelming. But this was not like any other fight, since Preacher was part of it.

Two unshaven, buckskin-clad men jerked back a little as pistol balls slammed into them. Preacher had hit both of them in the chest. Their momentum carried them forward, but their legs got tangled up and they fell. They were out of the fight now, nothing more than bleeding, dying heaps.

That still left two enemies for Preacher to deal with. One of them, a towering, broad-shouldered brute, lunged ahead of his companion. Preacher tossed the empty pistols aside, grabbed the tomahawk from behind his wide leather belt, and uncoiled from his kneeling position. The tomahawk flashed upward and caught the man under the chin, inflicting a hideous wound that sprayed blood in Preacher's face. The man's shoulder hit him anyway and drove him off his feet.

Preacher twisted desperately to avoid having the man's body fall on him and pin him to the ground. He didn't quite make it. The man landed on his left arm and left leg. Preacher needed a second to pull free.

Not wanting to give him that second, the remaining man from the quartet of would-be killers skidded to a halt, brought his rifle to his shoulder, and fired almost instantly.

Preacher threw himself to the left as much as he could, rolling halfway onto the man with the ruined face, who was shaking in his death throes with half his face cut off. The rifle ball hummed past Preacher's head and smacked into the ground, throwing up dirt and pine needles. Preacher put the hand holding the tomahawk on the dying man's back and used it to lever himself over. As he rolled and came up, he threw the tomahawk.

The remaining attacker was trying desperately to reload his rifle since he'd missed his first shot. He had luck on his side. Just as the tomahawk turned over in its spinning flight and was about to split his skull open, the rifle's barrel struck the weapon and knocked it off its path. The tomahawk went over his shoulder and past his head, but the impact also jolted the rifle out of his hands.

That didn't really matter. Preacher wouldn't have given him time to finish reloading, anyway.

The mountain man sprang to his feet and charged. The man yanked a knife from a sheath at his waist and slashed frantically at Preacher, who ducked under the blade and reached up with his left hand to grab the man's wrist. He wrenched at it and bones snapped. The man gave a shrill cry of pain as he dropped the knife.

The next second, Preacher's right fist crashed into the man's jaw with the force of a piledriver. The man went down hard, but as he landed on the ground, he used his other hand to fumble out and cock a pistol at his belt.

Preacher grabbed the barrel and shoved it up and back just as the man's finger jerked the trigger. The man's eyes had barely widened in horror before the lead ball smashed into his cheek and bored on into his brain. Preacher let go of the gun and straightened to look around and see how the rest of the fight was going.

Eight men had attacked Preacher and his companions as they got ready to break camp on the fine spring morning. They must have known who Preacher was, because four of them—fully half their force—had concentrated on the mountain man, leaving the odds even for the remaining members of Preacher's party.

That was a mistake, of course, but no matter what else the men might have done, this attack wasn't going to work out well for them. Hawk That Soars, the young, half-white, half-Absaroka warrior who was Preacher's son, had inherited some of the legendary mountain man's fighting ability, so he was quick to take on two of the enemy and give a good account of himself. He had downed one of them with a pistol shot and struggled hand-to-hand with the other, the early morning sun flashing on the knife blades they sought to plant in each other's bodies.

Unfortunately, Charlie Todd and Aaron Buckley, two young men from Virginia who had a couple of seasons of trapping behind them, weren't the tough, experienced battlers that Preacher and Hawk were. Their rifle shots had gone wild, and they'd been forced to dive behind a log for cover.

The remaining two attackers were circling that log in an effort to get clear shots at Charlie and Aaron.

The final member of Preacher's group, an elderly Absaroka named White Buffalo, stood off to one side, jumping up and down and screeching imprecations at the attackers, but that was about all he was good for.

Preacher figured Hawk stood the best chance of defeating his own opponent, so he ran toward the log where Charlie and Aaron had taken cover, leaped into the air, pushed off the thick log with one foot, and flew toward the two men stalking them. Jumping off the log in that way had given Preacher some height, so the men had to jerk their rifle barrels up at an angle as they both instinctively fired at him.

One shot came close enough that Preacher felt the ball's heat next to his cheek, but the other went way wide and high. He snapped a kick at the man on his right, catching him on the jaw with his moccasin-shod heel and sending him flying backward. Preacher grabbed the other man and dragged him down. They sprawled on the ground, but Preacher recovered first. He snatched his own knife from its sheath, raised it, and brought it down, burying the blade in the man's chest. He pulled it free, let his momentum carry him over in a roll, and surged back to his feet with a lithe vitality belying the fact that he had spent more than two decades on the frontier.

Hawk was rising from the body of his opponent, wiping his knife's bloody blade on the man's buckskin shirt as he rose. He and Preacher quickly circulated among the sprawled figures littering the campsite to make sure they were all dead.

They were, except for the man Preacher had just kicked in the face. His jaw was broken. He made agonized, incomprehensible noises as the upper half of his body twisted and jerked on the ground. His bleating took on a frantic, terrified note when Hawk grabbed his hair, jerked his head up, and got ready to cut his throat.

"Hold on there," Preacher said to his son.

Hawk looked up with a surprised frown on his face. "They attacked us," he said in excellent English. "Now that they are defeated, they have no right to expect that we would let them live."

"Go ahead and kill him," White Buffalo urged. "Never let an enemy live to fight another day if it is in your power to take his life."

Aaron and Charlie didn't say anything, but both young men looked pale and shaken by their close brush with death. They had come to the mountains as complete greenhorns, and even though they had gained some experience and seasoning, civilization hadn't rubbed off them completely yet.

"Wait just a dang minute." Preacher hunkered on his heels in front of the man with the broken jaw.

Hawk remained behind the man, ready to let his knife drink deep of the prisoner's blood.

At first glance, Preacher had thought all eight attackers were white, but he saw he'd been wrong. This one came from south of the border, or at least had a lot of Spanish blood in him. *"Habla Inglis?"*

The man made more choked, meaningless sounds as blood trickled from the corners of his mouth.

"Can't make out what you're sayin', hombre," Preacher said. "Just nod if you understand what *I'm* sayin'."

The man nodded, although the motion must have hurt like blazes. He whimpered.

"Good," Preacher said. "Listen to me, now. Ol' Hawk there's got his self a powerful hankerin' to cut your throat, and if I think you're lyin' to me, even for a second, I'm gonna go ahead and let him. *Sabe?*"

The man nodded again. Tears ran down his cheeks, either from pain, fear, or both.

"You and these other fellas"—Preacher waved a hand to indicate the dead men—"are you the only ones in your bunch?"

The man didn't respond instantly. Even under the circumstances, evidently he had to think for a couple of seconds as he tried to decide if he wanted to cooperate. Then, slowly and carefully so as to diminish the pain, he shook his head.

"How many?" Preacher asked.

Propped up the way he was against Hawk's kneeling leg, the man was able to lift both trembling hands. He opened and closed them three times.

"Thirty in addition to you fellas?"

Another slow shake of the head.

"So, thirty countin' you, which means there's twenty-two left somewhere."

The man nodded.

"Why'd you jump us like this?"

The man pointed a shaking finger at the pile of bundled and tied pelts to one side of the camp. Preacher and his companions had made a good haul already, and the season still had a long time to run.

"You were gonna steal our furs?" Preacher said. "You're just a bunch o' no-account thieves?"

The man closed his eyes, nodded, and whimpered.

"Well, I can't say as I'm surprised," Preacher mused. He waved a hand at the wild, majestic Rocky Mountains rising around them and went on. "There are millions of beaver in these streams. Plenty to go around. If a fella's willin' to work hard and don't mind runnin' a few risks now and then, there just ain't no way he can fail to be successful out here. But I reckon there's always gonna be a certain amount of lowlifes who want somebody else to do all the work and run all the risks while they sit back and reap the rewards. Takes a mighty sorry varmint to do that, if you ask me."

"Can I get this over with now?" Hawk asked.

"Not just yet." Preacher looked intently at the prisoner again. "Which way is your bunch's camp?"

Again the man hesitated. Preacher raised his eyes to Hawk, and the prisoner realized Preacher was about to nod, a signal to go ahead and cut his throat. He raised his arm quickly and pointed to the north.

"We could have backtracked and found them," White Buffalo said. "No sign can escape the keen eyes of White Buffalo."

Stocky, brown-bearded Charlie Todd said, "Wait a minute. We're going to try to find the rest of the group this man came from?"

"That's right," Preacher said.

"Why in the world would we do that?" Aaron Buckley wanted to know. Clean-shaven, taller and slimmer than his best friend Charlie, he had black, curly hair.

"When these fellas don't come back, the rest of the bunch will come lookin' for them. Chances are, we'll have to deal with 'em sooner or later, so it might as well be on our own terms. Anyway, they're thieves and killers, and if we don't stop 'em, there ain't no tellin' how many innocent trappers they'll rob and murder before they're through." Preacher shook his head. "Comes to that, there ain't no tellin' how many they've *already* killed, and I can't abide lettin' 'em get away with that."

"Well, I suppose I can see your point," Charlie said with some reluctance. "We're going to be outnumbered more than four to one, though."

Aaron chuckled. "You're forgetting that when it comes to a fight, Preacher and Hawk count for more than ordinary fellows like us."

"That's true," Charlie admitted.

Preacher turned his attention back to the prisoner. He lifted his knife, a move that made the man's eyes widen in terror.

Preacher lowered the blade, rested the tip against the man's left thigh, and pushed. The razor-sharp knife cut through the man's buckskin trousers and went a couple of inches into his leg. The man didn't try to jerk away. Didn't react at all, in fact.

"You didn't feel that, did you?" Preacher asked. "Hawk, let loose of his hair so he can look down here."

Hawk released his grip. The man bent his head forward enough to see Preacher's knife in his leg. He made mewling sounds of horror.

"I thought the way you was holdin' your legs meant that you couldn't move 'em. You can't, can you?"

The man's chest rose and fell frenziedly, but his legs didn't budge.

"Yep, when I kicked you and knocked you over, you busted somethin' in your back when you fell," Preacher went on. "You won't ever walk again. We can leave you alive here, but I reckon that ain't somethin'

I'd want if I was in your place. I'd rather get it over with quick-like."

The man closed his eyes. More tears ran down his cheeks. He nodded. Sounds came from him. Preacher could tell he was trying to form words—curses, maybe, or prayers—but his broken jaw wouldn't let him. He kept his eyes closed, so he didn't see it when Preacher stood up and nodded to Hawk.

They finished breaking camp and departed not long after that, heading north and leaving eight dead men behind them.

CHAPTER 2

Jefferson Scarrow lifted his head and listened. He thought he heard faint reports of gunfire drifting in from a good distance away to the south, but in the mountains, being sure of such a thing was difficult. The steep slopes and the narrow, wooded valleys played tricks with sound.

If he was right, though, quite a bit of shooting was going on. The thought of that put a faint smile on the man's slightly lantern-jawed face. His men would return later in the morning bearing a good load of pelts . . . if all went according to plan.

Scarrow knelt beside the fire and poured himself another cup of coffee. Men went busily about their tasks around him, but he didn't pay much attention to the bustle of activity. He was thinking about money, and when such thoughts occupied Jefferson Scarrow's head, not much room remained for anything else.

"Damn it, Jeff. The fellas are gettin' impatient. They can understand you wantin' first crack at that squaw, but you ain't lettin' anybody else enjoy her nor havin' sport with her yourself."

The gravelly voice broke into Scarrow's mental

ciphering. He had been trying to add up how much money they would make by selling all the pelts they planned to gather this season, once they got back to St. Louis. As the enticing figures evaporated from Scarrow's brain, he turned his head to glare up at his unofficial second in command, Hogarth Plumlee.

With a name like Hogarth, folks just naturally called him Hog, and in one of life's appropriate coincidences, the name suited him. He was short and broad and pink-skinned—he had never tanned despite years of being outdoors—and his large, tipped-up nose resembled a snout. Also like a hog, Plumlee would eat anything put before him, and a thick layer of dirt caked his clothes and his body. Bristly, rust-colored hair stuck out from under the broad-brimmed felt hat he wore.

Scarrow straightened to his full height, nearly a head taller than Plumlee. His voice held just a hint of a British accent these days, since he had jumped ship in Boston more than ten years earlier and had been in America ever since.

"There's one squaw and thirty of us. We either all take turns, in which case she gets worn out and probably dies within a day or two . . . or we all leave her alone and suffer our deprivation equally. That's only fair, Hog."

In the two years Scarrow had known him, Plumlee had never shown any signs of disliking the name Hog. He just shrugged. "When you say it, it makes sense, Jeff. It always does, no matter what. But good common sense don't have nothin' to do with the gnawin' a fella feels in his guts when he looks at a gal like that Injun."

Plumlee was right about that. The young Indian woman who had stumbled into their camp two nights earlier was very attractive. Not just attractive for a squaw, either. Matched up against the women back in

St. Louis or even farther east, she still would have been pretty enough to take a man's breath away.

She had been running away from something or some*one*. That was obvious. But as she stopped short and looked around at the circle of roughly dressed, hard-bitten men made to look even more harsh by the garish wash of firelight, she must have realized her situation wasn't going to be any better. She'd tried to turn and flee, but one of the group, a young man called Clete, had been too fast for her. He'd lunged and caught her with both arms around her waist. She kicked her legs and cried out as he swung her off her feet, but she was no match for his strength.

"Hey, fellas!" he had shouted with a big grin on his face. "Look what I found!"

Scarrow hadn't let that stand. His quick brain told him he couldn't allow Clete to claim the Indian girl for his own. That would just cause hard feelings and trouble, maybe even a fight. He didn't want anybody cut or shot. He had stood up and said in a flat, hard tone that allowed for no argument, "I'm sorry, Clete, but she's not yours."

Clete had looked at him, started to protest that he was the one who had grabbed the girl before she could get away, then thought better of it. Like the rest of the men, he respected Jefferson Scarrow and was more than a little scared of him. Scarrow had killed at least nine men, not counting Indians, and nobody wanted to cross him. He was the unquestioned leader of this bunch that had drifted together and headed west to make their fortunes the old-fashioned way—by stealing and killing.

Since then, the squaw's hands and feet had been tied so she couldn't run away, and usually she was roped to a tree as well. Scarrow had tried to talk to her, using the bits and pieces of Indian languages he had picked up, but she wouldn't respond to him. Either she didn't understand what he was saying, or she was just too stubborn and prideful to cooperate.

He would have liked to know what she had been running from, but if she wouldn't tell him, he wasn't going to worry too much about it. He had a large, well-armed force and would pit it against almost any enemy.

However, he had never seen the point in fighting when he didn't have to, which prompted him to say to Plumlee, "There's another reason to hang on to her and not mistreat her, Hog. So far we've been fortunate and haven't encountered any bands of hostiles. Sooner or later, though, we're bound to, and perhaps when we do, we can use the girl to help us negotiate with them."

"She ain't friendly enough to want to help us," Plumlee said. "Fact is, she looks at us like she'd be mighty tickled to lift our hair."

"I wasn't talking about that. I meant we might be able to trade her for safe passage or something like that." Scarrow smiled again. "I imagine some wrinkled tribal elder, or even a young buck of a war chief, might want such a delectable morsel warming their buffalo robes at night."

Plumlee rubbed his bristly jaw, frowned in thought, and finally nodded. "Could be you're right about that. I'll have a talk with the boys and let 'em know why you're doin' what you're doin'. I ain't sayin' that'll fix everything, but it's worth a try."

"To tell the truth," Scarrow said, "I'm more concerned about Lopez and the men who went with him."

"They ain't hardly been gone long enough to worry

about 'em yet. I ain't really expectin' 'em back until the middle of the mornin'."

"I know, but I suddenly had a feeling that everything might not be right with them. I heard shooting a little while ago, or at least I believe I did, and enough of it that I know it didn't come from some trapper hunting his breakfast."

"You did? You got good ears, Jeff. I didn't hear a thing." A puzzled frown creased Plumlee's grimy forehead above his bushy eyebrows. "But shootin's good, ain't it? It means Lopez and the other boys found that bunch our scouts spotted the other day and wiped 'em out. Don't it?"

"It should," Scarrow agreed. "We sent eight good men to deal with five, and one of them was an old Indian who looked feeble and not able to put up much of a fight, according to the scouts. The odds definitely should have been on our side. And yet . . ." He shrugged.

"Oh, Lord," Plumlee breathed. "You've got a hunch, don't you?"

Scarrow nodded and said, "Yes. It came out of nowhere just now, while we were talking."

"I ain't never knowed one o' your hunches to be wrong," Plumlee said, shaking his head. "What do you reckon we should do?"

Scarrow considered the question for a moment, then said, "Pack up. I hate to abandon this camp. It's been a good one. But I think I'd be more comfortable if we were on the move."

"What about Lopez and the others? If nothin' bad has happened and they do come back—"

"We'll leave a man here to keep an eye on the place, and if Lopez and the others return successfully from their mission, he can tell them which direction we went and they can follow us. If they don't come back . . . if someone else shows up instead . . . he should be able to slip away without being spotted. So pick someone dependable for the job."

"Gordie Hemming will do," Plumlee said. "He don't spook easy, and he's good at sneakin' through the woods."

"All right. Pass the word to the men."

"If you're sure."

"I am," Scarrow said. The certainty had been growing inside him as he and Plumlee talked, and he had no doubt about it. Something had gone wrong.

Plumlee hurried off to give orders and get the men busy as Scarrow looked around with regret at the camp. Located on the western bank of a fast-flowing creek, the site provided plenty of good water and also an abundant supply of trout. Steep, talus-covered ridges to the north and south made it impossible for anybody to sneak up from those directions without setting off enough of a clatter to warn the occupants. A sheer cliff rose to the west. Across the creek to the east was a large, open meadow, making it impossible to approach from that direction without being seen.

Scarrow couldn't have asked for a better spot to make his headquarters. For several weeks, his men had been spreading out from there, ambushing small groups of trappers and the occasional lone man, killing them and stealing their pelts. The operation was simple but profitable. Men who remained in camp dried and bundled the furs, and a large pile of them had already grown up. If Lopez and the men who had gone with him were successful, the number of pelts soon would grow significantly, because the five men they'd targeted appeared to have done quite well so far.

Scarrow tried to tell himself that he was worrying

for nothing, but better to be careful, he supposed. While the other men began loading the furs in the canoes, along with the supplies that had been taken out, Scarrow walked across the camp toward the tree where the captive was tied.

The Indian woman noticed him coming toward her and glared at him. Scarrow wasn't sure how old she was, but no more than late teens, certainly. She was slender, not running to fat like so many of the savages did, and the long buckskin dress she wore clung to a good figure. Her hair, dark and slicked with bear grease, was long and straight.

Scarrow knelt in front of her, but not so close that she could kick out at him with her bound feet. He searched for fear in her eyes but didn't see any, only anger and defiance.

"We're going to be leaving here soon, and you're coming with us," he told her. "No one will harm you as long as you behave and don't give us any trouble. You're safe . . . for now." He paused. "I wish I knew whether or not you understand a word I'm saying to you."

She gave no sign that she did. He was convinced that she didn't understand the white man's tongue.

He smiled at her and said, "I know your secret, girl. None of the others have noticed, because they're too busy lusting after you, but *I* know. And I'm starting to have a hunch that perhaps *you* don't even know. It's been too long, hasn't it?"

She turned her head, glared away from him, and refused to look back at him.

After a moment, he laughed. "All right. Be that way. It doesn't really matter. You're ours, and you'll stay ours until we can make some good use of you. Better use than what most of those louts would like to do. A girl like you, out here on the frontier . . . you have some real value, whether you know it or not. Someday you'll see. You probably won't like it, but you'll see."

He wasn't going to waste any more time talking to her when there were things to be done. He straightened and walked to the stream's edge to peer southward along it. Lopez and the other men had gone that direction last night, to work their way close to the camp they were going to attack early this morning. The shots had come from that direction . . . if Scarrow was right and he truly had heard shots.

Gazing that way, he felt a chill go through him, and he turned away from the creek and snapped at Plumlee and the other men. "Keep moving. I want to get out of here while we have the chance."

CHAPTER 3

Preacher and his friends were traveling by horseback rather than using canoes like some trappers did. They had built a couple of travois on which to carry the pelts they'd taken and could easily put together more of the conveyances if they needed to. However, before much longer, Preacher had intended to head for a trading post he knew of so they could sell the furs and then head out again to trap more.

Unfortunately, the grim errand on which they were bound was going to interfere with that plan.

He led the way on a rangy gray stallion he called Horse. Aaron Buckley and Charlie Todd rode a short distance behind him, with their horses pulling the pair of travois. White Buffalo was next in line, and Hawk brought up the rear. The riders were arranged that way for a good reason. Preacher and Hawk had the sharpest eyes and the keenest senses, so if trouble approached from either in front or behind, they would spot it sooner than the others. White Buffalo liked to boast of being eagle-eyed, but in truth his eyesight was not what it once was.

"She was brokenhearted," the old man was saying as the party rode north along the eastern bank of a creek.

Charlie turned his head to look back at White Buffalo. "Who?"

"Yellow Sky."

Aaron joined the conversation by asking, "That's the Crow woman you married, right? The widow?"

"The woman I made very happy," White Buffalo said with a smirk on his wrinkled face. "So happy that when I told her I felt the need to say farewell, her heart was broken. But the lure of the far trails and the call of the eagle soaring high in the sky were too strong for me to resist any longer."

"Are you sure that's the reason you left?" Charlie asked. "Or was Yellow Sky just tired of listening to your boasting so she kicked you out?"

White Buffalo glared and drew himself up in an offended stance on his pony's back. "Boasting?" he repeated. "Boasting? Not one word has ever passed these lips that was not truthful!"

"No?" Aaron said. "How about the time you told us you killed a whole pack of wolves bare-handed?"

"I would show you their pelts, but I long since passed them out to all the women who have shared my robes."

"Now, that's another thing," Charlie said. "Yellow Sky is pretty young, you know."

"Twenty-five summers," White Buffalo agreed.

"And you really expect us to believe that you were able to, uh, satisfy all her needs . . . ?"

White Buffalo sniffed. "Never were tears of disappointment shed in the lodge we shared."

Aaron was about to make some rejoinder to that, but Preacher hipped around in the saddle and lifted a hand to motion for silence. He reined in. The others followed suit.

Up ahead, a shaggy gray shape emerged ghostlike from the shadows under some trees and then trotted toward them. At first glance, the creature resembled a wolf, but Preacher knew better. The newcomer was Dog, the big cur that had been one of his trail partners for a long time.

Dog had been off hunting somewhere when the men attacked the camp that morning, or he would have been in the thick of the fight, wreaking havoc with his sharp, flashing fangs.

He bounded up to Preacher and the others, stopped, sat down on his haunches, and turned his head to look toward the north. A low growl rumbled in his throat.

White Buffalo nudged his horse forward. "Dog, my old friend," he greeted the cur. "Tell us what you have seen."

The elderly Absaroka claimed to have the ability to speak to animals, and to have them speak to him in ways that each could understand. Preacher had his doubts about that, but sometimes he wasn't sure.

In this case, however, he didn't see any need for White Buffalo to translate. He communicated pretty well with Dog himself and knew what the big cur's actions meant. "You saw some enemies up there, didn't you?"

Dog had an uncanny ability to sniff out evil men. He barked, sprang up, whirled around, and ran about ten yards back from the direction he had come. Then he stopped and looked at Preacher and the others.

"He says we should follow him, and he will lead us to the men we seek," White Buffalo announced.

"Yeah, I got that idea," Preacher said dryly. He looked at Aaron and Charlie. "I've been thinkin'. Maybe it'd be best if you two took those pelts and headed on to the tradin' post I had in mind where we'd sell 'em. I can tell you how to find it, and I figure you could get there all right. You boys have spent some time out here in the mountains by yourselves. You know what you're doin'."

"I'm not so sure about that," Charlie said, frowning. "True, we managed to survive while you and Hawk went back to St. Louis and White Buffalo stayed with Yellow Sky and her people, but I wouldn't say we ever felt all that comfortable about it."

"Anyway," Aaron said, "you know what that man said. The bunch he and the others came from still numbers more than twenty men. That's too many for you and Hawk to take on by yourselves."

"They will not be alone," White Buffalo said. "They will have a great warrior with them, a warrior worth more in battle than ten white men!"

Preacher ignored the old-timer's immodest comment. "I'll leave it up to you boys, but if you want to come with us, we need to find somewhere to cache them pelts. We can't be haulin' around a couple of travois full of furs if we're gonna have a big fight on our hands."

Charlie nodded. "That makes sense. Do you know of a good place?"

Preacher leaned forward in the saddle and looked around. After a moment, he said, "It's been a while since I've been through these parts, but I seem to recollect there's a cave over east of here a ways. Won't be no bears denned up in it this time of year, so I reckon that'd suit us."

Hawk said, "Hiding the furs will delay us."

"Not that much. Anyway, Dog's got the scent of those varmints. Ain't nowhere they can go that he can't find 'em."

Hawk shrugged to show his acceptance of Preacher's

statement. Even without Dog's keen nose to follow their scent, twenty-two men couldn't move through the wilderness without leaving enough sign so that Preacher and Hawk could follow them easily.

The riders turned east, away from the creek, and Preacher led them a couple of miles to a spot where a cliff reared up. He searched through the thick growth at the cliff's base for several minutes before he uncovered a roughly square opening about four feet on a side.

"I hoped my memory wasn't playin' tricks on me," he said as the others gathered around. "I crawled up in there about fifteen years ago when some Blackfeet were after me. Had one o' their arrows in my side, so I figured I was crawlin' in there to die. I didn't."

Aaron asked, "What about the Blackfeet?"

"They did, after a spell. I had to heal up a mite first before I went lookin' for 'em."

Preacher didn't go into any more detail than that. Recounting his previous adventures would take more time than they had, and besides, he had always been the sort to look to the future, rather than the past.

He fashioned a torch from a branch and some dried grass, lit it with flint and steel, and crawled into the cave to make sure it was unoccupied. Twenty feet in, the chamber widened out slightly and the ceiling rose enough for Preacher to stand up. The place was empty, just as he'd hoped.

He returned to the others. Charlie and Aaron unloaded the bundles of furs and pushed them up the short tunnel, then cached the two travois in the cave, as well.

Preacher arranged the brush to cover the entrance

again. "We'll come back and collect 'em when we're finished with this little chore."

"How long do you think that will take?" Charlie asked.

"No tellin'. Might be later today, if we're lucky."

"You think we'll have dealt with those brigands that quickly?" Aaron said.

They all knew what he meant by "dealt with." They would have to kill all the thieves, or at least most of them, to eliminate them as a threat to the honest trappers on the frontier.

"Well, I said we'd need some luck," Preacher responded with a faint smile. "Let's go."

They returned to the creek and resumed their northward trek. It seemed likely to Preacher that the gang they were hunting for would be camped somewhere close to the stream. He counted on Dog to alert them before they got too close.

As they reached the edge of some trees bordering a long, open meadow that ran along the creek's eastern side, Dog sat down and whined. Preacher brought Horse to a stop and the others halted behind him.

Preacher swung down from the saddle and dropped to a knee beside Dog. "We're not far from where you saw 'em, huh?" he said quietly. "Let's you and me go take a look." He stood, hung his hat and rifle on the saddle, and told the others, "Dog and me are gonna do some scoutin'. The rest of you stay out of sight here in the trees. We'll be back in a spell."

"I can come with you," Hawk offered.

Preacher shook his head. "Nope, I'd rather you stay with Charlie, Aaron, and White Buffalo."

Hawk nodded. He understood that Preacher didn't want anything happening to both of them. The other three would stand a better chance of surviving if either he or Preacher was still alive.

Preacher and Dog bellied down and crawled out into the meadow. At that time of year, the grass was tall enough to conceal them, and the breeze blowing through the valley made the stalks sway back and forth enough that their movements weren't too obvious. They just had to make their approach slow and careful-like.

The sun was at its height, and the heat from it was uncomfortable as they inched along through the tall grass. Preacher hoped they wouldn't come nose to nose with a rattlesnake. Most rattlers preferred rocky dens, but it was possible to run across one in a meadow. Not wanting to risk a pistol shot, he drew his knife. Pitting his speed against that of a striking rattlesnake would be a good contest, if it came to that, with the stakes being life or death on both sides.

If any of the scaly varmints were around today, they stayed out of Preacher and Dog's way. Preacher angled toward the creek but stayed far enough back in the grass that they wouldn't be spotted easily. The little whining noises Dog made told him they were getting close.

When Dog stopped and didn't want to go on, Preacher whispered, "This must be the place." He parted the grass just enough to peer across the stream.

As soon as he saw the wide hollow between the two talus-covered ridges, backed by a cliff, he knew he had found the enemy's camp. Actually, their former camp. The place was empty. He spotted the remains of a good-sized campfire.

"They've lit a shuck," he told Dog. "Must've got

worried when the bunch that jumped us didn't come back. Their leader must be a cautious man."

He was about to stand up, thinking he would wade across the creek and have a better look around, when from the corner of his eye he saw a split-second flash atop the ridge to the north. The sun had glinted off something metal up there, and that likely meant something man-made.

"The varmints left somebody to watch over the place," he breathed. "And I almost went and told him we were here. Chances are he ain't spotted us in this grass, but he would have if we'd kept goin' much farther. Come on. Let's doodlebug outta here."

Crawling backwards was even slower than their approach had been. Preacher figured Hawk was getting impatient. The boy had an impulsive streak in him. Preacher couldn't blame him for that. Hawk came by it honestly. Preacher's own reckless nature had gotten him in trouble more than once, especially in his younger years. He had mellowed some since then—a mite, anyway.

After what seemed like a long time, they reached the meadow's edge, and as soon as they were back in the concealment of the trees, Preacher stood up. It felt good to be on his feet again, instead of his belly.

"They were there, all right," he told the others. "Looks like they abandoned the camp earlier today."

"Because they feared that the men they sent after us failed," Hawk said.

"More than likely. They left at least one man behind, though, in case their friends showed up . . . or to keep an eye out for pursuers, if they didn't." Preacher pointed. "See those two ridges on the other side of the creek? The fella I spotted is on top of the one to the north."

"I can reach him," Hawk declared. "I can circle around, and he will never see me until it is too late."

Preacher scratched his beard-stubbled jaw and nodded. "That's sort of what I was thinking. There's just one thing. Don't kill him unless you have to. He'll likely know where the rest of the sons o' bitches are headed, and we might as well let him tell us."

CHAPTER 4

Hawk went all the way around the meadow to the east, using trees, rocks, and brush for cover so the man on the ridge across the creek wouldn't see him. The open stretch was about a mile long, so it took the young warrior a while to circle it. Stealth was more important than speed, at this point.

When the trees grew all the way down to the creek's edge again, Hawk slipped through them, then crossed the stream. The ridge where the watcher was posted lay to the south of him. The slope on his side was not as steep, nor was it covered with loose rock like the other side. Hawk made his way in that direction in almost complete silence, moving like a phantom through the trees.

As he approached his quarry, he thought about the stories he had heard of how in the past, Preacher had slipped into the camps of his mortal enemies, the Blackfeet, in the middle of the night and cut the throats of several warriors before gliding back out. Those deaths weren't discovered until the next morning, but when they were, the Blackfeet knew that Preacher was responsible for them, even though none had seen him

at his grim work. The fact that he could kill them
with impunity struck fear into the hearts of even the
fiercest warriors.

Those incidents had led the Blackfeet to dub Preacher
the Ghost Killer. Some called him the White Wolf, as
well, but the other name was more common among
that bloodthirsty tribe.

Not that Preacher ever boasted of such things, at
least not around Hawk. No, the stories Hawk had
heard came from other men. Preacher possessed no
false modesty. He just didn't see any reason to brag
about his own exploits.

Hawk wondered if someday men would speak of his
adventures in admiring tones, if he would be remembered and known by names such as Ghost Killer. He
was just young enough, and just touched enough by
the vanity of youth, to think about that sometimes.

He put such thoughts out of his mind and concentrated on the task at hand. He had reached the ridge's
base and started stealing up it, darting from rock to
bush and back to rock as he climbed.

Within minutes, he spotted the man he was looking
for. The watcher had settled down in a nest of boulders atop the ridge. He wore buckskin trousers, a
homespun shirt, and a brown felt hat with an eagle
feather sticking up from its band. A flintlock rifle
leaned against the rock beside him. He probably had
a knife and at least one pistol, too, but Hawk couldn't
see those from his position.

The man leaned forward at his post, resting his
arms on a rock as he watched the abandoned campsite
below, clearly waiting for something . . . or some*one*.

Hawk stopped to study the ridge crest in both directions and make certain no other enemies lurked
nearby. After several long minutes, he was convinced

this man was the only one who had been left behind. The young warrior's moccasin-shod feet made no sound as he climbed onto a slab of rock behind the watcher. He stood up and drew back his rifle's hammer.

The metallic sound made the man stiffen and start to straighten from his casual pose.

Hawk said, "Stop! Do not move. I will kill you if you do."

Preacher had told him not to kill this man if at all possible, but of course the watcher didn't know that.

"Hold on," the man said. "I ain't done nothin'."

"Then why do you stand here, watching like a carrion bird waiting for something to die?"

"You got me all wrong—"

"Step away from your rifle and turn around," Hawk ordered. "Slowly. Keep your hands where I can see them or I will fire."

The menace in Hawk's voice was unmistakable, just as the sound of his rifle being cocked had been. With his hands raised to shoulder height, the man sidled to his left and then turned. His eyes widened in surprise when he saw Hawk standing on the rock slab.

"A redskin! I figured you for a white man. You don't sound like an Injun."

Hawk ignored that. "Use your left hand to take out your pistol and knife and toss them away from you. Do it now, or I will go ahead and shoot."

"Sure, sure. Don't get antsy, mister. Ain't no need for you to point that rifle at me, though. I'm not lookin' for any trouble."

"Then why do you watch that campsite below?"

"I'm waitin' to see if those fellas who were there before are gonna come back. I thought I might camp there tonight myself. It's a good place. But I don't want to go crowdin' in where I ain't wanted, especially with that bunch."

Hawk frowned. "You are not one of them?"

"What? You reckon I'm . . . one of them?" The man shook his head vehemently. "Good Lord, no, Injun. I come on 'em earlier and seen that they was a bad bunch. I could tell just by lookin' at 'em that they was all murderers and thieves. I didn't want nothin' to do with 'em. That's why I stayed hid up here where they wouldn't see me. They looked like they were packin' up to leave, so I figured I might wait 'em out and take over the camp once they was gone."

To Hawk, this man looked like he could be a murderer and a thief himself. His dull, heavy-jawed face had more than a hint of brutality to it. But such things couldn't always be judged by appearances, Hawk knew, and the things the man said not only made sense, they sounded sincere.

"You are a trapper?" Hawk asked.

"I sure am. Hemming is the name. Gordie Hemming. Who might you be?"

"I am called Hawk That Soars. These men you saw, how many of them were there?"

Hemming frowned. "I ain't rightly sure. Maybe about twenty?"

That matched what the mortally injured Spanish man had told them earlier, before Hawk had mercifully ended his life.

"And then there was the girl," Hemming added.

Hawk's frown darkened as he asked, "What girl?"

"Some Injun gal. It looked like she was a prisoner. They had her tied hand and foot. They didn't abuse her none, at least while I was watchin', but that's really all I can tell you about her, mister. You're not lookin' for a missin' gal, are you?"

"I did not know they had a woman with them," Hawk answered honestly without thinking about it.

"But you *are* on the trail of those fellas?"

Hawk's mouth tightened as he realized the man was trying to get information out of him, rather than the other way around as it was supposed to be. He began to think that he should take Hemming with him as a prisoner and let Preacher question the man. Preacher would be able to determine whether or not Hemming was telling the truth.

At that moment, Hawk realized Hemming had distracted him with all the talk, especially the surprising mention of a female captive. The man hadn't discarded his pistol and knife as ordered.

In fact, Hemming's hand had stolen closer and closer to the pistol as they were talking, and the man suddenly closed his hand around the butt and yanked the weapon free. He threw himself to his right as he jerked the pistol up and fired.

Hawk squeezed the rifle's trigger, but the ball missed Hemming by a whisker and whined off the boulder behind him. Hemming's hurried shot hummed past Hawk's left ear. Hawk dropped his rifle and made a leap toward Hemming before the man could grab his own rifle.

Hawk crashed into Hemming and drove him back against the rock. Hemming grunted from the impact. He still held the empty pistol and slashed at Hawk's head with it. The barrel struck the young warrior a glancing blow above the left ear and stunned him for a second.

That gave Hemming a chance to push him away. He tried to hit Hawk with the pistol a second time, but Hawk ducked under this blow and rammed his shoulder into Hemming's midsection. Hemming went down with Hawk on top of him.

Hawk's pistol was loaded, and he also had his knife and tomahawk he could have used. Preacher had told him to take the watcher alive, though, so that was what he was going to do. He had fired the rifle at Hemming out of instinct, because Hemming had shot at him. Now Hawk tried to subdue the man with his bare hands.

That proved to be difficult. Hemming was bigger, outweighing Hawk by at least thirty pounds, and he was a vicious, unscrupulous fighter. He tried to ram a knee into Hawk's groin, and even though Hawk twisted aside from what would have been a momentarily crippling blow, the man's knee landed in his stomach and drove the air from his lungs. Hemming got a hand on Hawk's face and clawed at his eyes.

Hawk jerked back, hammered a punch into Hemming's prominent jaw that rocked the man's head to the side. Hemming hit him on the left ear with enough power to make Hawk's head ring. Hemming grabbed the front of Hawk's buckskin shirt and threw him to the side, then rolled after him.

Hawk tried to catch himself and get back to his knees, but just as he did, Hemming plowed into him again. The man's greater weight sent Hawk backward. Hawk's head thudded against one of the boulders Hemming had been using for cover. Red explosions burst behind his eyes. His muscles went limp. His eyesight cleared just in time for him to see that Hemming had yanked out his own knife and raised it high for a killing stroke aimed at Hawk's chest.

Desperation forced Hawk to cast off his momentary paralysis. He got his crossed arms raised to block Hemming's thrust at the last instant. The knife's tip stopped a mere inch or two from Hawk's chest. Hawk bucked up from the ground and dislodged Hemming's weight.

Hemming rolled and recovered enough to surge to his feet, but Hawk grabbed a fist-sized rock from the ground beside him and threw it with unerring aim. The rock smacked into Hemming's wrist and the knife flew out of his fingers.

Hemming snarled a curse and charged at Hawk again, just as Hawk made it to his feet. For a big man, Hemming was quick and agile, no doubt the product of a rough-and-tumble, no-holds-barred life on the frontier. Hawk realized the man had to be a member of the gang he and the others sought. If Hemming was really an innocent trapper who had stumbled upon the thieves, likely he wouldn't be trying to kill Hawk.

Hawk didn't have time to reach for his pistol before Hemming was on him again. The two men grappled, and as they did, Hawk suddenly felt the ground shifting underneath him.

No, not the ground, he realized. In their struggle, they had staggered through a gap in the clump of boulders and were at the talus slope's edge. Hawk tried to keep his balance, but the small, loose rocks were too unstable. His feet and legs shot out from under him.

As he went over backward, he grabbed Hemming and took the man with him. Hemming yelled in surprise and alarm as they fell and started to slide.

Rocks flew in the air and pelted Hawk as he tumbled over and over with Hemming beside him, going through the same punishment. It was an avalanche in miniature, and both men were trapped in the middle of it.

Sliding down the ridge seemed to take an eternity. A thick dust cloud rose from the rockslide and clogged Hawk's nose and mouth, blinding him as well as choking him. He thought he heard Hemming yelling, but with the loud clatter of falling rocks all around him, he couldn't be sure.

Finally, Hawk came to a stop, but he was disoriented and gasping for breath, not to mention stinging and aching from all the rocks that had pounded him on the way down. He knew that if he had survived the slide, Hemming probably had, too, so the danger wasn't over. Hawk pulled himself up to hands and knees and raised his head to look around.

A couple of yards away, Hemming was trying to get up, too. He planted his feet underneath him enough to launch himself into a diving tackle that caught Hawk around the shoulders. They rolled over several times.

Sharp rocks gouged into Hawk's flesh, adding to the pain that enveloped him. Hemming's face loomed over him, and Hawk jabbed a punch into it. At the same time, Hemming dug a knee into Hawk's belly. Hawk didn't have any more breath to lose, however. His head spun wildly, and he knew he was on the verge of passing out.

Hemming straddled him and snatched up a sharp-edged piece of rock about a foot wide. A hate-filled snarl pulled the man's lips back from his teeth as he used both hands to raise the rock high above his head.

Hawk was about to die.

CHAPTER 5

Preacher, White Buffalo, Aaron Buckley, Charlie Todd, and Dog were waiting in the trees while Hawk circled the meadow to take the watcher from behind.

Tired of waiting, Aaron broke their silence and asked Preacher, "How do you intend to attack the men we're after when they outnumber us almost five to one?"

"Takin' 'em by surprise will make a lot of difference. If we can put half a dozen or more of 'em out of the fight before they rightly know what's goin' on, that'll make the odds look a whole lot better."

"But in order to do that," Charlie said with a frown, "we'll have to shoot them from ambush. That means not giving them any warning."

"I reckon," Preacher said, nodding.

"That kind of bothers me. It seems like that would make us . . . well, just as bad as they are. After all, that's what they tried to do to us, isn't it?"

White Buffalo said, "They tried to kill us first. That makes whatever we do in defense of our own lives acceptable."

"But we killed the men who were trying to kill us,"

Charlie argued. "With them, it was self-defense, sure. That just makes sense. But we'll be attacking these other men before they've done anything to us."

"I can see why that'd bother you," Preacher said. "I really can. But you got to think about it like this, Charlie. Crawlin' through that field put me in mind of rattlesnakes, because I thought I might run into one. What would you do if you came on a whole nest o' rattlesnakes?"

"I'd kill them," Aaron answered without hesitation. "I'd blast away until they were all dead."

"Yeah, I suppose I would, too," Charlie admitted.

"But if you found 'em in their nest, they wouldn't have struck you yet," Preacher said. "They probably wouldn't have even tried to, if they were denned up."

Charlie shook his head. "It would still be too dangerous to let them live. They might bite one of us or somebody else in the future." He began nodding slowly in understanding. "They might have struck and killed other people in the past."

"Yep. To change the talk from snakes to dogs, the time to shoot a mad dog is before he bites somebody."

"But you're still assuming that every one of those men is just as bad as all the others," Charlie said. "You can't know that they're all mad dogs. Some of them might be redeemable. They might not have ever hurt anybody."

"There's that chance, all right. But if you throw in with a bad bunch, you got to figure that you might come to a bad end, too. Life ain't always black and white on the frontier . . . nor anywhere else, Charlie. A fella does what he has to in order to see that he and the folks he cares about get through it. In the end, that's all anybody can do."

"That's a hard way of looking at things."

"Yeah, I reckon it is. But if you do what seems right, it all balances out in the end . . . if you're lucky."

Before that philosophical discussion could continue, a pair of shots suddenly shattered the midday peace and quiet. They came so close together the reports almost sounded like one blast, but Preacher's keen ears picked out the difference. One rifle and one pistol, he thought . . . and no more shots followed as the echoes of those two rolled up the valley.

"Hawk!" Aaron exclaimed softly. He took a step toward the edge of the trees.

Preacher put out an arm to stop him. "Hold on there. You don't need to go chargin' out into the open while we don't know what's goin' on. Could be Hawk had to kill that varmint to save his own life. If that's what happened, we'll know soon enough."

"And if the man killed Hawk?"

"We'll know that, too." Preacher left unspoken the fact that if his son was dead, he would wreak a terrible vengeance on whoever was responsible for that.

The two shots had come from the direction of the northern ridge. When no more gunfire erupted, Preacher moved to the edge of the trees where the shadows still partially concealed him but he could see across the creek into the abandoned camp and the ridges that rose around it.

Movement caught his eye. Atop the ridge, two roughly dressed figures came into view, struggling with each other. Only a couple of heartbeats passed before one of the men slipped, fell, and dragged the other down with him. Both men began sliding down the loose rock that covered the steep slope.

"Hawk's in that rockslide!" Preacher burst out of the trees, his own advice to Aaron forgotten. There was no question. He *knew* his son was in danger. He had gotten a good enough look to recognize Hawk before the two men fell.

With his rifle held at a slant across his chest, Preacher raced toward the creek. Dog bounded alongside him. The others probably followed, but Preacher didn't look back to check on them. All his attention was focused on reaching Hawk and making sure the young warrior was all right.

A cloud of dust followed the two men down the ridge and rolled over them as they reached its base. Preacher could no longer see them. He splashed into the creek, which flowed swiftly but was no more than two feet deep. Water flew high around him, the droplets sparkling in the midday sun.

As he bounded onto the stream's western bank, the dust thinned and he saw Hawk and the other man again as they fought among the talus that had slid down the slope with them. The other man was easy for Preacher to pick out because he wore a lighter-colored homespun shirt instead of buckskin like Hawk.

Preacher was still a hundred yards away when he knew the man was about to bring a large rock crashing down on Hawk's head in a death blow.

Preacher couldn't reach the two men in time, but a rifle ball could. Stopping short, he brought his rifle to his shoulder and took only an instant to aim. The weapon boomed and spewed flame and smoke from the long barrel.

Through the white smoke, Preacher saw the man lurch as the ball struck him. The rock flew from his hands as he toppled forward. Preacher broke into a run again and hoped that the rock hadn't fallen on Hawk and injured or killed him.

The sight of Hawk struggling to push the larger man's body off him dispelled that worry as Preacher approached. The mountain man pulled a pistol from his belt in case the stranger wasn't dead and still had some fight left in him.

That didn't appear to be the case. When Hawk shoved the man away and the man flopped over loosely onto his back, Preacher saw the large, bloody splotch on the front of the homespun shirt. He knew his shot had struck the man in the back and blasted a hole clean through him.

So much for the idea of taking the man alive. Saving Hawk's life was more important, though.

Hawk was sitting up, coughing, and rubbing dust and grit from his eyes by the time Preacher reached him. He stopped and looked over his son. Dust coated Hawk's hair, face, and clothes, and a few drops of blood leaked from cuts and scrapes here and there. Otherwise he appeared to be all right.

"Thank you," Hawk said, his voice hoarse from the dust he had breathed in. "That was a good shot."

"Glad I was here to make it. This is the fella that was spyin' on the camp?"

"Yes."

Preacher tucked his pistol away and extended a hand to Hawk. The young warrior lifted his arm, and they clasped wrists. Preacher pulled Hawk to his feet.

"He was by himself?"

"Yes," Hawk said. "I made sure of that before I tried to capture him."

"He didn't want to be took alive, though, I reckon."

"He put up a fight," Hawk said. "He was a good fighter, too. But before that, I spoke with him for several minutes. He tried to distract me with talk. He claimed he was a trapper and not part of the group that had been camped here."

Charlie, Aaron, and White Buffalo came trotting up in time to hear what Hawk said.

Aaron asked, "You didn't believe him, did you?"

"He was convincing. I was not sure whether to believe him. But he lied. I know that now. If he had been telling the truth, he would have had no reason to try to kill me." Hawk nodded. "He was one of them, all right. I have no doubt of that."

"Me, neither." Preacher looked at the man's lifeless eyes staring up at the sky and added, "At least he won't sneak off and warn the rest that we're after 'em."

"He said something else," Hawk told them. "He claimed that the others have a prisoner. A young Indian woman."

"A woman?" Charlie repeated in a surprised exclamation.

Hawk nodded.

"Was he telling the truth about *that*?" Aaron asked.

"There is no way to know," Hawk replied. "Perhaps it was just another attempt to distract me. But it seems an odd thing to make up."

Preacher scraped a thumbnail along his jawline and frowned. "Yeah, that's right. But it wouldn't be the first time a bunch of lowlifes grabbed an Injun gal. I don't reckon it really matters."

"If she's their prisoner, I think it probably matters to *her*," Aaron said.

Preacher shook his head. "That ain't what I meant. We're still goin' after those varmints whether they've got a prisoner or not. If they do, and they've been mistreatin' her, that's just one more reason to kill them." He looked at Charlie Buckley. "Like a whole den o' rattlers."

* * *

Jefferson Scarrow hoped the uneasy feeling that had come over him would dissipate once the men broke camp and moved on. That didn't happen. His nerves grew more tense as the day wore on and he searched for a new place to make camp. In case of trouble, they needed somewhere that would be easy to defend.

That turned out to be a high, beetling bluff on the western bank that bulged out over the creek. The overhang was so great that it formed a cavelike area underneath it. Scarrow spotted the place and pointed it out to Hog Plumlee, who occupied the lead canoe along with Scarrow. Plumlee dug his paddle into the water and angled toward the bank. Scarrow, behind him, paddled hard against the current as well. The creek had widened and become deeper as they proceeded upstream. By this point, it was almost big enough to be called a river.

The other ten canoes trailed behind them, some riding lower in the water because they were loaded with pelts as well as the men who rode in them. The Indian girl was in one of the canoes, as well, trussed up and lying in the bottom of the craft so she couldn't throw herself out into the water and drown. Scarrow had a feeling she would have preferred that fate to remaining a captive, so he wasn't going to risk her making such a desperate move.

As he and Plumlee came up to the bluff, he saw that the space underneath it was a good twenty feet deep, perhaps more, and fifty or sixty feet long. Room enough for a fire and the supplies they would need to unload, and the overhang would disperse the smoke. A brushy stretch of bank nearby would provide a place where they could pull the canoes ashore and conceal them. This location wasn't perfect, Scarrow thought, but it would do nicely enough for a time. Long enough for them to determine if any pursuers were on their trail.

Gordie Hemming was supposed to stay on the ridge overlooking their old camp for the rest of this day and another day after that. If Lopez and the other men hadn't returned by then, it wasn't likely they ever would. If no pursuers had shown up looking for the rest of the group, Scarrow figured he didn't have to worry about that threat. It would have been nice to know what had happened to Lopez and the others, but it wasn't a necessity.

Scarrow pointed to the brushy stretch and told Plumlee, "Let's paddle on up there and go ashore. There's a ledge that leads back down here."

"We're gonna fort up in that cave?" Plumlee asked over his shoulder.

"For the time being."

Plumlee's massive arms and shoulders made the paddle cleave the water with considerable power. The canoe breasted the current and moved up to the bank. He lifted the paddle and reached for a branch that hung out over the water. He held the canoe in place while Scarrow climbed out, found some good footing, and took hold of the canoe. Then Plumlee got out as well and the two of them dragged the craft ashore.

The other men repeated the process, and within minutes all eleven canoes were pulled up on the bank with brush around them, making them hard to see.

When they were secure, Scarrow said to Plumlee, "Bring the girl."

Plumlee bent over and reached into the canoe where the prisoner was. The young woman flinched away from him, but she didn't have anywhere to go.

Wedged into the bottom of the canoe the way she was, she couldn't retreat.

Plumlee picked her up like a doll and draped her belly-down over his left shoulder. She kicked at him with her bound feet until he smacked her sharply where her buckskin dress was stretched tight over her rump.

"Stop that, gal," he rumbled at her. "You best behave yourself, if you know what's good for you."

With the girl on his shoulder, he walked along the ledge behind Scarrow, who led the way into the big hollow under the bluff.

Scarrow stopped, put his hands on his hips, and looked around, assessing the place. When he was satisfied, he nodded and said, "This will do for now."

Plumlee lowered the captive to the ground. She glared up at him, and he chuckled.

"Don't worry, darlin'," he told her. "I'll gather some pine boughs and use a blanket and make a little bed for you. You'll be as comfortable as if you were in some fancy hotel back in St. Louis."

CHAPTER 6

Preacher and his companions didn't take the time or go to the effort of burying the man Preacher had shot. The wilderness was remarkably efficient when it came to disposing of dead bodies. Preacher always figured he would wind up the same way someday, even though he was so stringy he would make a tough meal for whatever scavengers got to him first.

Instead they headed north, following the stream. Preacher had spotted the marks where canoes had been drawn up on the shore, so they knew the men they were after were traveling that way, rather than by horseback.

Because their quarry had to follow the creek but could leave it on either bank, Preacher split his group. Hawk and White Buffalo stayed on the stream's western side while Preacher and the two young trappers took the eastern bank. As long as they didn't come across cached canoes or any other sign that the men had left the creek, they knew they were still on the trail.

They could rely on Dog, too, to alert them if he caught the scent on either side of the creek. The big cur ranged back and forth on both banks.

It was only a matter of time, Preacher thought as he moved Horse along at an easy walk. Although the possibility that the thieves had a female prisoner with them added a layer of urgency. There was no telling how much of an ordeal she had already suffered, but the sooner she was free, the better.

"How long will it take us to catch up to them?" Aaron asked as he urged his horse up alongside Preacher's mount.

"Maybe tonight, maybe tomorrow," the mountain man replied. "The ashes of that campfire were still a mite warm. I reckon they broke camp sometime around the middle of the mornin', which means they're only a few hours ahead of us."

"They're going upstream. Won't that slow them down?"

"Sure. Some, anyway."

"Then if we hurry, we might even catch them by the end of the day," Aaron suggested.

"We can't afford to rush too much. They might've left the creek somewhere and we don't want to miss it if they did. Out here on the frontier, there are times you need to hurry, and times you need to take things more slow and careful-like." Preacher's mouth curved in a smile under his dark, drooping mustache. "Knowin' which one is which is a big part of bein' able to stay alive."

Charlie said, "We'll never know as much as you, Preacher. Not if we stayed out here twenty years."

"Been longer than that since I came west. Thing is, twenty years from now, the frontier's gonna be tamed down a whole heap. Anybody with eyes can see that. More and more immigrants are headin' west these days. Whole dang wagon trains full of 'em. Civilization's like a weed. You can't stop it from growin', no matter how much you stomp on it."

"I don't think most people regard civilization as something to be stopped or stamped out," Aaron said.

"Maybe not . . . but most folks have never seen this high country the way it was in the beginnin', when fellas like John Colter first come out here, or even a little later when I came along. It was the cleanest, freshest place anybody ever saw, just the way God made it. Dangerous as hell, of course . . . but that's the way God made it, too." Preacher shook his head. "Anyway, what I was gettin' at, is that in twenty years, you won't have to know as much to survive out here as you do now. Shoot, by then there'll probably be things that *I* don't know, but fellas like you two will. Old mountain men like me will be . . . what do you call it? Obsolete, that's it. I'll be obsolete, even if I'm still drawin' breath." He chuckled. "Which ain't all that likely, come to think of it, considerin' how I'm always gettin' tangled up in so much trouble."

It was a long speech for the usually taciturn mountain man, and he was glad that Hawk abruptly signaled to them from the other side of the creek. The young warrior had found something.

The stream had gotten deeper as they rode north, but the horses were still able to cross it without having to swim. As Preacher, Charlie, and Aaron came up onto the western bank, Hawk pointed to some marks in the grass.

"They pulled the canoes out here," he said.

"And then pushed them back in," Preacher said as he studied the sign. "Must've stopped to rest a spell, then pushed on. Spot any footprints?"

Hawk shook his head. "You are thinking about the

woman. I saw no footprints of any kind, let alone any small enough to belong to a female."

Preacher nodded. "That doesn't really mean anything. If they have her tied hand and foot, like that fella told you, there's a good chance they didn't even take her out of the canoe she's riding in."

"You mean they didn't even allow her to get up and move around any?" Charlie asked.

"Probably not."

"That's inhumane treatment!"

"Fellas like we're talkin' about ain't known for bein' nice to folks," Preacher said.

"I'm starting to think you're right about how we should deal with them."

In the long run, it didn't really matter whether Charlie agreed with his plans or not, Preacher thought, but he didn't point that out.

"If they rested here for a while," Aaron said, "that means we can cut into their lead if we keep going."

"That's right," Preacher agreed. "And that's another reason not to push the horses too hard. If we wear 'em out, we'll have to stop and stay stopped for a while to let them rest."

"We will have to, anyway, sooner rather than later," Hawk pointed out.

"Yeah, but not just yet," Preacher said as he lifted Horse's reins. "C'mon, Dog." He rode back across the creek and headed north again.

Charlie Todd and Aaron Buckley followed, and Hawk and White Buffalo continued on the western bank.

Jefferson Scarrow ordered his men to keep the campfire small, so as not to attract attention, even though it was unlikely anyone would spot it in the

cavelike area underneath the bluff. Scarrow wasn't
convinced yet that no one was on their trail, but he felt
a little better now that they had found this place. It
would do for a camp until they knew whether the
other men were coming back.

He posted a guard on the canoes, a man at each
end of the bluff, and another in some trees across the
river. No one would sneak up and surprise them. As
dusk settled down over the wild landscape, the smells
of frying salt pork, pan bread, and coffee filled the air
under the bluff.

As Plumlee had promised the girl, he had made her
a bed from pine boughs and a blanket. That was probably the most comfortable she had been since she'd
stumbled into their camp, Scarrow thought as he
looked at her. She didn't return his gaze. Her face was
still set in a hostile mask.

He wondered again why she had been fleeing
through the night. Was there another threat lurking
out there in the gathering darkness? Scarrow believed
he and his men were ready for whatever might happen,
but it would be nice to know what to expect.

While the men were getting ready to eat supper, he
went over and sat down cross-legged beside the girl.
"You've eaten almost nothing for two days now," he
said to her in English. "You're not hurting anyone
except yourself, you know."

He tried to translate that into the several different
Indian dialects he knew bits and pieces of. He was sure
he made a mess of it but thought he conveyed enough
of the idea for her to understand, and she had to speak
at least *one* of those tongues. She knew what he was
saying, all right, she was just too blasted stubborn to
acknowledge it.

Suddenly angry, he reached out, took hold of her

chin, and roughly turned her face toward him. He leaned closer to her and said, "I don't appreciate being treated this way. I've done better by you than you had any right to expect, girl. I could have given you to my men that first night. If I had, you'd be just about used up by now. You'd be hoping for death to deliver you from that ordeal, I imagine. I'm sure being tied up has been uncomfortable, but that's all you've had to deal with. Well, I'm running out of patience."

He didn't bother trying to put that in words she understood. He could tell by the fear he saw in her eyes, mingled with the defiance, that she understood enough from his expression and his tone of voice.

A little irritated with himself, he let go of her and sat back. She was breathing harder than usual. He couldn't help but glance down at the way her breasts rose and fell under the buckskin dress. He prided himself on his control of his own emotions, but he was human, too. Maybe he ought to abandon his plan of using her as a bargaining chip in future negotiations if they encountered hostile tribes.

Not yet, Scarrow decided. He trusted his instincts. He pushed himself to his feet, looked down at her, and shook his head, then turned and walked away.

Later, Hogarth Plumlee went over to Scarrow. "I tried to get her to eat some, but she wouldn't do it. I stuck some pan bread in her mouth anyway. She might've swallowed a little of it."

"That's all right, Hog," Scarrow told him. "I appreciate the effort."

"The boys are sure gettin' antsy—"

"Let them," Scarrow snapped. "I don't care how disturbed they are as long as they do what they're told."

Plumlee looked like he wanted to say something

else, but after a moment he just shrugged his massive shoulders and walked away.

Scarrow had spread his bedroll near the back of the cave. He lay down and looked around in the dim, flickering light from the fire. He could see the girl lying on the bed Plumlee had made her, but her figure was indistinct in the poor light. Scarrow supposed she had dozed off from exhaustion and weakness brought on by barely eating for several days. She was only punishing herself, he thought.

The guard shifts were already established, so Scarrow didn't have to worry about that. He dozed off, and he wasn't sure how long he had been asleep when a sharp cry suddenly jolted him out of his slumber.

He sat up, and by the time he was upright his hand had closed around the butt of the pistol he had placed beside him. The fire was just embers, casting light so faint Scarrow could barely make out the shapes of sleeping men scattered around.

He saw the struggling figures on the other side of the camp, though, and knew instantly what was going on.

He threw his blankets aside, stood up, and stalked toward the spot where one of the men wrestled with the girl as she tried to squirm away from him.

The man had one hand clapped over her mouth to stifle any more cries while he tried to bring her under control with the other hand. "Stop it!" he hissed at her. "I ain't gonna hurt you, you crazy little fool. I just want to have some fun with you. Hell, you might even like it! Now settle down and let me get this dress up—"

"Step away from her, Clete," Scarrow ordered, his voice loud and harsh enough to wake any of the men who hadn't been roused already by the girl's cry.

The young man called Clete stopped struggling with the prisoner, but he didn't let go of her. He turned his head and said over his shoulder, "I ain't tryin' to cause any trouble here, Mr. Scarrow, but it ain't right you keepin' all of us away from this gal. It ain't fair! A man's got needs—"

"So does an animal," Scarrow said coldly. "I've explained that I have a potential use for this prisoner and until we know whether or not we'll have need of her in that fashion, we're *not* going to use her in any other fashion."

"Damn it!" Clete spat. "It wouldn't hurt her. It wouldn't make one damn bit o' difference. You reckon there ain't already been a dozen redskin bucks straddlin' her, boss? A gal that looks like she does? You know there have been!"

"It doesn't matter," Scarrow grated. "I've given you an order, and I expect you to follow it." He lowered the hammer on his pistol and stuck it behind his belt again. He didn't want gunshots to announce their location to anyone who might be out there looking for them. As he moved closer, he went on. "Now let go of her and step away from her, or I'll be forced to thrash you."

Clete muttered some curses, but he released his hold on the girl and allowed her to slump back on the blanket-covered pine boughs. Scarrow relaxed. Clete straightened and turned away from the prisoner.

"Look out, Jeff!" Plumlee yelled.

Without that warning, Clete might have succeeded in what he was trying to do. He had slipped out his own pistol and brought it up swiftly as he cocked it. Scarrow dived aside. The gun boomed, and the report was deafening under the overhanging bluff.

Something whipped through the air. Clete gasped and staggered back a step. The empty pistol in his hand sagged toward the ground as he looked down at the knife buried almost to the hilt in his chest. Scarrow, lying on the ground where he had landed after diving out of the line of fire, recognized the knife's bone handle. It belonged to Hog Plumlee, an expert in its use.

He had just proven that by splitting Clete's heart with the blade.

Clete's knees buckled. He thudded to the ground.

Plumlee came up beside Scarrow, took hold of his arm, and helped him to his feet. "You all right, Jeff?"

"Yes. The shot missed, thanks to you."

"Maybe I shouldn'ta killed the varmint, but when I seen him take that shot at you, I didn't stop to think about it. I just throwed my knife."

"And I appreciate that." Scarrow turned to the other men, who were all on their feet, looking shocked and uneasy in the light from the embers. "This is what happens when someone doesn't obey orders. I trust there won't be any more such incidents."

The men mumbled agreement, but Scarrow wasn't completely convinced of their sincerity. They were shocked at Clete's sudden death, but give them a day or two and their lust would rise up again, blinding them to logical thought. When that time came, Scarrow didn't know what would happen, but it wasn't likely to be anything good.

Of course, he might not have to worry about that, he reminded himself. Clete had fired his pistol, and there was no way of knowing how far the sound had traveled.

Nor could Scarrow know if anyone was out there in the darkness to hear it . . .

CHAPTER 7

Preacher and the others had followed the creek until nightfall. Preacher called a halt. The horses needed rest, and to be honest, so did Charlie, Aaron, and White Buffalo. The two young trappers couldn't go on tirelessly like Preacher and Hawk, and White Buffalo's advanced years had taken a toll on his stamina, no matter how much he might deny that.

"We won't stay here the whole night, though," Preacher told them. "Once the moon rises after a while, there'll be enough light for us to see where we're goin'. We got Dog to tell us if he catches a scent where they veer off from the creek."

"How likely is it that will happen?" Aaron asked.

"Not likely. Fellas who travel by canoe pretty much have to follow the streams. They might stop and venture off a ways to do some huntin' or somethin' like that, but they always have to come back to the water sooner or later."

Charlie said, "Then we're assured of finding them."

"There's a pretty good chance of it," Preacher said.

Aaron and Charlie stretched out to rest. White Buffalo sat cross-legged on the ground, closed his eyes, tilted his head back, and started chanting in a low, soft voice. The sound was a monotonous drone that put the two young men to sleep very quickly.

Preacher and Hawk stood watch. Preacher said quietly to his son, "If the varmints we're after really are holdin' a girl prisoner, Charlie and Aaron are gonna be more worried about rescuin' her than anything else."

"Yes, I know," Hawk replied. "They are kindhearted." He said it as if that were some sort of flaw in their personalities, which came as no surprise to Preacher.

He knew that Hawk had a . . . well, not exactly a bloodthirsty streak . . . but Hawk was extremely practical. He did what had to be done, and if that involved killing, it didn't bother him the least little bit. He wasn't cruel, but he didn't shy away from spilling blood.

Of course, neither did Preacher, so he figured the old saying about how the apple didn't fall far from the tree had a lot of truth to it. But Preacher knew he didn't really fit in with the sort of society that spawned Charlie and Aaron. He had known that from the time he was a boy, which was one reason he had left home and headed west at such a young age.

"They'll want to save the girl even if it means lettin' those bastards go," Preacher said.

"That would be a mistake," Hawk said. "We need to kill them to avenge the evil they have already done and prevent the evil they will do in the future."

Preacher scratched his jaw and tugged at his earlobe. "Varmints like that, one of the first things they'll do when the fightin' starts is to cut that girl's throat."

"Better for one girl to die than for all the innocent lives that will be taken if we spare those men. And we do not know for certain that they even *have* a female prisoner," Hawk added.

"That's true, we don't. I'm just sayin', if they do, those two youngsters are liable to give us trouble."

Hawk shook his head in the darkness. "It does not matter. You and I will do most of the killing, Preacher. Perhaps all of the killing. It is always that way."

"Yeah," Preacher said. "I reckon it is."

They fell silent as the minutes stretched past. White Buffalo continued to chant. A snore came from Charlie Todd. The horses blew out air and cropped at the grass on the creek bank. Preacher didn't know where Dog was, but the big cur would be somewhere close by. Probably hunting himself a rabbit for a snack before they pushed on. Might be a good idea if the rest of them followed suit and gnawed on a little jerky to keep their strength up, he decided.

That thought was going through his mind when he heard a gun go off.

Hawk heard the shot, too. His breath hissed between his teeth. Then silence hung between the two men. White Buffalo had stopped chanting, but the two young trappers still slept.

No more shots sounded. After a moment, Preacher said, "Might not be them. Could be a lone trapper scarin' off a wolf or a bear."

"You do not believe that," Hawk said.

"Well, seein' as it sounded like that gun went off about a mile upstream, no, I reckon it's more likely it belongs to one of the fellas we're after."

"Why only one shot?"

Preacher shook his head. "No tellin'. Even if it's

them, they might've been tryin' to spook some critter, like I said."

"Or perhaps they killed someone," Hawk suggested. "Like that prisoner."

"Only one way to find out," Preacher said. "Let's wake up Charlie and Aaron and go see."

The two young men were nervous and excited, now that they were closing in on their quarry. Both of them had been involved in battles before, but it was still a fairly new experience for them. A frightening experience, as well. But they knew enough to keep quiet as Preacher carefully led the group upstream.

When they had covered close to a mile in Preacher's estimation, he signaled for a halt and Hawk slipped down from his pony's back. Without having to be told what to do, the young warrior melted into the shadows cast by the trees along the eastern bank. Preacher hadn't been able to tell from the sound of the shot which side of the creek it came from, but when the men had pulled the canoes from the stream earlier in the day it had been on the western bank. That was as good a guess as any.

Either way, Hawk would find out.

"Do we just wait?" Charlie whispered.

"That's right," Preacher told him. "No more talk."

Charlie opened his mouth to say something, probably an apology, but caught himself in time and just nodded.

Long before, Preacher had learned how to wait. Sometimes a man had to stay in one place, silent and motionless, for hours in order to save his life. White Buffalo had that ability as well, although Preacher figured it was more difficult for the old-timer to keep his mouth shut for long periods of time. Charlie and Aaron were restless, though. They fidgeted, but at least they didn't make much noise about it.

A three-quarter moon was rising over the mountains to the east by the time Hawk reappeared like a ghost from the darkness. Charlie and Aaron both jumped a little when they realized he was there.

The others all gathered around Hawk as he whispered, "One guard, two bowshots ahead on this side of the creek. On the other side, in a cave underneath a bluff, a campfire that has died down. Many men, most sleeping. Two guards on that side."

"What about a prisoner?" Preacher asked.

Hawk shook his head. "I could not tell. I can kill the guard on this side of the creek, then cross over and kill the others. That way I can get close enough to see."

"Or we could wait until morning," Aaron said, "when there's some light."

"If the guards are dead, we can take the others by surprise," Hawk argued. "The five of us can line up across the creek and open fire. With each of us armed with a rifle and two pistols, we can fire fifteen shots before any of them know what is going on. Many will be killed."

"Including the prisoner, more than likely!" Charlie objected.

"We do not know there *is* a prisoner. We have only the word of a man we know to have been a liar and a killer."

Preacher thought about it for a long moment, then said, "There's another way. We get a man into that camp."

"How in the world can we do that with guards all

around?" Aaron asked. "Even if the guards are dead, nobody can just walk in there without being noticed."

"You have not heard the stories about Preacher," White Buffalo said. "The Blackfeet call him Ghost Killer, because he can go among his enemies and never be seen until it is too late."

"Preacher can do this," Hawk said, "but so can I."

Preacher cocked an eyebrow at his son, although Hawk couldn't see that in the dark shadows. "Are you volunteerin'?"

"I can cross the creek without them knowing I am there," Hawk said. "The men are probably all asleep except for the guards. Even if one woke, he would take me for another of his companions. I can see whether there really is a prisoner, and if such exists, perhaps free her."

"You'd be takin' a mighty big chance," Preacher said.

"There is no other way to be sure."

The boy was right about that, Preacher thought. He considered for a moment, then said, "I'll take care of the guards. Charlie, Aaron, White Buffalo, you'll be posted directly across the creek from the cave. You keep the place covered with your rifles while Hawk checks out the camp. Hawk, if you're about to get caught, light a shuck outta there and dive into the creek. The rest of you open fire. That'll give Hawk enough cover to swim back over here.

"All that make sense?"

Murmurs of agreement came from the others.

"If there *is* a prisoner, I will free her and try to slip out of the camp with her," Hawk said. "If you can dispose of the guard at one end of the bluff, as well as the one on this side, we can flee in that direction."

"I'll try to take care of all of 'em, but I'll get rid of

the one at the south end first, after the one on this side of the creek."

Strategically, it was a sound but risky plan. A lot depended on Hawk's stealth. However, Preacher knew how capable the young warrior was. Hawk stood a chance of succeeding, and on the frontier, a chance was all a man could ask for, most of the time.

"Wait here," Preacher told the others. "I'll come back and get you once there ain't no guard on this side of the creek."

Hawk felt no impatience as he waited for Preacher to return, only anticipation for the task at hand. He still thought the most reasonable approach would have been to fill that cave with rifle and pistol balls and kill as many men as they could, but even though he wouldn't admit it, the arguments advanced by Charlie and Aaron—and by his own father—had swayed him somewhat. The man called Hemming had sounded like he spoke the truth when he mentioned the young woman, and if such a prisoner *did* exist, she didn't deserve to die.

"I still don't see how you're going to do this," Charlie said as they waited. "You can't make yourself invisible."

"There are always shadows in life, and a man who knows how can blend into them," Hawk said. "One who knows when to move and when to be still can go anywhere and not be seen."

Aaron said, "I hope you're right. If they do discover you, get out of there as quickly as you can. We'll cover you."

Hawk smiled grimly in the darkness. "Just be sure not to strike me with your covering fire."

"Do not worry," White Buffalo said. "I will instruct these two on what they should do."

"That is a great weight off my mind," Hawk said, knowing that White Buffalo would never hear the dry tone in his voice.

A few minutes later, Preacher returned and told them that the plan's first part was complete. "The guard on this side of the creek's taken care of. If none of the others show up to relieve him any time soon, we won't have to worry about that. Come on."

After reminding Charlie and Aaron to move as quietly as possible, Preacher led the way along the bank toward the spot directly across from the bluff and the cave underneath it. To Hawk's eyes, the moonlight was almost like the middle of the day. He had no trouble seeing where he was going, but he reminded himself that the vision of his white friends was not as sharp as his.

A short time later, they were in position behind a thick log that lay on the bank parallel with the stream. Hawk propped his rifle against the log, then drew out his pistols and laid them on top of it. Since he would be crossing the creek underwater, the firearms were of no use to him on this mission. He would be armed only with his knife and tomahawk.

"You fellas keep your eyes open," Preacher told White Buffalo and the two trappers. "Hawk, are you ready?"

"I am."

"I'll go after those other guards, then." Preacher clasped his son's upper arm for a second. "Good luck."

"And to you, Preacher," Hawk replied. They didn't need any more sentiment than that between them.

Preacher drifted back off to the south and disappeared. Hawk swung his legs over the log and catfooted toward the creek, which was about ten yards away. He dropped to hands and knees and then onto his belly. He crawled to the water's edge and slipped into it, disturbing it no more than a sleek beaver would have as he entered the stream.

CHAPTER 8

Like all mountain streams, the water in this one was cold and flowed swiftly as it closed over Hawk's head. He had taken a deep breath just before he slid into the creek. It was about five feet deep, so he was able to swim underwater without touching the bottom. The moonlight was a wavering, silvery glow on the surface above him, but otherwise he was surrounded by darkness.

The creek was no more than thirty feet wide, so he swam across it with strong strokes in a matter of moments. His hands, reaching in front of him, touched the western bank. Under the bluff, no grass or brush grew, so he didn't feel any roots brushing his fingers. Only dirt and rock. He found some rough spots to hang on to and pulled himself closer.

He eased his head above water where the bank rose a couple of feet. He could pull himself up onto it with ease, but water would stream from his body and buckskin garments, and that would make some noise. He needed to take it slow in order to be as quiet as possible. With that thought in mind, he reached higher and found another handhold.

Hawk heard several men snoring as they slept under the bluff's looming overhang. One man muttered, evidently talking in his sleep. Another rolled over restlessly. That one might pose a problem, Hawk thought as he pulled himself up higher. His head came above the bank so he was able to look into the camp.

It wasn't really a cave, he saw, because it was open at both ends, but in other ways it might as well have been. The overhang provided shelter from the elements, along with concealment. It hadn't been able to hide these men from Hawk and his companions, though.

Only a few embers still glowed in the campfire, and the orange light they cast was swallowed up quickly by the shadows. Hawk lifted himself all the way out of the water and rolled onto the bank. He lay on his belly, head raised, using his finely honed senses to the utmost.

He smelled the lingering scent of woodsmoke from the fire, the food these men had eaten for supper, the unwashed flesh of their bodies mingled with pipe tobacco and the tang of whiskey. White man's smell, Hawk thought with more than a little disdain. He inched forward.

He was able to pick out the dark shapes that told him where the men were sleeping as he charted a path among them then moved into the cave.

As he passed within a few feet of some of them, he thought again of the stories he had heard about Preacher. It would be easy to slip the knife from the sheath at his waist, clap a hand over an enemy's mouth, and slit his throat, cutting deep so the hot rush of blood could be felt on his hand. Hawk was tempted, but there was always a chance something could go wrong and an alarm might be raised, and he hadn't determined yet whether these men really did have a woman prisoner—or not.

If they didn't, perhaps on his way back out of the camp he could send a few of them over the divide, as Preacher called it.

A faint crackling and rustling came from up ahead, near the place where the rear wall of the cavelike area met the ground. Hawk paused in his exploration and frowned. He had heard noises like that before. They were the sort of thing that came from a pile of pine boughs being used as a bed when whoever was sleeping there moved around a little. As far as he could tell in the poor light, all the thieves had bedrolls and were using them. Of course, one of them could have piled up some branches to sleep on them instead . . .

Or they could have done that for a prisoner, who wouldn't have a bedroll. Hawk certainly couldn't rule out the possibility.

He crawled forward again, heading toward the sound he had heard.

A shape became visible ahead of him. The right size for a human being, he thought, and not an overly large one, at that. He watched as the person shifted around, evidently searching for a comfortable way to lay. Again the rustling sound accompanied the movement.

Hawk was only a couple of feet away. He pushed himself up on his left elbow and reached out with his right hand. He wanted to see if the person was bound.

Before he could touch the figure, it jerked back and gasped. The prisoner, if that's who it was, must have been awake enough to see him close by. Hawk acted swiftly, lunging forward and following the sound of the gasp to clap his hand over the person's mouth.

"Shhh," he hissed, adding in a barely breathed whisper, "I am a friend." He spoke in the Crow tongue.

The Crow and the Absaroka were related, and so were their languages.

Hemming had said that the prisoner was an Indian woman, and in this region that meant there was a good chance she was Crow. Even if she wasn't, she might understand enough to know what he meant.

She started to thrash around anyway. Hawk knew she was going to make so much noise she would rouse the others, so he did the only thing he could to keep her still and quiet until he could convince her he meant her no harm. He pushed himself even closer and lay on top of her, crushing her against the pine boughs underneath her.

Without even thinking about it, he had known she was female as soon as he put his hand over her mouth. The smooth skin of her face told him that much. Now, the soft curves of the body molded against his offered unmistakable proof. Hawk had been with a few girls before, back in the days before his people had been wiped out, so he knew what they felt like in such an intimate position.

However, it was not the time to be thinking about such things. He lowered his head until his lips brushed against the soft folds of her right ear. The smell of the bear grease in her hair filled his nostrils. He breathed, "My name is Hawk That Soars. I am Absaroka. I have come to free you from these evil men."

She was still squirming some, as much as she could with his weight holding her down, but when he spoke those words, she stopped. She lay there without moving except for the rise and fall of her chest. Hawk felt a fluttering and knew that was the wild beating of her heart.

"Are you bound?" He didn't take his hand away from

her mouth because he didn't fully trust her not to make any noise.

She nodded under his touch in reply to his question.

He used his other hand to explore and found that her arms were pulled back in what had to be a miserably uncomfortable fashion. Her hands were tied behind her back, he thought. Hemming had been telling the truth about that. About everything where the prisoner was concerned, evidently.

"I have to move my hand. You will not cry out."

A shake of her head. He hoped she meant it. He lifted his hand, and other than a soft exhalation of breath, no sound came from her.

Hawk paused to listen intently to the snoring and the other small noises from the rest of the camp. So far his daring incursion seemed to have gone undiscovered. The men were sleeping peacefully.

If he could free this girl and slip out of the camp with her, Preacher, who had probably killed the other guards already, and the others could open fire on the thieves.

"I will cut you loose," Hawk whispered into her ear. "Lie very still." He slid his knife from its sheath.

The girl raised her left shoulder and turned slightly. A soft grunt came from her as she twisted her arms around so he could reach them. He felt along smooth, warm flesh until he came to the rawhide thongs around her wrists. Then, very carefully—he didn't want to cut her—he worked his blade under the bindings and began to saw at the tough rawhide.

His jaw clenched tightly. He knew how important stealth was, but eagerness to be out of this thieves' den welled up inside him. He worked at the bonds and gradually they began to part and fall away. Finally her wrists were free. She made a tiny mewling sound as she moved her arms, and he knew she must have suffered greatly from being tied.

He sat up and turned to find her feet. More rawhide thongs were lashed around her ankles. He sawed on them for what seemed like an eternity before cutting through them at last. He put his knife away and spent several minutes rubbing her feet and calves because he knew that more than likely, they were numb from the circulation being cut off. The girl whimpered again as the blood began to flow.

Hawk regretted causing her pain, but it was necessary. If they had to make a run for it, Hawk didn't want her to stumble and fall because she couldn't feel her feet.

As he rubbed her calf, he became aware that his heart was beating faster. That was because he knew how much danger surrounded them, he told himself. He switched to the other calf and felt the taut muscles under the smooth skin.

When he thought that enough feeling had probably returned to her feet and legs, he bent close to her ear again and told her, "I will crawl toward the creek. You come right behind me and go everywhere I go. I will keep you safe, but you must be as quiet as you can."

"I will, Hawk That Soars," she said.

It was the first time he had heard her voice. As Hemming had said, she was young . . . but fully grown. Hawk already knew that, of course, from lying on top of her.

He didn't want to start thinking about that again, so he turned, stretched out on his belly, and began crawling through the camp toward the creek. The girl followed him. He felt her touch him on the foot now and then, probably to make sure she was still right behind him in the darkness.

The men continued to sleep. Hawk covered five

feet, then ten. He began to believe they would reach the creek and slide into its icy embrace without being discovered.

Preacher had long since lost count of how many men he had killed in his life . . . not that he was the sort who would keep track of such a thing, anyway. What he did know was that he had never killed a man who didn't have it coming.

He was confident that was true of these guards as well, but he wished he knew a little bit more about who they were. Still, they were part of the same group that had tried to kill him and his friends, and they had left behind that fella Hemming to watch for any pursuit, and Hemming had done his damnedest to blow a hole in Hawk.

That might not be enough evidence to hold up in a court of law back east, but it was more than enough for the court of mountain man justice. Getting far away from such strictures was another reason Preacher had headed for the tall and uncut.

So he came up behind the varmints without them ever knowing he was there, looped his arm around their necks, and drove his knife into their backs, right between the ribs and into the heart. Each of the guards died without ever knowing what was happening until too late. And even then, they'd probably been scratching their heads in puzzlement when the Devil greeted them with a big ol' grin on his face and a pitchfork ready for the proddin'.

Preacher killed the guard at the south end of the bluff first, then circled the massive upthrust of rock and did for the varmint at the north end. The way was clear in both directions for Hawk if he had to make a hurried exit from the camp.

Preacher had just lowered the body of the guard at the north end to the ground and was straightening from that task when a branch snapped somewhere behind him.

The explanation for that unexpected sound flashed instantly through his brain. *Hawk had missed a fourth guard.* The fella had been posted somewhere upstream, probably where the canoes were cached. He had spotted Preacher, realized trouble was afoot, and was sneaking closer so he could see what was going on.

Preacher turned, crouching, and hoped he could fade into the shadows so maybe the varmint would decide his eyes had been playing tricks on him.

No such luck. The man stiffened, rasped a curse, and a second later orange flame spurted from a rifle muzzle as a shot blasted. Pretty good shooting for bad light, too, Preacher realized as he heard the ball hum past his head. The fella hadn't missed by much.

But even a narrow miss was usually fatal on the frontier. Preacher jerked the tomahawk from his belt and threw it. His aim was deadly. He heard the *thunk!* of razor-sharp steel striking flesh and biting deep into it, followed by a clatter that had to be the guard dropping his rifle. He had given a warning shout as soon as he fired, but he wouldn't be yelling again. Preacher felt pretty confident of that.

The damage had been done, though. More yelling erupted in the camp under the bluff. Preacher hoped Hawk had the good sense to get out of there, mighty quicklike.

* * *

Hawk heard the shot and the shout but didn't know what had happened and at the moment didn't care. He and the girl were surrounded by men who would kill both of them without a second's hesitation. He surged to his feet, grabbed her arm, and hauled her up beside him. "Run! Into the creek!"

They dashed toward the water. Around them, yelling men struggled out of their blankets and leaped up from bedrolls. Because of the thick shadows underneath the bluff, Hawk and the girl were just more shadows flitting through the darkness.

Somebody was keen-eyed enough to spot them, however, and bellowed, "Stop him! He's stealing the girl!"

Hawk didn't let go of her arm. She panted and gasped as she ran alongside him. A man on his knees reared up and made up a grab for Hawk, who barely slowed down as he kicked the man in the head.

The girl cried out and jerked back against Hawk's grip. Someone had hold of her and was trying to pull her away. Hawk twisted around, drew his knife, and thrust at the shape. He felt the blade bite into flesh. The man screamed and fell back. Hawk jerked the girl toward the creek again. She stumbled and started to fall.

Hawk's arm went around her. Still gripping his knife in that hand, he was careful not to slash her as he swept her off her feet. Cradling her against him—not that easy because she was a substantial girl despite her slenderness—he rushed toward the creek.

As he dived from the bank, he shouted, "Now!" hoping his friends on the eastern bank would know what he meant.

CHAPTER 9

Preacher saw the muzzle flashes from the other side of the creek as Charlie, Aaron, and White Buffalo opened fire on the camp. He had heard Hawk's shout an instant before that, followed by a big splash, so he knew his son was in the water, below the line of fire. Preacher hoped the prisoner was with him—if there actually had been a prisoner.

Either way, Preacher wanted those sons of bitches in the camp to keep their heads down until Hawk had a chance to get away. He pulled his pistols from behind his belt, leveled them at the dark area under the bluff, and pulled the triggers.

Orange flame spurted in the darkness as some of the men in the camp returned fire. Preacher had left his rifle across the creek, knowing he was bent on an errand that required close, quiet work, and since he had emptied the pistols and didn't want to take the time to reload them while he was out in the open, he backed off quickly. A few rifle and pistol balls came close enough for him to hear them, but none found their target.

When he reached the spot where the fourth guard had been, he looked around until he found the body lying on its back with a tomahawk planted in the middle of its face. Preacher wrenched the weapon free, wiped the bloody blade on the dead man's shirt, and faded farther into the shadows, away from the camp. Shots still rang out from both sides of the creek.

Preacher had crossed downstream where the water was shallower. He held his pistols and powder horn above his head as he waded across, then he headed back down the eastern bank toward the log where he had left White Buffalo and the two youngsters. When he got there, he saw two more figures kneeling behind the log—Hawk and the prisoner he had freed from the camp.

"Everybody all right?" Preacher called softly as he came up behind them.

Charlie yelped in alarm. "Preacher, you scared me out of five years of my life, sneaking up like that!"

"We're fine," Aaron said. "Since Hawk freed the young lady and they got back here safely, I think we should retreat while we have a chance."

That was the reaction Preacher expected. He had said as much to Hawk earlier. But Aaron had a point. Judging by the amount of gunfire coming from the camp underneath the bluff, most of the men over there were still in the fight. Preacher and his companions were still considerably outnumbered. Circumstances hadn't allowed them to strike a devastating surprise blow as they had hoped.

The mountain man was a little surprised, though, when Hawk said, "Yes, we should go while we can."

Hawk was the one who had wanted to wipe out the gang of thieves, even if it meant that the prisoner would be killed in the fighting. Clearly, he had changed his mind, now that the prisoner was an actual, flesh-and-blood young woman, rather than just a possibility.

"All right." Preacher picked up his rifle, which was right where he had left it. "Hawk, you head back to the horses first. Take the girl with you. White Buffalo, you go after them. The rest of us will follow, but we'll keep those varmints across the creek occupied for a few more minutes."

Hawk didn't argue. Holding the former prisoner's arm, he led her into the shadows under the trees. Horse and the other mounts were tied about fifty yards away, on the other side of the thick growth that protected them. As soon as Hawk and the girl were gone, White Buffalo fired a last shot at the enemy camp and then hurried after them.

Preacher, Aaron, and Charlie kept up a steady fire for another few minutes. The two young men had been coolheaded so far. Charlie cursed under his breath as a rifle ball from across the creek chewed into the log and sent splinters jabbing into his face.

"You all right?" Aaron asked.

"Yeah, yeah. I'm fine." Crouching low, Charlie rammed a ball and patch down the barrel of his rifle. "Just a little tired of being shot at."

"Reckon you'd better get used to it," Preacher told him. "It seems to happen pretty regularlike."

Finished reloading, Charlie raised up, thrust his rifle over the log, and squeezed off the shot. As his weapon boomed, he yelped again and fell over backward, landing hard on his rear end.

"Charlie!" Aaron exclaimed. "Are you hit?"

Charlie sat up, put a hand to his cheek, and said, "I'm bleeding!"

Aaron knelt beside him. "I can't see very well, but I don't think it's too bad. A shot must have just nicked you."

"You boys get on outta here while you can," Preacher told them. "I'll be right behind you. And keep your heads down!"

Aaron helped Charlie to his feet. They hurried off through the trees. Preacher waited until he had a muzzle flash to aim at, then triggered his rifle again. A howl of pain from the other side of the creek rewarded his patience.

Quickly, he reloaded the rifle, then leaned it against the log. He sat there with his back against the fallen tree for a moment while he reloaded both pistols, making sure they were heavily charged and double-shotted, as usual. It was a good thing he had so much practice at chores like this, he thought, because he didn't have any trouble reloading in the dark.

When he was ready, he raised up and swung around to blast away with both pistols. Then he stuck them behind his belt, grabbed his rifle, and ran into the trees as return fire began to pelt into the trunks around him. None of the lead touched him.

Moments later, he reached the spot where they had left the horses. The others were all mounted, Preacher saw in the moonlight. He also noted that the girl was on Hawk's pony, sitting behind the young warrior with her arms wrapped around his waist.

Preacher swung up onto Horse's back and whistled for Dog. The big cur bounded out of the darkness.

"Which way are we going?" Hawk asked.

"We'll head north first, then cross the creek and

circle west," Preacher said. "Those fellas are on foot, so it ain't likely they'll catch us, but we'll put enough distance between us and them that we don't have to worry about it."

He heeled the rangy stallion into motion and took the lead with the others stringing out behind him. Preacher figured they would travel west for a day or two, then swing back south and make a big loop back to the place where they had cached the furs. He didn't want to give up on all the work they had done to gather those pelts.

And when they stopped, he planned to have a talk with the young woman Hawk had freed. They might as well find out who she was and where she came from, so they could get her back home if at all possible.

Fury filled Jefferson Scarrow's heart and mind, crowding out any other emotion and not leaving much room for rational thought. He wanted to lash out, to punish, to kill. That rage was directed at the strangers who had dared to venture right into camp and steal away the prisoner. Not only that, but six of his men were dead, as well, and a couple more wounded.

Hogarth Plumlee gave him that report on the casualties, then said, "You reckon those were some o' the girl's people who came to rescue her?"

Scarrow forced himself to calm down and think about the question Plumlee had just asked him. "I doubt it. I distinctly heard the man who invaded the camp shout in English to his allies, just before he and the girl dove into the creek."

Plumlee grunted. "White men, then. Say, do you reckon it might've been the same bunch Lopez and the others were supposed to kill? They never came back, and you were worried they might've been wiped out, instead o' the other way around. You thought those fellas might come after us if that happened."

"It's logical," Scarrow said. "But how would they have known we had a prisoner? That has to be the reason one of them slipped into our camp. To free her."

"Hemming," Plumlee said. "They caught him somehow and made him talk. Probably tortured him plumb to death."

"Serves him right for getting captured," Scarrow snapped, then immediately thought that he shouldn't say such things, at least not around the other men. It would be bad for morale. With Plumlee, it didn't matter so much. Plumlee was doggishly devoted to him.

The two of them stood at the edge of the creek while the others tended to the wounded men and carried the dead ones out of the cavelike space underneath the bluff.

"I thought I heard hoofbeats in the distance after the shootin' stopped," Plumlee went on. "I reckon that means they rode off and took the girl with 'em. Well, she's lost to us now, so there ain't no point in worryin' about it, I guess."

Scarrow turned sharply toward him. "What do you mean, she's lost to us?" he demanded. "We're going after them."

The words came out of his mouth without him actually thinking about them, but as soon as he realized what he had just said, he knew it was right. The outrage he felt would never be satisfied until he had reclaimed the girl and avenged himself on the men who had dared to take her.

Plumlee stared at him in the light of the fire they

had built up. Disbelief was on the piggish face. "Goin' after 'em?" he repeated. "Dang it, Jeff, we can't do that. They're on horseback, and we're afoot. We'd never catch 'em."

"In country this rugged, a man on horseback can't move much faster than a man on foot," Scarrow argued. "It's not like they're out on the plains. We can find them. We need to be persistent, that's all."

"But she's just one Injun gal! We got a good start on a small fortune in furs, and there's plenty more out there for the takin'. You can't figure on throwin' all that away just because of one squaw."

"She's more than just one squaw. She's . . . a symbol of those men who dared to defy us."

Plumlee shook his head. "Sorry, Jeff, but I don't give a damn about symbols, and neither do the other fellas, I'm bettin'. If you just want her for herself . . . Well, hell, you shoulda taken her while you had the chance!"

Scarrow knew that, and he regretted his decision. But it wasn't too late to set things right. Besides, he knew something that none of the others did.

"She's not just a squaw," Scarrow said quietly. "In fact, she's not an Indian at all."

Plumlee frowned and asked, "What in blazes are you talking about?"

"Despite her appearance," Scarrow said, "that girl was every bit as white as you and I, Hog."

They rode north a ways, swam the horses across the creek, and then headed west through rugged foothills. Towering peaks loomed ahead of them, blotting out some of the night sky, but Preacher knew a pass that would take them through the mountains. He didn't think he would have any trouble finding it the next day.

He kept them moving at a fairly brisk pace for several miles. The terrain was so rough that often they had to dismount and lead the horses. Preacher didn't like that delay, but he remained convinced the thieves wouldn't come after them. Chances were, that bunch would hunker down and lick their wounds and decide it just wasn't worth it to give chase and probably lose more men.

When he was convinced that they had covered enough ground for the night, he led the group up a slope onto a ridge that was topped by trees and littered with boulders. They would be able to fort up there if they needed to, even though he considered the likelihood remote.

"We'll stay here until morning," he told the others as he dismounted and gestured for them to do likewise.

Hawk took hold of the girl's arm and helped her slip down from the pony's back. He dropped lithely to the ground beside her.

Preacher joined them and asked Hawk in English, "Have you had a chance to find out anything about this girl?"

"I spoke to her in the Crow tongue, and she seemed to understand it," Hawk replied.

Preacher nodded. In Crow, he told the young woman, "We are your friends, and we mean you no harm. This young man is Hawk. The others are Charlie and Aaron, and the old man is White Buffalo, an Absaroka like Hawk. I am called Preacher."

"Preacher!" Clearly, the girl recognized the name.

"That's right. If you've heard of me, you know that

I'm a friend to the Crow people. You can stay with us for a spell. You'll be safe, and when we can, we'll take you back to the village you came from."

She looked down at the ground and shook her head. In a voice almost too soft to be understood, she said, "There is nowhere to go. The Blackfeet raided my home. They killed all the warriors and many of the women and children as well. The others they took as slaves. I was forced to live among them until, finally, I was able to escape."

"You were running away from the Blackfeet?" Hawk asked.

She nodded shyly.

"Then how did you wind up with that bunch of white men?" Preacher wanted to know.

Before the girl could answer, Hawk said, "She is tired. She should rest. There will be time for talk in the morning."

"I want to know what we're dealin' with," Preacher said.

The girl lifted a hand and said, "It is all right. I can speak. I was fleeing from the Blackfeet when I saw a campfire. Some of them were close behind me, so I ran, hoping the fire belonged to friendly hunters, Crow or Absaroka or some other tribe, who would help me." She paused. "But the men were *white*. They were evil. They caught me and would not let me go."

"What happened to the Blackfeet who were chasin' you?" Preacher asked.

The girl shook her head. "There were only a few of them, scouts from the main party. They must have feared the large group of whites and turned back to get the others. They will come after me, if they have not started already."

"How do you know that?"

"Because their war chief has decided that I am to be his woman," she answered bluntly, "and he will not give up and turn back. When Angry Sky wants something, he will kill anyone who gets in his way."

CHAPTER 10

"Angry Sky," Preacher repeated.

Aaron and Charlie had been listening to the conversation, even though they understood only a few words of the Crow language. Aaron must have noticed something about the tone in Preacher's voice because he asked in English, "Is something else wrong?"

Preacher rubbed his chin. "We got more to worry about than just that bunch we just took the gal away from. There's a Blackfoot war chief named Angry Sky who wants to find her, and she's convinced he'll keep lookin' until he does."

Charlie said, "Angry Sky is his name? That sounds rather . . . ominous."

"For good reason," Preacher said with a nod. "I've heard of the varmint. Supposed to be one hell of a fighter, and when the Good Lord was handin' out mercy, ol' Angry Sky was behind the door and didn't get nary a drop."

"He sounds like a dangerous man," Aaron said.

"From what I know of him, he is. And more than likely he'll have a bunch of warriors just like him backin' his play."

Hawk blurted out, "We cannot let him get his hands on Butterfly."

Preacher turned his head to look at his son and cocked an eyebrow. "Butterfly?"

"As I told you, we spoke some while we were riding," Hawk said with a glare. "She is called Butterfly."

"All right, fine," Preacher replied. "Nobody said anything about leavin' her behind for Angry Sky to find. We took her away from those other fellas, so I reckon she's our responsibility now."

The girl sounded scared as she asked in Crow, "What is all this talk?"

"Nothing for you to worry about," Hawk immediately assured her. "We will not let anything happen to you. We will find a village that will take you in, where you can be safe."

He looked at Preacher as if daring the mountain man to contradict him.

"We'll talk about all that in the mornin'," Preacher said. "For now, I reckon we should all get some rest. We'll need to post guards, though." Usually, he could count on Horse and Dog to function as sentries in such situations, but if an enemy with a reputation like Angry Sky's was out there somewhere, searching for them, Preacher was going to be extra careful. "Hawk, you and I will each take a shift."

"Fine." Hawk put a hand on Butterfly's shoulder. "You should sleep. We will watch over you."

"This is . . . so different from what those white men did. They kept me tied all the time, and the way they looked at me and spoke about me . . . Even though I could not understand most of the words—"

"Put those things out of your mind," Hawk told her. "You are safe now, with us."

Impulsively, she threw her arms around his neck

and hugged him. Hawk stood there stiffly for a second, then raised a hand and awkwardly patted her on the back. He looked over her shoulder at Preacher and the others, and in the moonlight, Preacher could see the glare on the young warrior's face. Despite the danger they were still in, he had to hold back a chuckle as he told Charlie, Aaron, and White Buffalo, "You fellas go ahead and turn in. Mornin' will be here before you know it, and there ain't no tellin' what it'll bring."

As soon as streamers of gray light appeared in the eastern sky, heralding the approach of dawn, Jefferson Scarrow had his men unload the rest of the supplies from the canoes. Also on Scarrow's orders, they carried the bundles of stolen pelts into the area underneath the bluff and stacked them against the rock.

"I don't understand this, boss," one of the men said as he paused in the work. "Shouldn't we be puttin' the supplies we unloaded last night *back* into the canoes so we can move on?"

"We're not moving on," Scarrow replied. "At least, not on the creek. We're going to find the tracks of those men who stole the girl from us and pursue them."

That was the first time any of the men except Hogarth Plumlee had heard what Scarrow intended to do. They all stopped in their chores and stared at him.

Finally, a man said, "We're goin' after those fellas? Why?"

"Because I won't allow them to get away with what they've done. It's as simple as that."

Another man spoke up, and his voice had an ugly tone to it. "You mean stealin' a squaw? Hell, there are hundreds of squaws out here. Maybe thousands. Sure, they ain't all as pretty as that one was—"

"That young woman was not an Indian," Scarrow said. "She was white."

That announcement got the same sort of surprised and disbelieving looks that Plumlee had given Scarrow earlier.

"She sure looked like a squaw to me," one of the men muttered.

"That's because none of you got close enough to look into her eyes." *None of you* care *enough about a woman to look into her eyes,* Scarrow thought. "They were blue. As blue as a clear mountain sky."

"I've heard that a half-breed Injun might have blue eyes. Shoot, there are probably trappers' brats scattered all over this part of the country." This from another man.

"No doubt, but I'm still convinced about this one," Scarrow said. "The girl was a white captive. Stop and think about it, for God's sake. Somewhere back east there's probably a wealthy family who'll pay a hefty sum for her safe return."

The men looked at each other. Scarrow's theory was possible, but even if the former prisoner was indeed white, she might also be from some family of poor immigrants who had long since given her up as lost and wouldn't have a dime to pay for her, even if they did want her back.

Scarrow didn't intend to stand there arguing. In a brisk tone of command, he said, "Three of you will stay here to guard the furs and the supplies we leave behind. You can choose who it will be by lots or some other way. I don't care. The rest of us will follow those men who raided our camp last night."

That would give him a party of a dozen men plus

himself, he thought. More than enough to deal with the handful of thieves who had taken the girl.

Some might consider it odd that he regarded *them* as thieves, when he and his companions had come to the mountains for the express purpose of murdering trappers and stealing their furs, but that was the way Scarrow felt. Those men had taken something that belonged to him, and he was going to get it back.

One of the men abruptly shook his head. His name was Denver, Scarrow recalled.

Denver stepped forward and said in a harsh voice, "This is crazy. I'm not gonna throw away everything we've worked for just to chase after some Injun gal. She's not worth it, Scarrow. No female ever born would be worth that."

Mutters of agreement came from several more men.

This was troubling, Scarrow thought. He didn't need a mutiny on his hands, and there was only one way to put a stop to that. He looked at Hogarth Plumlee.

The second in command stepped up to Denver with a friendly smile on his ugly face. Denver had no idea what was about to happen, so he didn't have a chance to block the hamlike fist that crashed into his face with no warning. Denver went over backward, blood welling in thick, dark red gouts from his broken nose.

Plumlee knelt beside him and held his knife to Denver's throat, pressing down just hard enough to make a few drops of blood ooze out around the blade. "All you got so far is a busted beak. You can keep arguin', in which case I'm gonna push down with this knife and not stop until it's scrapin' your backbone. Or you can shut your trap and do what the boss tells you. You oughta know by now that whatever he does, he's got a mighty good reason for it. He ain't steered us wrong so far, has he?"

Denver was afraid to move. It wouldn't take much pressure for Plumlee's knife to slice his throat open.

"Let him up, Hog," one of the men said.

His name was Taylor, Scarrow recalled. He and Denver were friends.

"He'll do like the boss says from now on." Taylor looked at Scarrow. "I give you my word, Mr. Scarrow."

"And I'll take your word," Scarrow said. "Hog, let Denver up."

Plumlee lifted the knife away from Denver's throat, straightened to his feet, and stepped back. Denver rolled onto his side, his breath bubbling and gurgling through the blood that filled his broken nose.

"One of you should set that nose for him," Scarrow went on, "or else it will heal crooked. There's no need for disfigurement. Right now, though, let's finish what needs to be done so we can start out on the trail of those thieves. I don't want to waste any more time."

Taylor helped Denver up. The men got back to work. Scarrow nodded his thanks to Plumlee. He didn't like the idea of ruling by fear—so far during this expedition, pure greed and ruthlessness had been enough to hold the men together—but if that was what it took to get the men to do his bidding, Scarrow was willing to take that step.

Anyway, Denver didn't know how lucky he truly was. For a moment there, Scarrow had given serious thought to pulling out his pistol and blasting a ball through the man's brain.

The night on the ridge passed quietly. Preacher took the first guard shift, then was able to sleep for a couple of hours while Hawk stood watch.

Instinct roused him early, before dawn. He stepped over to where Hawk stood beside a boulder and asked quietly, "Any sign of pursuit?"

"Not yet," Hawk replied. "Do you believe they will come after us, Preacher?"

"I wouldn't, if it was me. We didn't take anything except the girl. I'd go on about my business. Of course, that's what I'd do if I was the same sort of no-account varmint those fellas are . . . which I ain't."

"In the past two days, we have killed a good number of them," Hawk pointed out. "Most men would want vengeance."

Preacher nodded in the shadows. "That's true. And dependin' on how attached they were to the girl, they might want to get her back, too, just like ol' Angry Sky. So, between the Blackfeet and that bunch o' murderin' fur thieves, we can't afford to let our guard down."

"There are always men who wish to kill you, aren't there?"

"Seems like it," Preacher said with a wry chuckle. "Been goin' on now for a long time, too. But I'd have to go back east to get away from 'em, and I sure as hell don't want to do that. Might not do any good, anyway."

"Evil is stubborn and would follow."

"That's been my experience, yeah." Preacher looked around at the still-sleeping figures of their companions. "Did Butterfly seem to be restin' all right?"

"I heard her make a few noises . . . as if she were having frightening dreams."

"I did while I was standin' guard, too," Preacher said. "And I wouldn't be a bit surprised if that's what was goin' on. From what she said, though, she was lucky. Things could've gone a lot harder on her. I don't think she was really mistreated so far, just handled kinda rough."

Hawk nodded. "Yes, I agree. If we can find a safe place for her, she can still have a good life." He paused. "But with a man such as Angry Sky after her, can anyplace truly be safe?"

"Reckon we'll find out. We'd best wake 'em all up. Horses'll be rested by now, and we can put some distance between us and anybody coming up behind us, red or white." He started to turn away, then stopped. "You might want to let Butterfly ride with White Buffalo today. That scrawny ol' man weighs less 'n you do. It'd be easier on his pony carryin' double."

The sky was light enough that Preacher was able to see the frown that appeared on Hawk's face. Obviously, the young warrior didn't like that suggestion.

"That old man cannot be trusted around young women," Hawk objected.

"Don't worry. We'll keep an eye on him. Anyway, he's feeble enough that if he gets too much outta line, Butterfly can just wallop him one. She'll probably be tradin' around and ridin' with everybody at one time or another before this is all over, so don't let it put a burr under your saddle."

"Fine," Hawk said, but he didn't sound like he thought it was fine at all.

He went to wake Butterfly. When he knelt beside her and lightly rested a hand on her shoulder, she gasped and bolted upright. Hawk had to grab her shoulders and say quickly in Crow, "It is all right! You are safe, Butterfly. It is only me, Hawk That Soars."

"Oh." She was breathing hard.

Preacher, standing a few yards away, could tell that she'd been terrified for a second. He supposed that was understandable, since she had gone directly from being a captive of the Blackfeet, bound for a life of slavery and degradation, to being the prisoner of a bunch of white murderers and thieves, where she wouldn't have any reason to expect much better.

She calmed down as Hawk continued kneeling in front of her and speaking in a quiet voice.

Preacher went over to Charlie and Aaron and nudged them awake with a foot. He didn't have to wake White Buffalo because Dog had taken care of that already. The big cur was licking the old-timer's wrinkled, leathery face.

"Dog tells me it is time to rise and face the new day and whatever dangers it may bring," White Buffalo said to Preacher.

"Maybe there won't be no danger."

White Buffalo looked over at Dog, who had sat down beside him. "You are right, my friend. Preacher has gone mad. A day without danger? Impossible!"

"He didn't say I'd gone loco," Preacher objected.

"Can you be certain of that?"

Preacher just shook his head and turned away to get a small fire started. He found Hawk standing in his way. The young warrior wore a puzzled and concerned frown on his face.

"What's wrong?" Preacher asked.

"I was talking to Butterfly just now . . ."

"I know. I saw how spooked she was when you woke her."

Butterfly was now on her feet, looking around as if in search of some brush where she could have a few moments of privacy.

"But you did a good job of calmin' her down," Preacher went on.

"It is difficult to say because the light is not good yet, but when I looked at her, I thought I saw something I did not expect, Preacher."

"What in the world was that?"

"I believe she has blue eyes," Hawk said. "I think she may be white."

CHAPTER 11

Hawk's theory was unexpected, but the idea that Butterfly might actually be white came as no real surprise to Preacher. Immigration from back east had increased in recent years, but for more than a decade, would-be pioneers had been heading west in search of new hopes and new dreams. Many brought their wives and children with them. It was inevitable that some of those families would encounter hostile tribes. Massacres had taken place, and white captives had been carried off to serve as slaves, or in some cases, to be taken into the tribes. White children, especially, were sometimes raised as Indians.

So it was entirely possible that Butterfly had been born to a white family, even though a person couldn't tell that by looking at her.

If that was the case, she had probably been living with the Crow for a long time. Her skin was deeply tanned like that of someone who lived a mostly outdoor life, and she was fluent in their tongue. When Preacher and the others spoke English around her, she gave no sign that the words meant anything to her. No matter what the circumstances of her birth, she was Crow now.

"That don't really change nothin'," Preacher said to Hawk. "She still has Angry Sky after her, and we can't rule out some of the bunch that was holdin' her prisoner comin' after her, too."

Hawk nodded. "I know. But I thought you would like to be aware of the possibility."

"Yeah, we'll check into it later," Preacher promised. "For now, don't say anything to the others, all right? I don't know how Aaron and Charlie would take it."

He could imagine, though. If Butterfly really was white and the two young trappers found out, they might think that she should be taken back east to live among her true people. They would have a harder time realizing that as far as Butterfly was concerned. The Crow *were* her true people.

Hawk nodded his agreement, then went to check on the horses. Preacher built a small fire, as he had started to do a few minutes earlier before the low-voiced conversation with his son. He boiled coffee and fried up some salt pork from their supplies. Hawk and White Buffalo had no use for coffee, but Charlie and Aaron certainly appreciated it. Preacher had developed a fondness for the strong black brew himself.

While they were having breakfast and preparing to break camp, Preacher noticed that Butterfly never strayed far from Hawk's side. He didn't know if the girl was already smitten with him or just trusted him the most because he was the one who had rescued her from the gang of killers and thieves.

She didn't like it when he told her that she would be riding with White Buffalo.

"I would ride with Hawk That Soars," she said with a frown.

"White Buffalo weighs less, so it'll be best to let his pony carry double for a while," Preacher explained. "You'll ride with Hawk again another time. If we can, we'll get you your own pony sometime."

A sullen look came over her face, but Hawk spoke to her quietly enough that Preacher couldn't make out the words, and she nodded. The boy could probably talk her into durned near anything, Preacher mused. He hoped Hawk was honorable enough not to try to take advantage of that.

They mounted up and headed west again, aiming for that mountain pass Preacher knew of. On the far side of it, the terrain wasn't as rugged and they would be able to make better time.

That was good. In that region of steep slopes, thick brush, and deep gullies, determined pursuers, even on foot, might be able to keep up with them. They needed to get through that pass in order to shake off, once and for all, anybody who might be after them.

Only one member of Jefferson Scarrow's group, an older man named Paulson, had much experience on the frontier. The others, including Scarrow himself, were more accustomed to the shadow-cloaked back alleys and smoke-filled taverns of cities back east. All of them had headed west at various times because the law was after them and had arrived eventually in St. Louis, the largest westernmost city. That was where Scarrow had gathered the group and proposed that they band together for the purpose of amassing a fortune in furs . . . illegally, of course.

Paulson was no more scrupulous than any of his companions, but he had been on the frontier longer and had made several legitimate trapping trips up the

Missouri River. Because of that experience, he could read sign better than any of the others.

"This here is where they crossed the creek," he said, pointing to marks on the bank that Scarrow might not have noticed. "And I can see from here where they came out on the other side."

"Are you certain?" Scarrow asked.

Paulson nodded. "I'd bet a coonskin cap on it, Jeff."

Scarrow didn't like it when the men called him Jeff. He tolerated the familiarity from Hog Plumlee since he had known Plumlee longer than any of the others. But he was willing to not make an issue of it with them. He wanted to save his authority for more important matters . . . such as going after the girl and the men who had stolen her away.

As planned, they had left three men back at the camp to watch over the supplies and pelts. The others had waded across the creek to the eastern bank and started up it searching for tracks. Plumlee was convinced he had heard the riders heading north the night before, and Scarrow trusted his second in command.

Paulson had confirmed that.

Scarrow asked the man, "Can you follow the tracks on the other side?"

"I reckon there's a good chance I can," the grizzled Paulson replied. "I expect they were hurryin', just tryin' to put some distance betwixt us and them, so they wouldn't have been takin' the time to cover up their trail."

"We can only hope," Scarrow muttered, then raised his voice to order the men across the creek.

They held their rifles and powder horns above their heads as they waded through the stream.

Once on the other side, Paulson had no trouble

following the hoofprints left by the riders' horses. As he had suspected, the men didn't seem to have been trying to make it difficult for anyone to trail them. Scarrow had a hunch that wouldn't continue to be true. Anyone smart enough to have stolen that girl away from them would soon realize that they needed to take some precautions.

Scarrow pushed the men as hard as he dared, keeping them moving at a brisk pace all morning. They had to climb in and out of arroyos, fight their way through clinging brush, and struggle up steep, hogback ridges.

Several times, Paulson pointed out tracks. "See, along here they had to dismount and lead their horses. They been leadin' more than they been ridin'. Looks like you might've been right about us bein' able to keep up with them, Jeff."

"We have to do more than keep up," Scarrow snapped. "We have to catch them." He looked around at the others and could tell by the expressions on the faces of some of them that they still considered this chase a fool's errand. His hold over them was precarious, he knew. "We'll take five minutes to rest."

That eased the looks of displeasure but didn't get rid of them completely. Scarrow thought about offering the men a little extra from his share of the money they would make from the sale of the furs, but he didn't want to take that step unless it became absolutely necessary. He liked money as much as any of the others.

Something about that girl compelled him, and he realized that he would do whatever he had to in order to get her back.

* * *

The men had drawn lots, as Scarrow suggested, to determine who would stay at the camp with the supplies and pelts. Most of them considered whoever stayed behind to be the winners in that competition, because they thought Scarrow's pursuit of the men who had taken the girl was a fool's errand. No woman was worth the money waiting to be made by continuing to murder any trappers they came across and steal their furs.

The three men left behind were Lew Merrill, Rex Norman, and Will Blassingame. All of them had been thieves for as far back as they could remember, and Blassingame had murdered several women in Kentucky, each of the killings committed with a knife. The three men weren't exactly friends, but they got along all right, which was good since they didn't have any idea how long they would be stuck there, waiting for the others to get back.

Norman had already started eyeing the bundles of furs stacked up at the back of the camp. "You know, if somethin' was to happen to the other fellas and they all die out yonder, we'd have to decide sooner or later what to do about those pelts."

"Scarrow and the others outnumber the bastards they went after," Merrill said. "Do you really think they won't come back?"

"You can't ever tell," Blassingame put in. "Hell, they could get caught in an avalanche or something and wiped out. We can't just sit here waiting for them forever."

Merrill protested. "It hasn't even been a day yet! We shouldn't be talking about this already."

"A fella's got to be prepared," Norman replied. "That's all I'm sayin'." He walked over closer to the pelts and studied the stacked bundles.

The other two joined him. Blassingame got a look of intense concentration on his face, and after a couple of minutes, he said, "You know, the money those pelts would bring amounts to a whole hell of a lot more if you divide it three ways, instead of thirty or even fifteen. I never was very good at ciphering, but I'm sure of that much, anyway."

"I had the same thought," Norman said. "Split three ways, it would be enough to make each of us a rich man, even if we didn't take a single pelt more than what's there right now."

Merrill glared and shook his head. "You boys are fools. Yeah, we could load up those furs and the supplies and head downstream. We'd be back to the Missouri River in a few days and in St. Louis is less than a month. And yeah, maybe we'd be rich." He paused. "But how long do you think it would be before Scarrow tracked us down and settled up with us for deserting him? Chances are, he'd have Hog with him, too. I don't want to have those two trackin' me down and looking for revenge."

"Who's to say they'd even be alive?" Norman demanded with a touch of impatience in his voice. "Anyway, I'm not sayin' we should go ahead and run out now. I just think that after a reasonable amount of time, we need to start thinkin' about—"

He never got to continue that argument. At that moment he made a gagging sound and stumbled forward a step. When Merrill and Blassingame turned their heads to look at him, they were horrified to see a bloody flint arrowhead and about four inches of the arrow's shaft sticking out from Norman's throat. The missile had struck him in the back of the neck and gone all the way through. Crimson blood welled out around the shaft and poured down over his chest as he dropped to his knees.

They knew that Norman was already as good as dead. Ignoring him as he pitched forward on his face and spasmed, they whirled around to see where the arrow had come from and cursed. They had left their rifles over by the campfire.

Not that they would have had a chance to reach the weapons anyway. Several buckskin-clad savages with painted faces stood at the edge of the creek with arrows already drawn back on their bows. They fired as the two white men turned.

Merrill staggered back as what felt like a hard punch with a fist struck him in the chest. He looked down and saw an arrow's shaft with fletching on the end protruding from his chest. Pain blossomed inside him. He roared in a mixture of agony and anger and managed to plant a foot and catch himself before he fell. He had a loaded pistol behind his belt and fumbled at the butt as he tried to drag it out.

Beside him, Blassingame screamed as arrows struck him in both thighs. Blood streamed from the wounds, and the muscles in his legs didn't hold him up anymore. He toppled over.

The Indians charged toward the two men. Merrill finally got his pistol free and struggled to hold on to it with both hands as he raised it and pulled back the hammer with his thumb. He was in too much pain to see straight, so he didn't bother trying to aim, just jerked the trigger and fired blindly.

One of the savages jerked as the pistol ball struck him in the upper left arm, missing the bone but tunneling through flesh and spraying blood when it came out. He dropped the bow he was carrying in that hand.

His right arm still worked just fine, though. He

grabbed a tomahawk that hung at his waist and threw it with force and skill. The tomahawk revolved once in midair, then the head struck Merrill just above the right eye, shattering bone and cleaving into the white man's brain. Merrill crumpled, dead by the time he hit the ground.

That left Blassingame. He screamed again and tried to scuttle backward, dragging his useless legs as the savages closed in around him. He had a pistol, too, and his terror-clouded mind cleared enough to prompt him into making a grab for it. Just as he pulled it from behind his belt, one of the Indians kicked it out of his hand.

Another savage struck Blassingame in the head with the flat of a tomahawk, knocking him down and stunning him. The world spun crazily around him. He flung his arms out to the sides and his fingers scrabbled at the dirt and rock underneath him. In his addled state, he felt like he would go flying off the earth if he didn't hang on.

A fresh burst of pain exploded in him and cleared his mind. He looked over and saw that an Indian had driven a knife through the back of his right hand and into the ground, pinning it there. Blassingame began to shriek in agony.

The thought that the women he had killed with a blade might have suffered just as much never entered his brain.

Blassingame closed his eyes and lay there whimpering, knowing that he was going to die any second. Merrill and Norman were already dead, and he would soon be joining them. It didn't occur to him that the savages might have a reason for sparing his life so far.

A foot smashed into his side in a vicious kick. The impact made Blassingame gasp, start to rise up, and then scream again as that movement caused even more pain in his impaled hand. He opened his eyes as the foot came down on his chest and held him still.

The Indian who loomed over him looked enormously tall from that angle. The savage's broad shoulders and thick chest testified to his power. He leaned over and said in good English that might have surprised Blassingame if he hadn't been so scared and hurting, "I am Angry Sky, white man . . . and before you die, you will tell me what I want to know."

CHAPTER 12

Preacher's memories of the area turned out to be correct, as they usually did no matter where he was. Once he had been in a place or followed a trail, he never forgot it. That afternoon he spotted the pass above them, right about where he had thought it would be. They continued climbing toward it as the day went on.

Any time they were walking and leading the horses, which was often, Butterfly headed for Hawk and walked beside him. Preacher wasn't the only one who noticed that, or the way the two of them spoke quietly to each other in conversations they didn't share with the rest of the group.

"The Crow squaw thinks to make Hawk her man," White Buffalo commented to Preacher. "And he likes the idea."

"Well, you can't blame him for that. She's a fine-lookin' gal, especially considerin' all that she's been through."

White Buffalo sniffed. "She would be happier with an older, wiser, more experienced warrior. One who knows how to deliver unto her true fulfillment as a woman."

Preacher grinned. "And that'd be you, I reckon."

"Many are the comely maidens who first knew pleasure in the lodge of White Buffalo! I remember one who swore that never before had she—"

"I'm sure you do," Preacher interrupted him, not wanting to listen to White Buffalo's boasting for the next ten minutes. "Have you seen any signs of anybody behind us?"

The old-timer shook his head. "No, but Dog is back there somewhere, making certain that we are not followed. He told me that you had ordered him to do so, when he said farewell to me before leaving."

"I don't have to tell Dog to do much of anything. He knows what needs to be done. Shoot, sometimes I think he's the smartest one of the whole bunch of us."

"I would not argue with that. Save for myself, of course."

"Of course," Preacher agreed dryly.

A short time later, Charlie Todd moved alongside Preacher and also brought up the subject of Hawk and Butterfly. "Those two seem to be getting along really well. Hawk's still as serious and solemn as ever, of course, but I think he likes all the attention."

Preacher smiled. "Are you feelin' a mite jealous, Charlie?"

"Me? No, not at all." Charlie shrugged. "Although it would take a blind man not to realize how attractive Butterfly is. There's something *different* about her . . ."

Preacher wondered if Charlie was starting to have his suspicions about Butterfly being white, too. All it would take was a good close look at her eyes. Preacher had been postponing that himself. He didn't see that it made any real difference. He was curious, certainly, but he would satisfy that curiosity when he got around to it and didn't see any point in hurrying.

"Actually," Charlie went on, "Aaron and I have always planned to return to Virginia once we've made our fortunes out here in the frontier. There'll be plenty of very beautiful young women back there to choose from, especially since by then we'll be rich businessmen."

"Got your eye on anybody in particular?"

"Well . . ." Charlie cleared his throat, and when Preacher glanced over, he saw that the young man was blushing. "There *is* one girl named Deborah who I'm quite fond of. She even has a sister who would be perfect for Aaron."

"Hope it all works out for you. I'm glad there won't be any squabbles amongst you and Aaron and Hawk over that Butterfly gal."

"No, I don't think you have to worry about that. But once we find a village where she can stay safely, what if Hawk decides to settle down and stay there with her?"

Preacher drew in a sharp breath. He honestly hadn't considered such a possibility before. The thought of Hawk taking a wife and putting down roots somewhere—at least as much as Indians ever put down roots—hadn't occurred to him. Since meeting Hawk a while back and discovering that the young warrior was his son, the two of them had shared a number of adventures and had saved each other's life on quite a few occasions. Hawk seemed happy to be partnered up with him, so Preacher had assumed that situation would just continue for the foreseeable future.

But it might not, he realized. Hawk might decide he'd had enough of Preacher's wandering ways. And father or not, Preacher didn't feel like he had any right to tell the boy how he ought to live. He hadn't even been aware of Hawk's existence for most of the young man's life.

Anyway, Preacher had never liked it when somebody told him what he ought to do, and he wasn't going to do that to anybody else.

"Hawk can do whatever he wants," Preacher said to Charlie. "Far as I can see, he ain't beholden to anyone."

"But he's your son."

"Young'uns grow up and strike out on their own. I reckon Hawk's bound to do that someday. If not now, then sooner or later."

With that settled, Preacher didn't think about it anymore. Hawk would make up his own mind what to do, when the time came.

But before it did, they had to dodge Angry Sky and maybe the gang of fur thieves, and find someplace where it would be safe for Butterfly to stay.

By late in the day, they were close to the pass. It had taken a long, grueling climb to reach the point, and even though they didn't have very much farther to go, Preacher could tell that the others, except for Hawk, were exhausted and in need of a breather.

He called a halt on a small, fairly level stretch a few hundred feet below the pass, and told them, "We'll rest here for a short spell, then push on and make camp for the night just on the other side of the pass."

"Do not stop on my account," White Buffalo said. "My muscles are like rawhide. They never tire or wear out."

Despite that protest, the elderly Absaroka's face held a faint gray tinge under its normal coppery hue.

"We're fine, too," Aaron said. "If you want to push on, Preacher—"

"We will stop to rest," Hawk declared in a flat tone that didn't allow for any argument. He stood next to Butterfly, who had sat down on a rock and was trying to catch her breath, something that wasn't always easy to do at higher altitudes, once a person was winded.

With that settled, Preacher moved to the edge of a nearby drop-off and peered back at the way they had come. From up there, it was apparent just how far they really had climbed during the day. The landscape fell away for a couple of thousand feet in a breathtaking sweep of green and brown and gray and tan. Far in the distance, Preacher spotted a sparkling, bluish-silver line and realized that was the creek where the thieves' camp had been. Carefully, he studied the territory between there and his current position, not looking at any one area too intently. He knew from experience that it was often easier to spot movement if a person wasn't looking directly at it.

That happened a few minutes later. At first he barely noticed a flicker. When he looked closer from that distance, the movement became a line of tiny dots, no bigger than ants crawling along a ridge which had to be close to a mile away.

Those "ants" were men, Preacher knew, and every hard-won instinct in his body told him they were following him and his companions.

Instantly, he was confident the pursuers were the survivors from the gang that had been holding Butterfly prisoner. A Blackfoot war chief would never allow himself and his fellow warriors to be visible like that atop a ridge. Angry Sky would be cautious all the time, even when he wasn't on the hunt.

White men, though, especially white men new to the frontier, made mistakes like that. Often such mistakes were fatal. Those fellas had survived so far, though, and they were a definite threat to Preacher and his friends.

He took a deep breath and swung around toward the others. "We need to get movin' again. They're back there. The ones we took Butterfly away from."

The girl said something to Hawk, and he answered her in the Crow tongue. Preacher couldn't hear any of the exchange, but he could tell by the sudden look of fear on Butterfly's face that she had asked Hawk what was wrong . . . and he had told her. She was scared that the men would catch up and take her prisoner again.

Preacher could tell that Hawk was trying to reassure her as they got ready to set out again, but Butterfly kept shaking her head and wouldn't be comforted.

The sun had set by the time they reached the pass, although the last red rays still slanted through the gap in the peaks. Preacher led his party through. The slope on the western side wasn't as steep. The tree line was about a hundred yards below the pass. Preacher led the others into the pines and kept moving until he found a good place to make camp.

A rocky knob thrust up from the mountainside. A spring welled from the stone and formed a pool at its base. The ground around the pool was fairly level and covered with grass for the horses.

Preacher nodded. "We'll make camp here."

In Crow, Butterfly said, "We should keep moving. We cannot let those men catch us."

"They're going to have to stop for the night, too," Preacher told her in the same language. "They can't keep moving in country as rugged as it is over there. They'll fall in an arroyo in the dark if they try to. They're bound to be smart enough to know that. We'll get an early start in the mornin', and the goin' should be a lot easier on this side of the pass. We'll pull away from 'em on horseback, and they'll never be able to close that gap."

"You are certain?" Butterfly asked with an anxious frown.

"I am," Preacher said.

Butterfly didn't look happy about it, but she didn't protest anymore. She helped set up the camp as dusk settled around them.

Preacher caught Hawk's eye and drew him aside. "I'm convinced that what I told the gal is right, but it might not be a bad idea for one of us to spend the night up yonder in the pass, just in case. Nobody can come through there without makin' some racket."

"I will do that," Hawk answered with hesitation, but Preacher shook his head.

"It oughta be my job," the mountain man said. "You stay down here with the others and keep an eye out for trouble."

Hawk didn't argue with him. That way he would be closer to Butterfly.

Preacher decided they would have a cold camp that night, just in case. They had enough jerky and pemmican to make a meal on, and the water from the spring was clear and cold. After everyone had eaten and full dark had fallen, he explained that he was heading back up to keep an eye on the pass.

"That don't mean I think anything's gonna happen,

because I don't," he told Butterfly. "I just figure it'd be better to be careful."

"And I will stand guard down here," Hawk said. "So there is nothing to worry about."

"I hope you are right," she said.

As Preacher walked back up to the pass, he reflected that the girl's nervous attitude was yet another indication that she might actually be white. Indian women got scared like anybody else, but often they didn't show it, especially around whites. A Crow woman would have been more impassive than Butterfly had been.

Of course, not all Indians were alike, any more than all whites were, Preacher reminded himself. Maybe Butterfly was just a mite more high-strung by nature. Considering everything that had happened to her, she had a right to be spooked.

With his rifle cradled in his left arm, Preacher sat down on a rock slab in the pass that had fallen from somewhere higher long ages earlier. He sat there, silent and motionless, with only the stars for company, for about an hour before he heard a soft padding sound that was very familiar to him.

"Been wonderin' when you'd show up," he said quietly to Dog when the big cur emerged from the shadows, sat down in front of Preacher, and wagged his bushy tail. "I'll bet you know those varmints are back there on our trail. Probably been watchin' 'em all day."

Dog growled low in his throat as if agreeing.

"Well, we'll outdistance 'em tomorrow. Don't suppose you saw anything of a Blackfoot war party, did you?"

Dog just cocked his head to one side.

"Don't worry about it. If they're back there, they'll

turn up sooner or later. I don't expect Angry Sky to give up as easy as those fur thieves are likely to."

It bothered Preacher, in fact, that the rest of the gang might get away. Right now, finding a safe haven for Butterfly was more important. Anyway, even if he missed them now, if the thieves continued to operate in this region there was a mighty good chance Preacher would run into them again later on.

And if he did . . . there would be a reckoning.

CHAPTER 13

Hawk found the most comfortable spot in the grass around the pool and spread a blanket there for Butterfly.

When he showed it to her, she said, "Stay here with me tonight, Hawk That Soars."

"I cannot," he said.

"We are not of the same clan. There would be nothing wrong with us being together." She put a hand on his arm. "But I speak not of that. Just . . . lie beside me. Your closeness will keep me from being frightened."

"I cannot," Hawk said again. "I must stay awake and stand guard."

"For the entire night? Will you not sleep at all?"

"I will wake White Buffalo later and then sleep for a short time."

"Come to me then," Butterfly implored. "I will not be able to sleep until you are beside me."

Hawk doubted if that was true. He knew Butterfly was exhausted, and he was confident that exhaustion would claim her almost as soon as she lay down, whether he was beside her or not. He just needed to convince her of that.

"I will not be far away," he promised her. "If you wake up and are frightened, or if anything bothers you, you need only call and I will be there in a heartbeat. This I swear."

She stepped closer and put her arms around him again, hugging him tightly to her. "You have delivered me from a terrible fate," she whispered. "Everything I have, everything I am, is yours, Hawk That Soars."

Discomfort and embarrassment stirred inside him. Never had he had a girl declare such devotion to him. It made him uneasy. At the same time, he couldn't deny the alluring nature of her face and figure. Crow or white, it didn't matter. She was a beautiful young woman, and he wanted her.

But with evil men on their trail, he didn't have time for such things. He put his hands on her shoulders and gently moved her back away from him. "Try to sleep," he told her. "In the morning we will talk again."

He felt a certain stiffness in her muscles under his hands as he touched her, as if she felt that he was rejecting her, but she nodded and turned to the blanket he had spread for her and stretched out on it. He moved part of the way around the pool, not wanting to be too close to her and hunkered on his heels next to the water. A few yards away, White Buffalo was already snoring, and Aaron and Charlie were rolling up in their blankets, getting ready to sleep, as well.

Even from where he was, he could hear Butterfly's breathing. It was a little rapid and uneven at first, but it soon settled down into a deep, regular rhythm, and he knew she was asleep despite her protests that she wouldn't be able to doze off without having him beside her.

Hawk looked up toward the pass where Preacher was standing guard. Knowing that the mountain man was up there made Hawk feel better. Did all sons feel that way about their fathers, he wondered? He doubted it. From what he had seen of the white man's world, some men were terrible despite having fathered children. Perhaps sometimes that experience changed what was in a man's heart . . . but not always.

Because he had never known Preacher while he was growing up, he didn't really think of the mountain man as a father, even though he knew that was true. Knowing Preacher was the best trail partner any warrior could have, Hawk was satisfied with that.

When the rest of the camp was asleep, Hawk moved over to a log and sat down. He rested his rifle against the log beside him, leaned forward, clasped his hands between his knees, and settled down to sit and listen to the night. His senses, not to mention those of the horses, would alert him if any threats came near.

The dark hours passed in peace and quiet. Butterfly shifted restlessly in her sleep a few times but never woke as far as he could tell. He kept track of time by checking the stars as they wheeled through their courses in the heavens. When he judged that it was a couple of hours until dawn, he roused White Buffalo to take his place. That would give Hawk enough sleep to stay alert and on a good fighting edge once they set out again in the morning.

"Did anything happen while I slumbered?" White Buffalo asked in a whisper.

"We fought a great battle against Angry Sky and the other Blackfeet, as well as the evil white men who pursue us. The slaughter was massive. Unfortunately, you slept through it."

White Buffalo sniffed. "There is no smile in your voice, but I know you are having sport with me, young warrior. You should respect your elders and not go . . .

what is the white man's word? . . . you should not go japing with them."

"Good night, White Buffalo. Stay alert."

"The senses of White Buffalo are as keen as those of any creature on the earth! White Buffalo's eyes are as sharp as those of an eagle!"

Hawk left the old-timer muttering boasts to himself and walked around the spring-fed pool to the area where Butterfly was sleeping. He didn't stretch out on the blanket beside her, although he felt confident she wouldn't mind if he did, but rather lay down beside her, within arm's reach. If she woke from a bad dream in the part of the night that remained, he would be right there for her.

Hawk didn't need anyone to wake him. Like many of those who lived on the frontier, he possessed the ability to awaken whenever he wanted to. He opened his eyes when the first faint streaks of gray were beginning to appear in the eastern sky. The stars were still bright over most of heaven's reach, and the moon still hung in the west, casting silvery illumination over the landscape.

That was enough for him to see that Butterfly no longer lay on the blanket close beside him.

He pushed up on an elbow and turned his head as he heard a slight noise that he recognized as water splashing quietly in the pool. When he looked in that direction, he saw Butterfly kneeling beside the water. The smooth sweep of her back told him that she had removed her dress, and as she leaned forward, he realized that she was washing.

Hawk looked at the other side of the pool, some twenty feet away. Aaron and Charlie were motionless in their bedrolls, still asleep if their regular breathing was any indication. White Buffalo had moved down to the ground and leaned his back against the log. His head drooped far forward. Despite his boasting, he had dozed off, too. His advanced years had betrayed his good intentions.

Thinking about those things served as a distraction for Hawk, so he wouldn't dwell on the fact that Butterfly was only a few feet away from him, as unclad as the day she was born. He knew he ought to close his eyes and pretend to still be asleep, but he found that impossible to do as she rose to her feet and stretched. The pre-dawn gloom made it impossible to see any details, but the slender, enticing shape of her figure was unmistakable even in the poor light.

She turned toward him, then lifted the buckskin dress over her head and pulled it on, smoothing the soft material down over her hips. Hawk's heart pounded so hard he was sure she was bound to hear it. She didn't seem to realize he was awake, though, and the only courteous thing to do was to allow her to continue with that mistaken assumption.

Or did she realize it? He thought he spotted a hint of a smile on her face. But again, with the bad light it was difficult to be sure.

Hawk sat up and pushed himself to his feet, unwilling to continue pretending. He said to her, "How did you sleep?"

"Better than I expected to," she replied. "I knew you were close by, even though you were not right beside me until late in the night. You should have shared my blanket for that time, Hawk That Soars."

"Perhaps another night."

"Tonight." Her tone told him she did not want him to argue.

He stiffened a little, not liking to be told what to do. "We will see." He turned and walked around the pool to White Buffalo and prodded the old man's foot with his toe. "Arise, one whose senses are as sharp as those of the animals."

White Buffalo didn't budge. Hawk caught his breath. Was it possible that White Buffalo had passed over to the spirit world during the night? He had seen many summers in his life, more than most of the Absaroka.

But then, with a sputter, White Buffalo came awake. He sat bolt upright, looked around wildly, then tipped his head back to gaze up at Hawk. "I fell asleep," he said in a tone of wonderment.

"I will tell no one," Hawk promised, knowing that White Buffalo was ashamed of his lapse.

"But I gave you my word that I would not. I boasted—"

"Say no more about it. Dawn will be here soon. It is time for all of us to rise and get ready to break camp." Movement in the trees caught his eye. "Here come Preacher and Dog now."

During the night, Preacher's eyes had searched the landscape that fell away dramatically to the east, looking for the orange dot of a campfire or any other sign of their pursuers. He never saw one, so he had to give the varmints credit for being smart enough not to announce their position that easily. He remained convinced they were still back there, however.

With the approach of dawn, he returned to the camp and found Hawk, White Buffalo, and Butterfly already up. Hawk woke Charlie and Aaron. They made a hurried breakfast of jerky and pemmican, like their supper had been, then got the horses ready to ride.

Hawk swung up onto his pony's blanket-covered back and extended a hand down to Butterfly, who clasped it eagerly. He lifted her to a position behind him. If it had been up to Preacher, he would have told her to ride with Aaron for the day, but he didn't figure it was worth arguing about.

He had sensed a subtle change in the way Hawk and Butterfly spoke to each other and looked at each other, as if they were even closer than they had been before. Preacher wondered briefly what had happened during the night, but he figured it was none of his business and put that out of his mind.

They set out, heading west again, before the sun topped the peaks behind them. A brilliant wash of orange-gold light filled the sky in that direction.

Preacher had been right about the terrain on that side of the pass. It was still rugged in places, but they were able to ride more often than they had to walk, and it had been the other way around the day before. The next mountain range rose about fifty miles ahead of them. Plenty of country in which they could lose their pursuers, Preacher thought.

He kept them moving at a good pace, stopping now and then to let the horses rest. During those brief halts, Preacher turned to study the pass behind them. At that distance, he didn't think he would be able to see anyone moving through the gap, but it wouldn't hurt to look. He didn't spot any of their pursuers.

At midday they stopped for a longer respite, and Preacher decided to go ahead and satisfy his curiosity. He walked over to Butterfly, who was close by Hawk, as usual. "Butterfly, let me take a look at you," he said in Crow.

"What is wrong, Preacher?" Hawk asked quickly.

Protectively, Preacher thought. "Nothin's wrong. I just want to take a good look at this gal. Haven't really had a chance to since she started travelin' with us."

Butterfly seemed nervous, but she stood quietly while Preacher peered into her face. After a moment, he cupped her chin with his hand and gently moved her head from side to side. Hawk bristled slightly when Preacher did that, but he didn't say anything.

Preacher let go of Butterfly's chin, smiled at her, and patted her on the shoulder reassuringly. "You're a very pretty girl," he told her. "But I reckon you knew that. I never ran into a pretty gal who *didn't* know."

He walked away, aware that Charlie, Aaron, and White Buffalo were watching him curiously. Hawk knew what Preacher had been doing, of course, but the others had no idea.

It was time they did, Preacher decided. He didn't want to ask them to keep on risking their lives when they weren't aware of everything that was going on. He motioned for Hawk to join him, then walked over to the other three.

Butterfly stayed where she was, watching them with a worried expression on her face. Dog was sitting beside her. Her hand strayed to the big cur's head. She rubbed his ears distractedly while keeping her attention on the five men.

"Figured it's time we had a talk," Preacher said quietly in English.

"What's this all about?" Aaron asked. "Is something wrong, Preacher? You and Hawk both seem . . . I don't know. Tense."

"We saw you looking at Butterfly," Charlie said. "Is there something about her we need to know?"

"I don't reckon Butterfly was the name she was given when she was born," Preacher said. "I don't know how she came to live with the Crow, but after lookin' at the shape of her face and seein' that her eyes are blue as they can be, there ain't no doubt in my mind that girl's white."

CHAPTER 14

Jefferson Scarrow had wanted to push on the night before, but as darkness fell, Hogarth Plumlee had talked sense to him.

"None of us have ever been in these parts before, Jeff, not even Paulson. Yeah, it's true the moon'll be up after a while, but moonlight ain't all that dependable. There's too big a chance somebody might fall off a cliff without ever seein' it, or somethin' like that." Plumlee had shaken his head dolefully. "We can't afford to lose too many more men."

He was right about that, of course, and Scarrow knew it. So he had called a halt and told the men to make camp, although with some reluctance.

It had been a cold camp, too. He didn't want the men they were chasing to know they were behind them.

"Paulson says it looks like they're headin' for a pass he spotted up above," Plumlee had said to Scarrow as they gnawed on two-day-old biscuits. "We'll get through there ourselves tomorrow, and then see what's what."

His second in command didn't sound very optimistic, Scarrow had thought, but that didn't matter. He had enough determination for all of them. Some of the men might believe that his resolve bordered on madness, but he didn't care about that. Let them think whatever they wanted as long as they followed his orders.

In the morning, he was anxious to break camp and get back on the trail even before the sun rose, and his impatience grew as the men seemed to take forever to get ready. They were finally just about prepared to set out when ghostly figures suddenly appeared from the shadows under the trees around the camp.

Paulson saw them first and let out an alarmed shout. Scarrow whirled around at the sound and spotted a buckskin-clad shape no more than ten feet away, holding a bow with an arrow nocked and drawn back. More Indians drifted out of the early morning gloom to menace Scarrow and his men.

"Hold your fire!" Scarrow called instantly, seeing that they were surrounded and the Indians could send a storm of arrows flying in at them before the white men could get off more than one or two shots. It would be futile to put up a fight. All of them would be pincushioned with arrows in a matter of heartbeats.

As he looked around, Scarrow estimated the war party, if that's what it was, numbered at least twice as many men as he had. Their fate was in the hands of the Indians, and he was certain they would die within minutes no matter what they did.

But they were still alive, so Scarrow was going to cling to the scant hope they would stay that way.

An Indian who didn't have a bow but carried a flint-lock rifle strode forward and surprised Scarrow by asking in English, "Who is chief here?"

"I'm the leader." Scarrow forced his voice to remain calm and level. If he was about to die, he wouldn't do it with hysterical pleas babbling from his mouth. "My name is Jefferson Scarrow."

"I am Angry Sky, war chief of the Blackfeet." The man was almost as tall as Scarrow, broad-shouldered and powerful-looking. His cheeks had alternating red and black stripes painted on them. "You are the men who made the girl Butterfly your prisoner."

Scarrow and Plumlee exchanged a glance. If this savage who called himself Angry Sky already knew that, what point would there be in denying it? But what was Angry Sky's interest in the girl? Scarrow wondered.

"We never knew her name because she wouldn't speak to us. But if she is a member of your tribe, we apologize, Angry Sky," Scarrow declared firmly. "We had no wish to harm her. True, we kept her tied, but that was so she wouldn't run off and hurt herself. She seemed out of her head when she wandered into our camp. We were simply trying to protect her."

It was an audacious lie, but there was a shred of truth to it, Scarrow thought. Butterfly, if that was her name, had spent a few uncomfortable days and nights, to be sure, but she hadn't been harmed in any real, meaningful way. Scarrow had gone to great lengths to make sure she wasn't molested.

That consideration might save his life and the lives of his men. It was probably the only thing that could.

"The girl is not Blackfoot," Angry Sky said. "She is a Crow slave. But she belongs to me, and I will not be stolen from."

That declaration struck a resonant chord within Scarrow. He felt the same way. "She was stolen from us, too, and we're pursuing the evil men who took her. If we had known who she belonged to, we would have returned her to you before now, Angry Sky. Let us help you get her back."

That was a bold suggestion, but when someone was backed into a deadly corner, often boldness was the only way out.

The light had become better . . . good enough for Scarrow to see the frown that appeared on Angry Sky's face as the Blackfoot war chief considered the proposal that they join forces.

After a moment, Angry Sky said, "Your men told us where to find you."

"The ones we left at our camp by the creek?" Plumlee asked.

Scarrow glared at him for a second. *He* was the one negotiating with Angry Sky for their lives. The addition of a second voice might just complicate things unnecessarily.

"One man answered my questions," Angry Sky said without really addressing what Plumlee had asked. "The other two were already dead. The third man said the girl was your prisoner."

"I've already explained that," Scarrow said. "Keeping her tied was for her own good. We fed her, protected her, kept her from wandering off again. As I told you, she was out of her head. Touched by the spirits, isn't that what your people say?"

Angry Sky grunted. "What you say may be true," he allowed, "but how can you be allies with us when we killed three of your friends?"

"That *is* unfortunate." Scarrow shrugged. "But I think we all understand perfectly well the notion of practicality. You outnumber us by a two-to-one margin. You can kill us with scarcely any effort, and I seriously doubt that we could kill more than one or two of you in return."

Plumlee said, "I, uh, don't know that I'd be pointin' those things out to him, Jeff."

"Nonsense," Scarrow responded. "Angry Sky is an intelligent man, obviously. He knows the situation every bit as well as we do." He smiled. "And he knows that we have a common enemy and a shared objective . . . that young woman."

"You talk too much," Angry Sky snapped. "But for now, you live. That is my decision. Tell your men not to test my mercy."

"We'll cooperate. I give you my word on that." Scarrow added, "You can consider us part of your war party now."

"White?" Charlie and Aaron exclaimed in surprise at the same time. They turned their heads to stare at Butterfly, who suddenly looked frightened, as if she wanted to bolt.

Hawk hurried over and spoke to her in a low voice, assuring her that no one was upset with her or intended her any harm.

"How is that even possible?" Charlie asked. "I mean . . . look at her."

"She certainly appears to be an Indian," Aaron added.

Preacher shook his head. "Like I said, she has blue eyes. I never saw an Indian who did, even a half-breed. Her cheekbones are pretty high, her hair is dark, and her skin is tanned mighty deep. Put all those things together, and she resembles a Crow, sure enough. But that don't make her one."

"Where did she come from?" White Buffalo asked.

"Ain't no way of knowin', unless she can remember enough to tell us," Preacher said. "Chances are, her family was on its way out here to settle somewhere when they got attacked, and she survived."

White Buffalo shook his head. "The Crow are a peaceful people, except when fighting the Blackfeet."

"Yeah, most of the time, but they've had some clashes with the whites. And the girl's family could've been jumped by a war party from some other tribe that took her prisoner. Slaves get traded around from tribe to tribe." Preacher shrugged. "Or maybe nobody took her prisoner. Could be she was the only survivor after a battle and wandered off on her own. The Crow could've found her and took her in."

"That is more likely to have happened," White Buffalo said. "The Crow are also a kind, generous people."

Aaron said, "Does any of that really matter? What's important is that if she's white, we should be thinking about taking her back to St. Louis instead of trying to find some Indian village where we can leave her."

"That's right," Charlie said. "We might even be able to find out her real name and where she comes from. She could have relatives who are worried sick about her."

That was exactly the way Preacher had expected the two young trappers to react to the news.

He said, "As far as she's concerned, Butterfly *is* her real name, and she comes from that Crow village the Blackfeet attacked. She's been out here long enough she probably doesn't remember anything else. As for any relatives . . . I reckon it's been long enough that they've given up on ever seein' her again."

"But shouldn't you at least try to find out what she remembers?" Aaron insisted. "It seems to me like the only decent thing to do."

Charlie nodded in agreement.

They still had to wait a while longer to let the horses rest more, so Preacher decided he might as well humor his two young friends. "I'll talk to her, but it's likely she won't remember nothin' except what she's already told us."

White Buffalo muttered, "It is best just to leave this be. No good can come of meddling when things cannot be changed."

Preacher sort of agreed with the old-timer, but he went over to Butterfly anyway. The girl looked apprehensive as she stood there with Hawk and Dog.

"Enough, Preacher," Hawk said in English. "She is frightened."

"I'm not gonna hurt her, and you know that. I'm just gonna talk to her, that's all."

Hawk frowned but didn't argue as Preacher looked intently at Butterfly and smiled. "I want to ask you a few things, Butterfly," he said in Crow. "Do you remember ever being called anything else?"

The question made her look confused as well as nervous. "You mean . . . before I was Butterfly? I have always been Butterfly, ever since I lived with the Crow people."

"No, I mean before that," Preacher said. "When you lived with white people like me and Aaron and Charlie."

Her gaze darted to the two young trappers for a second, then back to Preacher. "I never lived with Aaron and Charlie."

"Not them, but people like them. An older man and a woman, maybe some kids about your age. A family. A white family that you were part of."

Butterfly shrank against Hawk, who put his arm around her shoulders as she said, "Why does he ask these things? I do not know what he's talking about."

In English, Hawk said to Preacher, "You are scaring her. You should leave her alone and let her be Butterfly."

White Buffalo nodded in agreement with that statement.

Preacher had seen a flicker of something in Butterfly's blue eyes, however, and it goaded his curiosity that much more. He said in Crow, "Don't be frightened, Butterfly. Nothing will change. You will stay with us, and we will protect you. But we need to know what you remember about the long-ago days before you came to live with the Crow. Before they were your people. When you were a little white girl."

She shook her head stubbornly and whispered, "That . . . that was a bad time."

"You *do* remember it?" Preacher prodded.

"I remember . . . a man. He wore . . . a long black coat. He shouted words I . . . I never understood. And there was a woman. She was kind, but . . . her words . . . I cannot recall them. I rode with the two of them in a . . . a lodge that moved. Big beasts . . . like buffalo . . . pulled it."

"A covered wagon," Preacher said in English. "Pulled by a team of oxen. She's rememberin' her folks." He went on in Crow, "What happened then, Butterfly?"

She shook her head, closed her eyes, pressed her face against Hawk's chest, and shuddered. "It was bad," she said, her voice muffled. "Very bad. Much shouting. Loud noises. And people . . . people being hurt . . ."

"That is enough," Hawk snapped in English. "You have proven that she was part of a settler's family, Preacher. What else do you need to know? Why does any of this matter?"

"It's important because we need to know where she came from," Aaron said before Preacher could reply.

"If we can find out where she belongs, we can see to it that she gets back there."

"She belongs here!" Hawk cried. "Even if she was white once, she is Crow now! She has no place in the white man's world. Look at her!" Bitterness came into his voice as he went on. "In their eyes, she is a filthy redskin. No one would want her."

Preacher had a hunch the boy was right about that. White children who had been raised as Indians had been returned to civilization before. Preacher had heard about a number of such cases. And very few of them, he recalled, had ended well for anybody. The young-sters couldn't give up Indian ways, and the whites, even their families, regarded them as unclean.

"It might not be the best thing for her to go back—" He stopped short when Butterfly whispered some-thing else.

Hawk, with his arm still around her shoulders, looked down at her and asked, "What was that? What did you say, Butterfly?"

"C-Caro . . . line. Caroline. I remember . . . the woman . . . she called me that." She lifted her eyes, looked at the circle of men around her, and asked, "Is that my name? Am I . . . Caroline?"

CHAPTER 15

Angry Sky and his party of searchers were mounted, and they even had a few extra of the sturdy Indian ponies they rode. Not enough for each of Jefferson Scarrow's men to have his own horse, but some rode single and some rode double, and that way they were able to keep up with the Blackfoot warriors.

The white men and the Blackfeet exchanged plenty of wary, hostile looks. The truce between them was a very tentative one, based solely on the shared obsession of the two leaders. Some of the men in both groups surely wondered what it was about the young Crow woman called Butterfly that would inspire anyone to go to such lengths to find her.

It wasn't just the desire for a woman that prompted this pursuit, though, Scarrow knew. Even more than that, it had to do with pride and respect. He and Angry Sky couldn't maintain their leadership positions if they sat back, did nothing, and allowed someone to steal from them. Such audacity had to be punished. Their followers had to know that anyone who dared to cross them was taking his own life in his hands.

Now that they had joined forces with the Blackfeet,

they didn't have to rely on Paulson to follow the trail anymore. The Indians would have scoffed at the idea that a white man could read sign as well as they could. They might have even been offended by such a suggestion, and Scarrow didn't want to give any offense to them until he had what he wanted.

After Angry Sky had talked to some of his men in their tongue, hopefully making sure they understood that the white men were not to be killed, he started riding toward the pass that was still several hundred feet above them. That was the way Scarrow's party had been going, so Scarrow knew the Blackfeet agreed with Paulson about where the trail led.

The warriors surrounded the white men as they rode, no doubt to keep them from trying to escape or any other tricks. As they moved along, Plumlee brought his pony alongside Scarrow's mount—as the leader and second in command of their group, they didn't have to ride double—and said quietly, "Jeff, have you given any thought to what we're gonna do once these heathens get their hands on that girl? They're still gonna outnumber us by a bunch, and then they won't have no more use for us."

"You're not telling me anything I haven't already considered, Hog," Scarrow replied, also keeping his voice low enough that the conversation wouldn't be overheard. Other than Angry Sky, who had already demonstrated that he understood English, Scarrow had no way of knowing which of the other savages also spoke the language of civilization, if any. "The only thing I was thinking about back there was keeping us alive for the moment."

"And I'm mighty glad you did, don't get me wrong about that. I just think our days are still numbered unless we think of some way to turn the tables on these redskins."

"I know," Scarrow said. "I have been thinking about it, and it seems the best way to preserve our lives is to make certain that *we* control the girl's fate, not the Blackfeet."

"You mean we're gonna steal her from the Injuns after they steal her from the fellas we've been chasin'?"

"Something like that . . . however we can manage it. But she's our path to freedom and safety, Hog, mark my words about that."

Plumlee scratched his bristly chin. "I hope you're right, Jeff. I surely do."

A short time later as they approached the pass, Angry Sky signaled for his men to halt, and surrounded by Blackfoot warriors as they were, Scarrow's party had no choice but to do likewise. Angry Sky sent a couple of men ahead as scouts. They disappeared into the pass.

"You reckon those fellas might've set up an ambush on the other side?" Plumlee asked Scarrow.

"Highly unlikely. I believe their main concern ever since they raided our camp by the creek has been to put miles behind them. But anything is possible, I suppose, and Angry Sky, obviously, is a cautious man."

After some time had gone by, the scouts returned. They weren't hurrying, which told Scarrow they weren't being pursued and hadn't really found anything on the other side of the pass except maybe some tracks left by their quarry. The warriors reported to Angry Sky, who listened gravely to them, then nodded and turned halfway around on his pony to wave the group forward. The large party, now over forty men strong, moved into the pass.

As they descended the tree-covered slope on the other side, Paulson pointed out a clearing with a spring-fed pool to Scarrow and Plumlee. "That was where they made camp last night, I reckon. I can see signs that horses were here, and it's a good place to stop."

"But they're not here now," Scarrow said.

"Nope. I figure they've been gone for a while, but they're up there ahead of us somewhere. We'll catch up to 'em." Paulson sighed and echoed the concern Plumlee had shown earlier. "And then there's no tellin' what'll happen . . . but I reckon there ain't much chance of it bein' good."

The stricken look on Butterfly's face as she asked if her name was Caroline touched Preacher, so his voice was gentle as he told her, "I ain't sure why you'd know that name if it wasn't yours. Unless maybe it was your ma's name."

Hawk still looked protective. "Leave her alone," he said bluntly. "This torturing her with memories serves no purpose."

Preacher supposed he was right, but it was Butterfly—or Caroline—herself who said in Crow, "No, I . . . I should know who I am." She must have been able to tell what Hawk was saying by the tone of his voice. Or else she understood more English than any of them had realized.

Maybe on some deep-down level . . . Preacher wondered. He said, "Think back. You know what happened to the man and the woman you remembered."

She gave a quick shake of her head. "No. It was bad. I do not want to remember. There was much blood, so much . . ." She took a deep, shaky breath.

"But after that, I was alone. I walked and I walked and I walked . . . And then the Crow were there, and I was one of them. I was Butterfly. My mother was Red Deer. My father was Iron Bow. Many summers went by, and I was happy. Then the Blackfeet came . . ."

All that talk was in the Crow tongue.

Charlie asked, "What is she saying? What does she remember, Preacher?"

"She thinks her name may have been Caroline," Preacher explained. "I don't know where else she would've ever heard that unless it was her name. Or maybe that's what her ma was called. Her real ma, not her Indian one."

"It doesn't seem likely that would have stuck with her for this long if it was her mother's name," Aaron said. "Surely it was what she was called."

"What else does she remember?" Charlie asked.

"A man and a woman . . . bound to be her folks . . . and from the way she described the man as wearin' a long black coat and shoutin' all the time, I can't help but wonder if he was some sort of preacher." The mountain man grunted. "I saw a fella like that on the street in St. Louis once, and seein' him had a lot to do with how come I'm called Preacher . . . But hell, you've heard that story more 'n once. Ain't no need to go into it again.

"Best I can tell from what the girl said, she and her folks started west in a covered wagon. She didn't say anything about other kids, so it may be that she was an only child. Then somethin' bad happened to the grown-ups. Jumped by hostiles, more than likely. Butterfly got away somehow and was on her own, wan-derin' around, when some friendly Crow came upon her and took her in. That was many summers ago, she said." Preacher rubbed his chin in thought. "Ten or twelve years, I'd reckon, but that's just a guess. She's lived with the Crow ever since. She *was* a Crow, as far as she or anybody else was concerned. That's the story."

"What a tragedy," Aaron said in a hushed voice.

"For her folks, it was," Preacher agreed, "but from the sound of it, things could've wound up a heap worse for her. She survived whatever happened, found herself another family, and lived a happy life for a long time."

"Lived a happy life? As a savage?" Charlie exclaimed.

With a chilly note in his voice, Hawk said, "I was raised in an Absaroka village and was content with my life until the Blackfeet came. More than content."

"Well, sure, but you're not—" Abruptly, Charlie stopped whatever he'd been about to say.

"Not white?" Hawk finished for him. "Should I have been happy as a savage only half the time because I am only half Indian? Does a person somehow know that without being told?"

"Stop this wranglin'," Preacher said. "It don't accomplish a damn thing. Anyway, it's time we were movin' on again."

"You don't think we should take her back to St. Louis and try to find out who she really is?" Aaron wanted to know.

"I don't think we should be worryin' about anything right now except stayin' ahead of a bunch of varmints who'd just as soon kill us and steal her back."

"Are you talking about those fur thieves?"

"And Angry Sky," Preacher said. "Don't forget about him. I'm more worried about his bunch, because they might have horses. We know those other fellas are afoot. The Blackfeet might still catch up to us."

White Buffalo said, "Then we should go. Talk, talk, talk. Just a waste of time."

That was a mite humorous, coming from the biggest talker in their group, Preacher mused, but even White Buffalo knew there was a time to shut up and get moving.

And it was one of those times.

Preacher kept them moving at a brisk pace the rest of the afternoon, checking their back trail from time to time to see if he could spot anybody back there. He didn't, but as a precaution, he told Dog to hunt, anyway. Dog knew what that meant and turned to lope back the way they had come.

Butterfly still looked a little shaken and subdued, and she didn't say much as she rode behind Hawk on the young warrior's pony. Preacher had to think for a spell before he came up with the phrase he was searching for to describe what his questions had done. They had opened a bag of worms, he finally decided was the right way to put it. He had opened up the past in the girl's mind and showed it to her in all its slimy, squirming unpleasantness.

And worst of all, Hawk was right. Knowing what they now knew about Butterfly didn't change a damned thing. They were still in danger from Angry Sky and maybe the band of fur thieves, too.

Late in the day, Preacher spotted a line of thicker vegetation up ahead and knew it probably marked the course of a river. That jogged his memory. There *was* a river that ran through that area, and the last time he had been there, several years earlier, a Crow village had been located on that river about twenty miles upstream from where they were. It might still be there or it might not. The Crow weren't as nomadic as some tribes, but they moved around from time to time. If it was, that would be the closest place he and his friends could find a new home for Butterfly. The village Preacher remembered was big enough that even Angry Sky might think twice before attacking it.

All they had to do was stay ahead of the Blackfeet for the day or two it would take to reach the village.

Preacher pointed out the trees that grew along the river and told the others, "We'll make camp up there. We've covered a lot of ground today, and the horses need to rest."

"What about the Blackfeet?" White Buffalo asked. "I feel . . . a disturbance among the spirits, as if they are trying to warn us."

"Blackfoot ponies have to rest just like ours do. Anyway, it ain't gonna do us any good if we ride these horses into the ground. Then those varmints would catch up to us for sure."

White Buffalo frowned and muttered something about disregarding the wisdom of the elders, but Preacher just waved the others on and led the way to the river.

If the stream had a name, he didn't remember it. It was shallow but at least a hundred feet from bank to bank, flowing swiftly in several channels that wound their way among sandbars and outcroppings of rock and gravel. Preacher seemed to recall that rapids ran in other stretches and could be challenging to somebody in a canoe if they didn't know what they were doing. He and his companions wouldn't have to worry about that, however.

The banks were grassy on both sides, but those open areas were narrow and beyond them the pines, spruce, and fir grew thickly. Aspens and cottonwoods dotted the banks in places. With snowcapped mountains in the distant background, it was as pretty a location as anybody was likely to find in the high country. Preacher could have stayed in a place like that for the rest of his life. Sometimes he wondered why he didn't do just that. Build himself a cabin, live off the land, just enjoy peace and quiet and the Good Lord's handiwork.

Problem was, tranquility never lasted. Some son of a buck always came along and messed it up, usually by trying to carve out Preacher's gizzard with a knife or bust his skull open with a tomahawk or blow a hole in him with a rifle or pistol. If it weren't for those things, he'd be a plumb peaceable man.

Sometimes when he told himself that, he even believed it.

Preacher walked Horse across the river with the others trailing behind him. The water came up about three feet on the stallion's legs in the deepest part. They emerged onto the western bank. "This'll be a good spot to camp. Charlie, Aaron, you boys gather some of those good-sized rocks along the edge of the river and we'll use 'em to build a fire ring. Be nice to have some hot food and coffee this evenin'. The flames won't show and the breeze is from the southeast, so it'll carry the smoke smell away from anybody who's followin' us."

He didn't say anything about the Crow village he thought might be relatively nearby. He could do that in the morning when they turned north again and followed the stream toward what he hoped would be Butterfly's new home. He couldn't think of her as Caroline just yet. As long as she wore buckskins and had bear grease in her hair, he probably never would.

CHAPTER 16

Preacher knew that Aaron and Charlie wanted him to try to find out more about Caroline's past. Hawk and White Buffalo thought he ought to leave her alone, though, and that evening by the fire, they sat on either side of her and glared protectively. Preacher didn't see any need to force the issue, so he just smiled across the fire ring at her and went on eating the salt pork he had fried up for their supper.

Caroline surprised all of them by saying, "I have been thinking about the things you asked me, Preacher."

"You do not have to talk about that," Hawk told her. "You should put all of it out of your mind."

She shook her head stubbornly. "No, it is part of me," she declared. "How can I be who I really am if part of me is missing?"

Hawk's frown made it clear that he didn't like the way the conversation was going, but he wasn't going to sit there and argue with her.

Preacher said, "Anything you want to talk about is all right with us, Caroline."

His use of her white name caused a troubled look

to pass over her face for a moment, but then she said, "I have been thinking about the man and the woman I remembered earlier. The man always had something with him. A thing with . . . with tanned hide on the outside . . . and inside many things that were thin like rubbed leaves. He did this with it, many times." She pantomimed opening a book and turning the pages.

Preacher had had a pretty good idea what she was talking about, and her actions confirmed his hunch.

Aaron and Charlie had been listening intently to the conversation, even though they didn't understand a word of the Crow tongue.

Charlie said, "What's she talking about? She looks like she's pretending to read a book."

"I reckon she is," the mountain man said. "She's talkin' about her pa, the one I figured might have been a preacher. She said he always had a book with him and read from it all the time."

"A Bible," Aaron said. "A minister would always have a Bible with him."

Preacher nodded. "Yep." To Caroline, he went on in Crow. "What else do you remember about him?"

"He never smiled or laughed." She glanced over at Hawk. "Like Hawk That Soars, only worse."

"I smile," he protested. "Whenever there is something to smile about." His solemn expression weakened his argument, though.

"The woman was much happier," Caroline continued. "I remember her singing. Not the kind of songs the Crow sing, but the sound was pleasing. I remember . . . a big lodge . . . with hard walls and floor."

"A house," Preacher said.

Caroline shook her head. "I do not know that word. But I think we lived there, although it was so long ago that I have almost no memories of it. I remember the lodge on wheels better. Hide was stretched over the top of it, to block the sun."

"A covered wagon."

"If you say that is what it was called, then so it is," she said.

"Did you ever see any more like it? Did any white settlers ever come to the village of your people?"

Caroline shook her head. "I never saw another lodge on wheels. Whenever I thought about it, when I was younger, I decided it must not be real. I believed that it had come to me in a dream, and perhaps I would see one like it someday, but mostly I just thought that it was not real."

"It was real, all right," Preacher assured her. "These days, immigrants use 'em to travel west. Folks have started talkin' about somethin' called the Oregon Trail and say it won't be long before thousands and thousands of people will be rollin' along it in wagons just like the one you described."

"Thousands and thousands," Caroline repeated. "What is this?"

"You saw the sandbars in the river?"

She nodded.

"Think of each grain of sand in one of those bars. Now think about that many white people headed west to farm and run stores and build houses . . . big lodges with hard walls and floors."

Caroline's eyes widened. She shrank back against Hawk's shoulder, and he put his arm around her again.

"That sounds . . . terrible," she said in an awed voice. "That is too many. Too many!"

Preacher smiled and told her, "I can't say as I disagree with you. But that's what's comin'. Shoot, it may already be here. And I don't reckon there's a blasted thing any of us can do to stop it."

"*Now* what are you talking about?" Aaron asked, a little impatiently.

"Civilization," Preacher said. He added dryly, "We ain't all that sold on it."

Jefferson Scarrow sat beside the fire and enjoyed the warmth radiating from it. Even at that time of year, nights in the high country were often quite chilly.

Actually, considering how close he and his companions had come to death, he was very happy to be feeling *anything*.

Hogarth Plumlee, wearing a perpetually worried scowl, looked around at the camp and said quietly to Scarrow, "If them heathens start doin' some sort of war dance, I'm gonna try to fight my way outta here, Jeff. I probably won't make it, but I'll be damned if I'm gonna just sit here and let 'em slaughter me."

"There's not going to be any slaughtering," Scarrow said with more confidence than he really felt. What if the Blackfeet had brought them along simply so they could torture and kill the white men at their leisure? That possibility couldn't be ruled out, but so far he hadn't seen any signs of it happening.

In fact, the Indians were ignoring the whites, other than a couple of warriors armed with flintlock rifles who stood nearby, obviously acting as guards. The rest of the Blackfeet had a separate, larger campfire a dozen yards away where they chattered to each other in their mostly incomprehensible tongue.

Scarrow would have been more worried, and Plumlee would have been spoiling for a fight even more, if they had been able to hear and understand the conversation going on between Angry Sky and Red Rock, the most senior and trusted of his warriors.

"The warriors believe you are making a mistake by trusting the white men," Red Rock advised Angry Sky as they hunkered at the edge of the light cast by the larger campfire.

"Why do they believe I trust the white men?" Angry Sky asked.

"You have not taken their guns."

Angry Sky grunted disdainfully. "They will not use their guns against us. There are too many of us and not enough of them. Their guts are like water. They know if they try to hurt us, we will kill them all faster than a hummingbird can beat its wings."

"Most believe we should have killed them when we first found them. I have heard many say as much."

Angry Sky finished gnawing the meat off the leg bone of a rabbit he had roasted over the fire earlier. He threw the bone into the flames. "Any who dare to talk against me should do so to my face. Any who wish to challenge me for leadership are free to do so."

"No one wishes to do that," Red Rock replied without hesitation. "You are our war chief, Angry Sky, and will remain so, but Blackfoot warriors have their own minds. They want to know why our sworn enemies remain alive."

"And so they sent you to find out."

"No one had to send me," Red Rock said. "I would like to know the same thing."

Angry Sky's lips drew back from his teeth in a snarl. "Because the white men are fools! When we find the ones who stole the Crow woman, *they* will be the first to attack. They will die while killing our other enemies. And any who survive will die as soon as the battle is over."

Red Rock drew in a deep breath. "Where is the

honor in that?" he demanded. "It is not the Blackfoot way to use others to slay our enemies!"

"It is not the Blackfoot way to be foolish, either," Angry Sky snapped. He jerked a hand in a curt gesture. "That may not be the way it happens, but there is no harm in keeping the white men alive to see if we can use them to our advantage."

Red Rock shook his head. "Every white man who continues to draw breath harms our people. Our warriors can never be content as long as one white man lives."

Then they were doomed to never be content, Angry Sky thought. He understood there were far too many white men for all of them to ever be slain. As war chief, he had accepted as his mission in life the killing of as many white men as possible. He could only hope that when his time came to enter the realm of the spirits, he would carry the lives of enough enemies with him to ensure happiness for the rest of all time.

Now practical matters occupied his attention. He told Red Rock, "Send two scouts ahead in the night to see if they can find the ones we seek. Choose good warriors, strong and fast."

"Tall Pony and Bent Finger," Red Rock said without hesitation.

Angry Sky nodded, satisfied with Red Rock's choices. "If they find the men who stole the Crow woman, they are not to attack. They will come back here and tell us where our enemies are."

"I will be sure they understand," Red Rock agreed. He started to stand up, then paused and chuckled softly. "Using white men to kill white men . . . It is an odd idea, but I can understand why you thought of it, Angry Sky. In the end, all the white men die."

Angry Sky nodded and repeated, "In the end, all the white men die."

Charlie Todd rolled over in his blankets and muttered something as he came half-awake. He wasn't alert enough to know what he said. He settled down again, using his saddle as a pillow, and tried to sink back into the welcoming darkness of slumber.

A few seconds later, his eyelids flickered open and he sighed quietly. His bladder wasn't going to allow him to go back to sleep right away. The pressing fullness of it urged him to get up and go off into the bushes.

He remembered his father back in Virginia complaining about how many times he had to get up during the night to use the chamber pot. That common malady got worse with age, according to Charlie's father. Charlie was starting to believe that was right, and he wasn't even old yet! He was still a young man. He shouldn't have the same problem.

But try arguing with a full bladder, he thought. It wasn't going to listen to reason. He had no doubt of that.

So he pushed his blankets back and sat up.

Charlie looked around the camp, which was dark and quiet except for the river bubbling along a few yards away and a few night birds chirping in the trees upstream. Hawk was on guard duty, sitting cross-legged on the ground with Dog beside him. The big cur was stretched out, chin resting on his paws, but his ears were up and alert. He had trotted into camp late that evening. White Buffalo talked with Dog, or at least claimed to, and reported that Dog had not found their enemies anywhere close behind them.

Charlie didn't believe for a second that White Buffalo actually could talk to animals or that they could talk to him, but the elderly Absaroka seemed convinced of it, and Charlie didn't see anything wrong with humoring him. He and Aaron had talked about it, and Aaron felt the same way. They liked White Buffalo, and if it made the old-timer happy to chatter away at animals, then more power to him.

Charlie stood up, and Hawk was on his feet instantly, too. "What are you doing?" the young warrior asked in a whisper.

"I have to relieve myself," Charlie explained.

Hawk nodded in the moonlight. "Then go."

Charlie made a face. "Not here, right out in the open."

"There is nothing to be ashamed of, Charlie."

"I'm not ashamed. I just like a little privacy, that's all."

"On the frontier, privacy can be dangerous," Hawk warned.

Charlie pointed and said, "There are some bushes right there, not twenty feet away. I'll just go in there and be right back. You know there's nothing around to be worried about or you and Dog would have noticed it by now."

Hawk considered, then nodded slowly. "This is true. Do not waste any time, and do not go farther than the edge of those bushes."

"Of course," Charlie agreed. In his sock feet, he walked over to the bushes, being careful not to make enough noise to wake anyone else. Behind him, Hawk and Dog settled back down to standing guard again.

Charlie parted the branches and stepped into the gap he had created. The brush closed in around him. Some of the branches poked at him uncomfortably, so he moved around, trying to find a better place.

He didn't really realize how far into the brush he was penetrating until he looked back and could no longer see the camp through the screen of vegetation. This spot would do as good as any, he decided. He lowered his buckskin trousers and sighed with satisfaction as he started going about the business that had taken him there.

An arm circled his throat, clamped down on it like an iron bar, and jerked him back a step. He felt something digging into his back, through the buckskin shirt just below his left shoulder blade, and knew the tip of a knife was poised to thrust all the way into his heart.

CHAPTER 17

Dog lifted his head and growled. The big cur's actions made Hawk's muscles stiffen with alarm. He looked around quickly but didn't see anything amiss.

Charlie hadn't come back from the bushes yet, Hawk realized. The young trapper hadn't been gone long enough to worry about him yet . . . but Dog was looking in that direction.

Hawk came lithely to his feet and whispered sharply, "Dog, hunt!"

Dog moved quickly and silently through the grass toward the bushes. Hawk wasn't far behind him.

He could have roused Preacher and alerted his father that something might be wrong, but Hawk had never lacked for confidence. He felt sure that he could handle whatever needed to be done. Chances were, in a moment he would encounter a sleepy Charlie Todd stumbling out of the brush and headed back to his bedroll for the rest of the night.

Hawk reached the thicket's edge without seeing any sign of Charlie. Dog disappeared into the growth ahead of him.

Hawk paused there and called softly, "Charlie! Charlie, are you all right?"

No answer came from the shadows.

Hawk heard Dog growling somewhere in the bushes. It wasn't the sort of urgent, angry snarl that would have heralded an imminent attack on something by the big cur, but rather the sound of him finding a scent that he didn't like.

Hawk thrust branches aside and pushed into the growth. He followed the sound of Dog's growls and found the animal standing stiff-legged in a small open area. Hawk ran his hand along Dog's backbone and felt how ruffled and bristly the fur was—another sure sign of anger.

Kneeling, Hawk studied the ground as best he could in the poor light. He spotted a slightly darker patch and leaned forward to sniff the air above it. The sharp, unmistakable scent of human urine was starting to fade already, but Hawk was still able to smell it. Charlie had stood there to relieve himself.

That fact alone wouldn't have been enough to make Dog react like he had. And Charlie wasn't there anymore, which worried Hawk even more. If it was the spot he had chosen, why had he moved on somewhere else?

And why hadn't he just gone a few steps away from the others and made water there, as Hawk had suggested, instead of being so stubborn? Hawk felt some annoyance mixed with the growing concern over Charlie's whereabouts. Time to worry about that later, though, after he had found what had happened to his friend.

Hawk straightened and started to turn, then stopped short as he saw the tall, broad-shouldered figure standing a few feet away. Hawk hadn't heard anyone come up behind him, so he had a pretty good idea who it was.

Only one man could move that silently.

"What's wrong?" Preacher asked.

"Charlie is gone."

"Gone?" Preacher repeated.

Hawk could imagine the frown on the mountain man's face, even if he couldn't see it. "He came out here to make water and never came back, and now Dog smells something he does not like."

"Blackfoot, I'll bet," Preacher said. "Dang it. Those varmints can slip up on a camp with anybody knowin' until it's too late. They always run me a good race when it comes to sneakin' around."

"Do you think they took Charlie?"

"He ain't here, so it seems like there's a mighty good chance of it."

"Why did they not just kill him?"

"Well," Preacher said, "maybe they think they got a better use for him."

"Torture?" Hawk asked. The word caught a little in his throat. Charlie and Aaron could both be a trial at times, with their inexperience and white man's attitudes, but Hawk had become fond of them anyway.

"Maybe," Preacher said. "Or could be they've got somethin' else in mind."

Jefferson Scarrow was caught up in a restless slumber when Hogarth Plumlee shook him awake. Scarrow sat up instinctively clutching his pistol and looking for somebody to shoot.

"Take it easy, Jeff," Plumlee said. "Somethin's up with them redskins."

"What is it?" Scarrow was still a little disoriented. He

ran his left hand through his tangled hair and blinked rapidly as he looked around. The hour was late, and the fires had died down to the point that they no longer put out much light.

Enough, though, for Scarrow to see the knot of Blackfoot warriors gathered about fifty feet away. They were talking among themselves in low, urgent voices.

The group broke apart abruptly. Several of the Indians strode toward Scarrow, Plumlee, and the rest of the fur thieves. One man pushed a rather hapless-looking figure ahead of them. The man struggled to keep his balance and stay on his feet. He wore buckskins, but he had a dark beard and Scarrow was a little shocked to realize that he was white.

This stranger had to be one of the men who had stolen the girl, Scarrow thought. He supposed that the Blackfeet could have come across some lone trapper and captured him, but Scarrow's gut told him that wasn't the case. This was one of the men they were after.

The stranger's arms were lashed together with rawhide thongs bound around the wrists. His feet were free. He looked frightened, which proved only that he was a sensible man. Only a fool or a lunatic wouldn't be afraid if he found himself the prisoner of a Blackfoot war party.

Scarrow and Plumlee got to their feet. Scarrow could see now that the man prodding the stranger along was Angry Sky. The war chief snapped, "Guard this white man. If he escapes, one of you will die. Maybe more."

"Who is he?" Scarrow asked. He looked at the stranger and added, "Who in the hell are you, man?"

"My . . . my name is Charles Todd. You're white men, you have to help me—"

Angry Sky's harsh laugh broke into the man's plea. "These white men are friends of the Blackfeet. They are your enemies."

Charles Todd stared at them, then said, "You're that bunch of fur thieves. How . . . how did you wind up working with—"

Angry Sky interrupted him again, kicking the back of Charlie's right knee and making his leg buckle. As Charlie dropped to his knees, Angry Sky planted the same foot in the middle of his back and shoved. Charlie slammed face-first to the ground.

"Guard him," Angry Sky said again. "My scouts captured him when they found the camp of our enemies."

"You know where they are?" Scarrow asked. He couldn't keep an excited edge from creeping into his voice. "We're going to catch up to them?"

"Tomorrow," Angry Sky said. "And then we will find out how much they value this one." He nodded toward Charlie, who still lay facedown on the ground, breathing heavily. "We will see whether they believe his life is worth more than that of a stolen Crow woman."

Dog wanted to follow the trail, but Preacher called him back.

"That scent'll still be there in a few minutes," the mountain man said. "We ought to let the others know what's goin' on."

He, Hawk, and Dog returned to the camp. Preacher woke up White Buffalo first, then Aaron. He didn't see any reason to disturb Caroline, so he let her sleep.

"What's going on?" Aaron asked as he rubbed the sleep out of his eyes. He looked around, blinked a few times, and then said, "Hey, where's Charlie?"

"It looks like the Blackfeet took him," Preacher said.

"What?" Aaron exclaimed. He took a quick step forward, then to the right, then froze and looked around as he realized he wasn't accomplishing anything with the erratic movements. "That's impossible!"

"He went out into the bushes to piss, and one of 'em sneaked up and grabbed him," Preacher said. "That's what I'm guessin' happened, anyway."

He went over to the fire ring, stirred up the embers inside it until small flames flickered, and made a torch by winding dry grass around a branch. Once he had started it burning, he walked quickly back to the brush and used the torch's light to study the spot where Charlie evidently had been captured. The other men followed him and crowded around to look. Caroline was still asleep.

The broken branches and the marks on the ground confirmed Preacher's theory. He pointed to a couple of parallel depressions and said, "That's where they dragged him off." He moved the torch around to study the scene more closely before the flames burned out. "But I don't see any blood, which is a good thing. I reckon Charlie had enough sense not to put up a fight."

"Are you saying it's better he didn't try to stop them?" Aaron asked.

"If he had yelled, they would have gone ahead and killed him. Wouldn't have been any reason not to. Then, if there was enough of the varmints, they would've attacked the camp. If there were just a few, a couple of scouts, maybe, they would have lit a shuck outta here instead of gettin' in a fight . . . but not without killin' Charlie first. So this way, at least he's got a chance of survival."

"They will still kill him," White Buffalo intoned solemnly. "The Blackfeet cannot stand to see a white man live if they have it in their power to take his life. His death merely has been postponed."

"Which means there's a chance to turn the tables on them before they kill him," Preacher said as he dropped the branch with its few bits of still burning grass. He ground the last sparks out under his moccasin. "They snuck up on us. Dog and me are gonna sneak up on them."

"I'm coming, too," Aaron said immediately.

"No, you ain't," Preacher told him. "I don't mean to insult you, Aaron, but you ain't nowheres near light enough on your feet for a job like this."

"I am," Hawk said. "I will go with you, Preacher."

The mountain man shook his head. "Nope, that ain't gonna work, neither. You need to stay here and look out for Aaron, White Buffalo, and Caroline."

White Buffalo sniffed. "I do not need some stripling youth to protect me. I am an Absaroka warrior, the mightiest warrior of my people!"

Preacher let that pass. He knew that Hawk had volunteered to accompany him out of habit, but the young warrior didn't really want to leave Caroline there with nobody but Aaron and White Buffalo to defend her.

With some genuine reluctance, Hawk said, "It would be best if I stayed, I suppose . . ."

"What are you going to do, Preacher?" Aaron asked. "Will you try to free Charlie?"

"Depends on what I find." It was possible the Blackfeet did intend to torture Charlie, and he might be dead by the time Preacher got there. "But if I can, I'll bring him back. You got my word on that."

They returned to the camp.

While Preacher gathered up his rifle, pistols, and a few supplies, he said quietly to Hawk, "As soon as it's light enough in the mornin' to move, you take the others and light a shuck outta here. Head north along the river. There used to be a Crow village up that way, maybe a day and a half from here. I don't know if it's still there or not, but there's a good chance it is. The last time I was through these parts, the chief was an old fella called Falling Star. He'll give you a hand, if they're still there. I saved his son from a grizzly."

He didn't repeat any of what he had said, knowing that Hawk would remember everything.

"You will be outnumbered, Preacher," Hawk said.

The mountain man chuckled. "Won't be the first time, by a long shot. And don't forget, I'll have Dog with me. But I don't aim to fight the whole bunch unless I have to." He lowered his voice so Aaron wouldn't have any chance of overhearing him and added, "Besides, there's a chance I'm wrong about what they got in mind and Charlie's already dead. If he is, I'll just turn around and come back." He reached out and gripped Hawk's shoulder for a second. "Take care o' these folks . . . and yourself."

"I will," Hawk promised.

"Come on, Dog."

Preacher trotted toward the trees with the big cur at his heels, and in a matter of moments, the two of them had faded away into the darkness.

CHAPTER 18

Charlie Todd had never been so frightened in his life. And he had been involved in a number of dangerous fights since he and Aaron had come to the frontier and met Preacher and Hawk.

But he had never been a prisoner, surrounded by hostile savages who wanted to make him die with as much agony and suffering as possible. He could see that bloodthirsty desire on their cruel faces every time they looked at him.

The white men didn't look as vicious, but they didn't seem to have any interest in helping him, either.

At least one of them, a lean-faced man with dark, bushy side whiskers, took enough pity on Charlie to tell the burly man next to him, "Pull that fellow over here, Hog. I want to talk to him."

The man called Hog grunted, stood up, and bent down to grab hold of Charlie's shirt. He hauled Charlie half-upright and dragged him over to join the other man. Clearly, Hog was extremely strong. He handled Charlie with ease, almost as if he were a child, despite the fact that Charlie was a rather hefty young man.

Hog helped Charlie sit down on the ground next to

the other man, who said, "I'm Jefferson Scarrow. This is my friend Hogarth Plumlee."

Charlie swallowed hard and nodded. He supposed Plumlee was called Hog both as a nickname and because of his appearance, which certainly fit the name. Charlie tried to respond, but his mouth was too dry with fear at first.

Finally he managed to say, "I . . . I'm Charlie Todd."

"I wish I could offer you some encouraging words, Charlie, but I'm afraid that fate has put us on opposite sides in this little affair." Scarrow's voice held a trace of a British accent. "We've thrown in our lot with Angry Sky and his men. It was that or lose our own lives."

"You called us fur thieves," Plumlee said coldly. "How'd you know about that? You're part of the bunch that Lopez and the others went after, ain't you?"

"I . . . I don't know anyone named Lopez," Charlie said.

Scarrow shook his head. "There's really no point in denying it, Charlie. Several days ago, some of *our* friends visited your camp with the intention of relieving you and *your* friends of the pelts you've harvested so far this season. That's the only way any of this makes sense. Señor Lopez was in charge of that party. But he and the others aren't coming back, are they?"

Charlie just looked down at the ground in front of him and didn't say anything.

"I told you," Plumlee said. "They're all dead, Jeff." He gave Charlie a hard shove on the shoulder. "But I don't reckon it was a fat greenhorn like you who killed 'em! Who else was with you? How many in your bunch?"

Charlie didn't want to answer the questions. He wasn't going to provide any help to these men. They were murderers and thieves to start with, and now they had allied themselves with a Blackfoot war party.

Plumlee drew his knife, grabbed Charlie's hair with his other hand, and jerked his head back. As he brought the blade toward Charlie's throat, Scarrow told him, "Angry Sky ordered us to keep this man alive, Hog, not kill him."

"I ain't gonna kill him," Plumlee growled. "But I reckon Angry Sky won't mind if I carve on his face a mite. I figure I can cut both cheeks down to the bone and write my name on his forehead without makin' him lose enough blood so he dies. I can write my name. Did I ever tell you that, Jeff? And I don't mean just carvin' an X, neither."

"I'm impressed with your education," Scarrow said dryly. "Charlie, you should cooperate with us. I don't believe my friend Hog is in any mood to listen to my advice. So you had better be willing to, if you know what's good for you."

"A . . . All right," Charlie gasped out. "I'll tell you. There are twenty of us—"

An older man who had been sitting nearby listening to the conversation leaned forward and interrupted Charlie by saying, "That's a lie. I found the tracks of five horses, that's all. And there wasn't anybody travelin' on foot except when they were leadin' the horses. There can't be more than four more of 'em, now that this fella's caught, plus the girl."

Plumlee ran the blade's edge along Charlie's throat just below the beard, leaving a tiny cut that welled a drop of blood. "The next lie will go deeper," he warned.

"So you have four companions, Charlie," Scarrow said. "Who are they?"

Charlie was completely convinced that Plumlee would go through with the threat to torture him. He couldn't see what harm it would do to answer their questions. Nothing about the situation would actually change if he did.

But an unexpectedly stubborn streak welled up inside him. He grimaced as Plumlee held the knife at his throat, but he got the words out that he wanted to. "You can all just go to hell!"

"That was the biggest mistake you ever made in your life, boy," Plumlee snarled at him. The blade lifted from Charlie's neck and came toward his face.

He saw firelight reflected in flickering glints from the steel.

Dog never wavered from the trail he was following. Once he had the scent, he wasn't just about to lose it. He could have bounded on through the night and outdistanced Preacher, but he knew the mountain man was following him and didn't go too fast, just trotted along easily.

Preacher's loping pace carried him after Dog. The big cur would let him know when they got close enough to their destination that they needed to slow down and be quieter.

Preacher thought back on all the times he had slipped into Blackfoot camps. Not just the Blackfeet, either. They were his mortal enemies and had been ever since capturing him as a young man and threatening to burn him at the stake, but he had clashed with other tribes in the past, too. And with white men from this country and numerous others. He had even run into a bunch of crazy folks from way down in Mexico who had their own hidden city up in the mountains.

Seemed like he couldn't get along with much of anybody, he thought with a wry grin as he followed

Dog. Folks just didn't realize he had such a peaceable nature at heart.

He estimated that they had covered about a mile and a half when Dog suddenly slowed. Preacher did likewise. When Dog stopped, Preacher dropped to one knee beside him and put an arm around the big cur's shaggy neck.

"They're close, I reckon, or you wouldn't be actin' like this," he whispered.

Dog whined quietly in response.

"Stay here, and I'll see what I can find out." Preacher stretched out on the ground and started crawling forward. He had a hunch the Blackfoot camp might be on the other side of the trees and brush making a dark line about a hundred yards ahead of him.

Again he thought about the possibility of crawling onto a rattlesnake in the dark but trusted to luck that he wouldn't. Also, any snake out hunting at that time of night would probably be alert enough to avoid a human coming toward it.

He reached the trees without any such encounters. He paused and put all his senses to work. The air was barely stirring, but it moved enough to carry a faint scent of woodsmoke to his nose. And as he listened, he thought he heard voices murmuring somewhere up ahead. Both things confirmed his hunch. The Blackfeet weren't far away.

A savage grin tugged at Preacher's mouth. Turnabout was sure fair play, as far as he was concerned. The Indians had snuck up on his camp, and now he was sneaking up on theirs.

He eased forward into the trees.

Minutes dragged by. He couldn't get in any hurry now. The voices grew louder. Preacher paused and stiffened on the ground as he realized that some words he was hearing were English. But some were undoubtedly Blackfoot.

What the devil was going on?

He eased ahead again. An orange glow appeared. The light from a campfire that had burned down some but was still casting enough illumination to spread through the trees. Preacher used his elbows and knees to work closer. He had his flintlock rifle beside him. He placed it carefully each time he moved.

He could see shadowy shapes moving around. The firelight had a flicker to it. He lifted his head, carefully parted the brush right in front of him, and peered through the gap he had created.

About twenty feet away, on the other side of a small fire, several white men sat on the ground. Others were stretched out nearby, evidently asleep.

Charlie Todd was one of the men Preacher saw. He sat between two strangers with his hands tied in front of him. The men flanking him weren't bound, though, and they still had their weapons, so they weren't prisoners even though Charlie obviously was.

Blackfoot voices made Preacher crane his neck and look to the left. A dozen or more warriors were within his range of vision. They were armed, too.

Well, hell, he thought. From the looks of this setup, the Blackfeet and the white fur thieves were working together. Unlikely though that seemed at first glance, it was really the only explanation for what he was seeing that made any sense.

That meant Charlie was in double trouble, and when Preacher looked toward the young trapper again, he saw that one of the white men, a thick-bodied varmint with a piggish face, had pulled a knife and was holding it to Charlie's throat. The other man was questioning Charlie. Preacher felt a surge of pride as the young trapper defiantly told them to go to hell.

But then that human hog moved the knife, and Preacher could tell he was about slice Charlie's face open.

Preacher didn't stop to think about what he was doing. He just raised himself on his elbows, thrust the rifle out in front of him, and fired. The boom was deafeningly loud in the night.

Just as Preacher squeezed the trigger, the hog-faced man twisted to get a better angle on the mutilation he was about to carry out, so the rifle ball struck him in the shoulder instead of the chest as Preacher had intended. The impact was enough to knock the man over on his back. The knife flew out of his hand without inflicting any more damage on Charlie.

In the blink of an eye, Preacher was on his feet. He shouted, "Charlie, run!" as he pulled out a pistol with his right hand and fired toward the Blackfeet on the other side of the camp. At that range, with the heavy powder charge and two balls loaded in the pistol, he couldn't miss.

The white man who had been questioning Charlie made a grab for him, but Charlie rolled out of reach and then struggled upright as quickly as he could with bound wrists.

"Dog!" Preacher bellowed.

Now that he wasn't hidden in the brush anymore, he had a much better look at the odds he was facing. Might have been better not to know, he thought wryly. Forty to one or thereabouts.

Forty to *two*, rather. At that moment Dog flashed out of the night and at the end of an eye-blurring leap clamped his jaws on the throat of a Blackfoot warrior. The big cur's weight slammed into the man's chest and knocked him down. By the time he hit the ground, Dog had ripped his throat out in a fountaining spray of blood.

"Kill them!" cried the white man who seemed to be in charge of that bunch. Shots blasted after Charlie, but he was already at the edge of the firelight and jerked back and forth as he ran to make himself a more difficult target. He was still moving fast as he disappeared in the shadows. Preacher hoped he hadn't been hit.

Rifle and pistol balls and arrows were whipping around him, too, as he drew his second pistol and fired it at the Blackfeet's white allies. One man stumbled and clapped a hand to his chest. Blood welled between his fingers. As he collapsed, several other men charging toward Preacher stumbled over him and fell, taking them out of the fight for a few seconds, anyway.

A warrior screamed as Dog's powerful jaws locked on his forearm and snapped it. Dog got another man by the ankle and jerked his leg out from under him, spilling him on the ground. The big cur's slashing teeth tore half his face off.

Preacher called, "Come on, Dog," and he whirled away from his victim to race after the mountain man. Preacher lunged into the darkness after Charlie, knowing the Blackfeet would be in hot pursuit within seconds.

The race was on. The stakes were life and death.

CHAPTER 19

"Charlie!" Preacher called as he ran. "Charlie, sing out!"

"Up here, Preacher!" came the response from up ahead. Preacher angled a little to the right and caught up with Charlie a few moments later. The young trapper was running as hard as he could, but he didn't have Preacher's speed. Preacher slowed down to pace him.

"They're going to . . . come after us . . . aren't they?" Charlie puffed.

Preacher heard shouts from behind them and said, "They already are. But we're gonna give 'em the slip!"

"How? There are . . . too many . . ."

Preacher grasped Charlie's arm and changed his course a little. "See that star low to the horizon right in front of us? Keep headin' toward it and you'll get back to our camp. I'm gonna slow those varmints down."

"Preacher, you can't . . . They'll kill you!"

"They'll have a hell of a time tryin'! Now go!"

Preacher gave Charlie a push to head him in the right direction, then stopped and swung around to face the pursuit. The Blackfeet were too close behind

him. He could already see their darting shapes. He
didn't have time to reload his rifle and pistols.

So he knelt, placed his empty rifle on the ground,
slid his knife from its sheath, and pulled the tomahawk
from behind his belt.

The grass was tall enough that the pursuers would
have a hard time spotting him until they were right on
top of him. They had to be expecting him to continue
fleeing, instead of waiting for them to catch up to him.
Only a madman would do that.

A madman . . . or Preacher.

As several Blackfeet raced past him, Preacher exploded up from the ground, swung the tomahawk into
the back of one warrior's neck, and thrust the knife
into the side of another. Both men went down in the
loose sprawl of death. Preacher whirled, and another
man's skull crunched under the tomahawk's impact,
after which came a slashing knife stroke too swift for
the eye to follow, and a warrior stumbled and gagged
as blood, black in the moonlight, flooded from the
gaping wound in his throat. Preacher ducked under
a sweeping tomahawk and swung his with enough
force that it almost decapitated the warrior who had
struck at him. In three heartbeats, maybe a shade less,
Preacher had killed five men.

Those five were the vanguard of the pursuit, but
more were coming hard on their heels. Muzzle flame
spurted redly from a couple of rifles. Preacher heard
the balls hum past his head. He drove hard into the
next bunch before they had a chance to reload, and
again blood fell like rain as he spun and twisted among
them, wielding the knife and tomahawk.

The Blackfeet were at a disadvantage. The poor
light made it difficult to tell friend from foe, but
Preacher didn't have that problem. Anywhere he struck,

the blow landed on an enemy. Four Blackfoot warriors were in the second group, and they all fell in a matter of seconds, dead or dying.

Other warriors shouted not far away, but Preacher had taken care of all the ones who had drawn close to him. He turned, ran back to where he had left his rifle, snatched it from the ground, and ran on, his long-legged strides eating up the ground.

He was moving at an angle toward the south, away from the direction he had sent Charlie. He thought that would draw the pursuit after him, and as he glanced over his shoulder from the crest of a hill, he saw that he was right. He spotted the dark shapes bobbing up the slope after him.

He entered the shadows under the trees at the top of the hill, and stopped. Not needing light to reload his pistols, his fingers performed that task with great efficiency without even thinking about what he was doing. He didn't take the time to double-shot them but put one ball in each pistol and waited for the warriors to come in range.

When they were almost at the top of the hill, Preacher swung out from behind the tree where he had taken cover, leveled the cocked weapons, and pulled the triggers. The double boom slammed through the night. The heavy lead balls smashed into two men, driving deep into their chests. One even went all the way through the first target's body and struck a warrior behind him in the head. With swinging pistols, Preacher met the other two in the bunch and felt skulls shatter as he struck to right and left.

He turned, grabbed his rifle from where he had leaned it against the tree trunk, and ran down the hill.

By that time, the other pursuers were stumbling over the bodies of their fellow warriors. Seeing the slaughter Preacher had inflicted on those luckless fellows had to give them pause. The shouts behind him weren't as loud, and as he continued running, he heard them falling even farther behind.

Several screams ripped through the darkness. Preacher grinned. Dog wasn't with him, so he suspected the big cur was harrying the enemies' flanks. Between the damage the mountain man had already done and the threat of those flashing teeth and powerful jaws striking out of the darkness with no warning, Preacher figured the rest of the bunch would turn back pretty soon, if they hadn't already.

Sometimes, outnumbering the man being chased didn't mean a damned thing.

It all depended on the man.

Jefferson Scarrow had just finished binding up Hog Plumlee's wounded shoulder when some of the Blackfoot warriors who had gone after the fugitives came limping back into camp. Angry Sky had ordered that the fires be built up, so plenty of light spilled over the ground and revealed the warriors' sorry shape.

"Good Lord," Plumlee muttered. "Looks like less 'n half of 'em came back. And they don't have no prisoners with them."

"I see that," Scarrow said tightly. He was glad he hadn't ordered any of his men to give chase.

Angry Sky had lost some of his warriors, but Scarrow's force was still at full strength, at least compared to what it had been when they fell in with the savages. Well, almost at full strength since Paulson had fallen with a pistol ball in his chest.

A warrior who was bleeding heavily from a thigh ripped open by what appeared to have been a wild animal spoke rapidly to Angry Sky. The war chief listened with a murderous scowl on his face. Then he turned and stalked toward Scarrow and Plumlee.

Scarrow got on his feet to meet the Blackfoot leader. Angry Sky snapped, "Preacher!"

That took Scarrow by surprise and left him puzzled. He had no idea what Angry Sky meant by that bitterly voiced word. With a shake of his head, he said, "I don't know what you mean."

"One of my men heard the fat white man call the name Preacher." Angry Sky put his dark face close to Scarrow's and snarled. "Did you know one of the men we sought was Preacher?"

"What does it matter if he's a preacher?" Scarrow asked. "What I want to know is how they managed to get away."

That was a bold thing to say, considering the murderous rage that obviously filled Angry Sky.

Plumlee muttered in a voice thin with pain, "Careful, Jeff."

"Not *a* preacher," Angry Sky said through clenched teeth. "There is a white man *called* Preacher. All the Blackfeet, from one end of our hunting ground to the other, know him, or know who he is. Mothers frighten their unruly children with tales of how Preacher will come for them. He is sometimes called Ghost Killer because he can come into one of our camps and kill half a dozen warriors in their sleep without ever being seen!"

"That sounds like a fairy tale," Scarrow said. "Such a monster can't exist."

"Preacher is no monster. He is a man . . . a man who has killed hundreds of Blackfeet!"

Scarrow still didn't believe that, but Angry Sky

seemed convinced of it, and arguing with him probably wasn't wise.

Not only that, but Plumlee said quietly, "I think I've heard of that son of a bitch, Jeff. They say he's all teeth and a yard wide, like an alligator gar. I've heard men say they'd sooner fight a grizzly b'ar instead o' Preacher."

"So that's the man we've been chasing, eh?"

"Makes more sense now that him and his friends might've done for Lopez and the others."

Angry Sky didn't like the fact that Scarrow and Plumlee were talking to each other instead of him. He brought Scarrow's attention back to him by saying, "You claim you did not know one of our enemies might be Preacher?"

"Of course I didn't know. I never even heard of the man until just now. But surely it can't make *that* much difference, can it? He's only one man!"

"Fourteen of my warriors lie out there in the night, dead. Five more were killed here in camp when he and his demon dog attacked. Nineteen brave, strong warriors wiped out! Preacher must pay for their lives with every drop of his blood!"

"We'll help you," Scarrow said. "We want this Preacher dead, too, Angry Sky, and all his friends. You have my word on that."

Angry Sky jerked his head in a nod and walked back to join his warriors.

As Scarrow sat down again, Plumlee said quietly, "I don't know about this, Jeff. Goin' up against Preacher ain't what you'd call safe."

"Nonsense," Scarrow said. "With losses like he's suffered tonight, Angry Sky needs us more than ever now. And here's something else to consider . . ." A cunning smile appeared on the man's face. "Unless I'm counting incorrectly, I believe that *we* now outnumber the Blackfeet. So perhaps in the long run, we owe this Preacher a bit of thanks."

Gray had begun to streak the eastern sky by the time Preacher reached the camp on the riverbank. He hoped to find Charlie and Dog there, and the sight of them coming toward him eagerly to greet him made satisfaction well up inside him. The others trailed behind them.

"Thank God you made it back, Preacher!" Charlie cried. "Are you wounded?"

"Nope. I reckon I got quite a bit of blood splattered on me, but I don't think any of it's mine."

White Buffalo said, "There will be wailing and grieving in the lodges of the Blackfeet when the news of this reaches them. This is good."

"It's true, I whittled 'em down some, with Dog's help," Preacher said. "How about you, Charlie? Are you hurt?"

"I'm just embarrassed." The rueful look on his face confirmed that. "I was a fool, Preacher, and I'm sorry. I could have gotten myself killed, and worse, I might have cost you your life."

"Shoot, I coulda let that fella cut you," Preacher said. "It was my choice to shoot him. But I reckon I'm glad I did."

"So am I," Aaron said. "Charlie can be extremely annoying, but I've grown accustomed to having him around."

Hawk hadn't said anything to Preacher by way of

greeting. "I was about to tell everyone to get ready to leave. We are still heading north for that Crow village?"

Preacher nodded. "Yep. The fellas chasin' me turned back—the ones who still could, anyway—but the rest of the bunch will be comin' after us. Charlie, I reckon you told them that gang o' fur thieves is workin' with the Blackfeet now?"

"Yes. The leader is a man named Jefferson Scarrow. The one who threatened to torture me is Hogarth Plumlee. Do either of those names mean anything to you, Preacher?"

"Nope. Reckon they're new to this part of the country. That ain't a surprise. More and more folks come out here every summer, and some of 'em are no-account thieves and killers like that bunch." Preacher sat down on a log to rest after his long run while the others made preparations to break camp.

They wouldn't take the time for coffee and a real breakfast. Starting to put distance behind them again was more important.

Caroline came over and sat down beside him. "I am glad you are alive, Preacher," she said to him in Crow.

"Yeah, me, too," he agreed, smiling at her.

"And that you saved Charlie. He is a good man, but this is not the country for him."

Preacher nodded. "You're probably right about that. Him and Aaron should go back to where they came from. They got good hearts and plenty o' courage, but they ain't cut out for this sort o' life."

"You said . . . this is a Crow village upriver?"

"There used to be. I don't know if it's still there or not. The chief was called Falling Star."

"I have heard the name. He is said to be an honorable chief. He will help us?"

"I think so, if he's still there."

"Even though it may put his people in danger?"

"Like you said, he's an honorable man." Preacher chuckled and added, "Anyway, I never knew a Crow warrior who'd pass up a chance to fight with some Blackfeet."

"Maybe . . . the men who are after us will give up and let us go on our way?"

Preacher grew solemn and shook his head. "No, I don't think so. Too much blood's been spilled. As stubborn as they were earlier, I can't imagine they'd give up now. No, Butterfly . . . Caroline . . . I figure one way or another, this is a fight to the death."

CHAPTER 20

Since the preparations were made already, Preacher waited only a few minutes to catch his breath before telling the others it was time to move out. They mounted up and started north along the river. Once again, Caroline rode with Hawk. Preacher didn't waste his time suggesting any other arrangement. That one seemed to be working, after all.

He took the lead, with Hawk and Caroline riding behind him, then Aaron and Charlie side by side, and White Buffalo bringing up the rear. Or rather, Dog brought up the rear, hanging back to check the trail. Preacher knew better than to think that their enemies, red or white, would give up.

The day passed without incident, however. The group moved at a good pace and covered quite a bit of ground.

Late in the day, the river curved more to the west, toward the next range of mountains. When Preacher saw that, it was familiar to him. The Crow village they sought was located where the stream entered the foothills. It was a good location, and he hoped Falling Star's band was still there.

He had no illusions that the Blackfeet weren't following their trail, and Angry Sky's war party was bound to have several good trackers in it. By now, the warriors would have realized that Preacher and his companions were following the river.

After thinking about the situation all day, Preacher reined in and told the others, "We'll rest the horses for a spell, but then we're pushin' on through the night. There'll be enough light for us to see that we're stayin' by the river where we need to be. If we make camp, there's a good chance those varmints will keep comin' and catch up to us during the night."

"You really think they're that close to us?" Aaron asked with a note of alarm in his voice.

"They sure might be. I saw a good-sized pony herd when I was in their camp, and Angry Sky lost enough men so that all of Scarrow's bunch ought to be mounted and probably won't even have to ride double. Some o' the Blackfeet were hurt and would've needed patchin' up, so that probably kept 'em from comin' after us right away. Angry Sky had to wait until it was light enough for his trackers to pick up our sign, too, but then they took out after us, hot and heavy. You can bet a hat on it."

They let the horses drink and rest and crop at the grass on the riverbank for a short time then Preacher told everyone to mount up again. The sun was down and twilight's gloom began to gather over the stream and the landscape around it.

They had ridden only a couple of hundred yards when Preacher heard a faint twanging sound from the other side of the river. Most men would have missed it entirely, but to Preacher it sounded clear as a warning bell.

He reacted instinctively and immediately, ducking

low over Horse's neck. Something slapped hard against his back. Preacher knew an arrow's shaft had just glanced off him. The head had barely missed him. If he hadn't moved when he did, it would have struck him in the side and probably skewered his right lung.

"Ambush!" he bellowed. "Everybody stay low and ride hard!" He kicked the stallion into a gallop along the bank.

If he and his companions could reach the cotton-wood trees growing close to the water up ahead, they would stand a lot better chance of surviving the ambush. The trunks would make it more difficult for arrows to find them, and the thickening shadows would conceal them.

Another arrow whipped past his head, another near miss, but close didn't count.

Hoofbeats pounded behind him. Preacher glanced back to see that Hawk and Caroline were close, but Aaron, Charlie, and White Buffalo had fallen back some.

As Preacher's head was turned so he could see how the others were doing, White Buffalo suddenly jerked and nearly toppled off his pony. Only a frantic grab at the horse's long mane saved the old-timer from falling. Preacher couldn't be sure in the fading light, but he thought an arrow's feathered shaft was sticking out of White Buffalo's side.

The possibility that the old warrior was hit made Preacher haul back on Horse's reins. He pulled the stallion aside and waved Hawk and Caroline on past him, calling to them, "Get to cover!"

He urged Charlie and Aaron on, as well. As they galloped by, Preacher caught a glimpse of movement on the far bank. He brought his rifle up with blinding speed and fired, letting instinct guide his shot instead of aiming.

He was rewarded by a harsh cry of pain. Then another arrow flew over his head as White Buffalo reached him. Preacher saw the arrow embedded deeply in the old-timer's side. White Buffalo swayed, still having trouble staying mounted.

Preacher fell in alongside him and guided Horse with his knees so he could reach over with his free hand and grasp White Buffalo's arm. Steadying the old Absaroka, he said, "We'll take cover in those trees!"

"Leave me!" White Buffalo cried. "I am dying!"

"The hell you say! I'll believe that when I see it, you tough old pelican!"

Two more arrows whistled around them as they raced toward the trees, but neither missile found the target. Horse and White Buffalo's pony weaved in among the cottonwoods. Preacher kept them moving until they were a quarter-mile deep in the woods.

Then he reined in, and White Buffalo was able to bring his pony to a stop, too. Preacher leaped to the ground and caught White Buffalo as the old-timer half-fell from his mount's back.

"Preacher! Preacher, where are you?"

The call came from deeper in the woods. That was Aaron, Preacher thought as he went to his knees and cradled White Buffalo against him. Hawk had more sense than to announce his location when enemies were nearby. Preacher didn't answer and hoped Aaron would shut up.

The shout didn't come again. Could be Hawk had found Aaron and told him to be quiet, or maybe Aaron had just realized it was a good idea. Either way, silence descended over the woods along the river. The small animals that would normally be out at dusk had gone to ground, and any birds in the trees had flown off.

Preacher listened to the bubbling rasp of White Buffalo's breathing and knew it wasn't good. White Buffalo hadn't moved or said anything since they had gotten down from the horses. Preacher wondered if he had passed out.

White Buffalo put that idea to rest by asking in a hoarse whisper, "Where is . . . Dog?"

"He ain't with us right now," Preacher said, answering in the Absaroka tongue White Buffalo had used. "If he had been, he would've warned us of that ambush."

"I wish he was here. I would have liked to . . . talk to him again . . . before I die."

"Ain't nobody said you're dyin'."

"The arrowhead is . . . deep within me . . . Preacher. Every time I breathe . . . I can feel it."

"We'll get it out," Preacher said, but even as he spoke, he knew it was impossible. He couldn't push the arrow on through to snap off the head, as he would have if it had been stuck in a shoulder or a leg, and pulling it out would just do more damage and hasten White Buffalo's death.

The old-timer wasn't going to make it. They both knew it.

Soft footfalls padded on the ground nearby. Preacher shifted his right hand and closed it around a pistol butt.

He relaxed his grip as he heard Hawk whisper, "Preacher?"

"Here," the mountain man said. "White Buffalo is with me."

Hawk emerged from the gathering shadows, followed by Caroline, Aaron, and Charlie.

"Any of you hurt?" Preacher asked.

"No, we reached the trees safely," Hawk replied. "The ambush failed."

"Not . . . entirely," White Buffalo said. He coughed, followed by a pained grunt.

"White Buffalo!" Hawk exclaimed. He dropped to his knees on the old-timer's other side. Charlie and Aaron crowded forward, too. They were very fond of the elderly warrior, just like Hawk was. Caroline hung back a little, uncertain.

Hawk went on. "We must get that arrow out—" then stopped abruptly as he realized that was impossible.

White Buffalo raised a trembling hand. As Hawk grasped it, the old-timer said, "I am proud of you . . . Hawk That Soars . . . as if you were . . . my own flesh and blood. You are . . . a mighty warrior. The mightiest . . . of the Absarokas."

"Grandfather," Hawk said softly. He and White Buffalo weren't related by blood, but Hawk respected him and treated him as if they had been.

"The girl Butterfly . . . she will bear you many fine sons . . . The two of you will be happy . . . for many years."

"You do not know—"

"I *know*," White Buffalo said. "The spirits . . . have told me." He tightened his grip on Hawk's hand.

Then a smile lit his face as Dog trotted out of the shadows and came up to the group gathered around White Buffalo. The big cur licked the old warrior's leathery cheek, and White Buffalo said, "Ah, my friend! You have come . . . to say farewell."

Dog whined quietly.

"Do not worry. We will . . . meet again . . . far on the other side of the mountains . . . where the hunting is good . . . and the sun always shines."

Dog whined again and leaned in closer to nuzzle against the old-timer, and Preacher could almost believe that he was talking to White Buffalo. Why not? Preacher sure as blazes couldn't say one way or the other.

White Buffalo got a skinny arm around Dog's neck and hugged him, then lifted his head and said in a stronger voice, "The Blackfeet will be coming."

"You let us worry about that," Preacher said.

White Buffalo shook his head. "Leave me here. Let them find me. I will . . . slow them down."

"We will not abandon you," Hawk declared.

"You will not be . . . abandoning me," White Buffalo argued. "I would fight . . . one more battle . . . against the hated Blackfeet . . . One more . . . great battle . . ."

Preacher wasn't sure White Buffalo had enough strength to even stand up, let alone fight, but he understood what the old warrior was asking. And White Buffalo had a point. All of Angry Sky's remaining war party wasn't on the other side of the river. If that had been the case, the ambush wouldn't have ended with a few arrows flying. Angry Sky, his warriors, and their white allies would have charged across the river to wipe out Preacher and his friends.

More than likely, there were only a few scouts sent ahead of the main bunch. The ambush was meant to kill them if possible, otherwise to slow them down and allow the rest of the war party to catch up. It would be happening at that very moment.

"White Buffalo's right," Preacher said. "We've got to get movin' again. Those varmints will be coming up fast behind us."

"We can't just leave him here," Charlie protested with anguish in his voice.

"He knows what he's doin'. And it's what he wants."

White Buffalo said thinly, "Help me stand. Put my back against . . . one of these trees."

Charlie turned to Hawk. "You have to talk some sense into them."

"A warrior can ask for no nobler fate than to die in battle," Hawk said.

"With the bodies of his enemies piled around him!" White Buffalo rasped.

Hawk took one of the old man's arms while Preacher held the other. They easily lifted White Buffalo to his feet and helped him to a nearby cottonwood. He braced his legs underneath him, leaned against the trunk, and faced the river with his bow in his hand and his quiver of arrows pulled around so that he could reach them easily.

"I am sorry," he said, "that I will bring pleasure to no more young women. That I will hunt no more with my friends. That I will speak no more to the beasts of the earth and hear their simple wisdom."

Dog licked the old warrior's hand.

"Yes, my friend," White Buffalo said. "I will die well."

"Come on," Preacher said to the others. "We got to get out of here."

"Go. Go with the wind and the night," White Buffalo offered.

Charlie and Aaron were choked up by emotion but managed to say good-bye to White Buffalo. Hawk grasped the old warrior's shoulder for a second and nodded to him. Caroline came up and brushed a kiss across his cheek. Then Hawk ushered them away, leaving Preacher as the last.

"I hope I can go out the same way when my time comes," the mountain man said. Full darkness had almost fallen, but he saw the faint smile that touched White Buffalo's lips.

"I do not believe you will die . . . for a very, very long time . . . my friend," he said.

"The string plays out for everybody, sooner or later."

"Perhaps . . . but you, Preacher . . . the spirits have spoken to me about you . . . They say you will roam this earth for many moons . . . You will see many sights . . . do many things . . . and your true greatness . . . still awaits you."

Like Hawk had done, Preacher gripped the old warrior's shoulder. "Good-bye, White Buffalo."

"Good-bye . . . Preacher."

Preacher turned and hurried off in the same direction Hawk and the others had gone. He knew they would be waiting not far away with the horses.

Dog trotted along with him, but the big cur turned his head to look back several times. A sound that was part whine, part growl came from his throat.

"I don't like it any better than you do, old son," Preacher told him. "But we all have things to do, and I reckon this is one of White Buffalo's."

The big shapes of the horses loomed out of the shadows. The others were all mounted and waiting.

Preacher swung up onto Horse's back. "We'll keep pushin' along the river. Let's go."

They rode in grim silence for several minutes before the sudden shrill yip of a war cry came from far behind them. The sound continued for long seconds, then stopped abruptly.

Silence reigned again in the night.

Dog bounded ahead onto a knoll that stuck out into the river. At the top of it, he looked back in the direction they had come from, tipped his head to the sky, and loosed a long, mournful howl that echoed in the souls of the five riders.

CHAPTER 21

Angry Sky's hate and rage made him tireless. He pushed the group all day in pursuit of their quarry, never allowing the men and horses to rest for more than a few minutes at a time.

That was all right with Jefferson Scarrow. As long as Angry Sky was thinking only about recapturing the girl and getting the revenge he so single-mindedly desired, he wasn't as likely to notice how the situation had changed.

Angry Sky had started out with more than thirty men in his war party. He was down to only a dozen now, including himself. Preacher and his friends had really wreaked havoc on them.

Of course, Preacher had whittled Scarrow's group down to less than half its original number, too, but Scarrow still had Hog Plumlee and eleven more, so they outnumbered the Blackfeet by two men. Not a comfortable margin, certainly, but far better than the roughly two to one odds in favor of the savages that had existed before Preacher's invasion of the camp the previous night.

The plan to trade the prisoner Charlie Todd for the

girl had fallen through before it could ever begin. Probably just as well, Scarrow thought. Preacher probably never would have agreed to it. Frontiersmen had ridiculous codes of honor and chivalry.

It was simpler for a man just to take what he wanted, by force if necessary, which was what Scarrow intended to do where the girl was concerned.

Night had fallen when Angry Sky called a halt to let the horses rest again. Scarrow was sure the war chief didn't care how tired the men were, but their mounts had to be protected.

Earlier in the afternoon, Angry Sky had sent three of his men ahead on the fastest horses in the bunch. Their job was to locate Preacher and the others, kill them if possible—except for the girl, of course—or slow them down, at the very least.

As they paused by the river, Scarrow thought Angry Sky might be waiting for those men to return.

Scarrow and Plumlee drank from the stream and then knelt on the bank.

Plumlee asked quietly, "When are we gonna make our move, Jeff?"

"Against the savages, you mean? As soon as the girl is back in our hands and our other enemies are dead."

"You ain't worried that'll be too late? You know those damn redskins will try to double-cross us as soon as they get the chance."

"Yes, I'm well aware of that," Scarrow said. "We'll just strike first, before the treacherous heathens have the opportunity."

"That's risky."

"All life is risky, Hog. That's what gives it the necessary spice!"

Plumlee just grunted, as if to say that he could do

without such spice. But he didn't press the issue and didn't have a chance to, anyway.

A moment later a commotion broke out among the Blackfeet. Scarrow and Plumlee stood up.

"I think them scouts are back," Plumlee said.

He and Scarrow walked along the bank toward the spot where Angry Sky and some of the other warriors were gathered around two men who had just ridden in. They dismounted and unloaded the body of a third warrior. The Blackfeet let loose a flood of obviously outraged words in their language.

Scarrow let the reaction go on for several minutes before he stepped closer to Angry Sky and asked, "What happened?"

The war chief swung around and glared at Scarrow. "I have lost another warrior," he spat. "And the other two are wounded. But the enemy lost a man, as well. An old dog of an Absaroka. They left him behind when they fled, because he was wounded. He killed that man"—Angry Sky nodded curtly toward the body stretched out on the ground—"and put an arrow in the leg of another, before he died." With grudging respect, he added, "It was a valiant death."

"But Preacher and the others got away," Scarrow said.

"For now. We know they are following the river. We will set out after them again as soon as the horses have rested more."

"In the dark?"

Angry Sky made a curt, dismissive gesture. "There has to be a reason they are staying so close to the river. I do not know what it is, but they have a destination in mind. If this were not true, they would have struck out across country by now. So we will do the same. The moon and stars will provide enough light for that."

What Angry Sky said made sense, Scarrow thought.

"All right. My men and I will be ready to ride whenever you say."

Angry Sky grunted as if to say that no one needed to tell him that. It was a foregone conclusion that everyone would follow his orders.

At least in *his* mind, it was a foregone conclusion.

But Jefferson Scarrow might have had other ideas.

The group felt incomplete with White Buffalo gone, but Preacher didn't dwell on the loss. He was a practical sort, not given to brooding, and he still had Hawk and the others to worry about. Mourning would come later. Anyway, he had lost friends before and was sure that he would again, if he lived long enough.

White Buffalo had seemed convinced that Preacher was going to live for a long, long time.

He put that prediction out of his mind, as well, and concentrated on keeping everyone moving. Hawk and Caroline led the way, with Dog ranging ahead of them on Preacher's command, to alert them to any more potential danger. Preacher rode behind Aaron and Charlie. The two young trappers were unusually quiet, probably because of White Buffalo's death.

When Preacher called a halt to let the horses blow, he hipped around in the saddle to peer back into the darkness behind them. Even though he couldn't see anything threatening, every instinct in his body told him the Blackfeet were still back there, coming on with their murderous white allies, bent on killing Preacher, Hawk, Charlie, and Aaron and then . . .

And then he suspected the two groups would have a falling-out over the girl. More men would die. But in the end, no matter which side won, Caroline would be just as bad off as before. Quite possibly worse, in fact.

That knowledge was why, after a few minutes, Preacher told the others, "Come on. We'd best get movin' again."

The moon had come up and cast its silvery illumination over the landscape, including rippling reflections on the surface of the fast-moving river. The air was warm, and it should have been a peaceful, pleasant night. It would have been without the specter of the enemy looming behind them.

They had traveled another mile or so upriver when Hawk suddenly reined in. Aaron and Charlie stopped behind him, while Preacher moved Horse up beside Hawk's pony.

"What is it?" Preacher asked quietly, but then he saw why Hawk had stopped. Dog had returned and was pacing back and forth restlessly on the bank in front of the riders.

"He has found something," Hawk said.

"Yeah, and there's a mighty good chance it ain't anything we'd like." Preacher looked around. Off to the left, three trees had fallen at some point in the past, and the logs laced together to form a possible defensive position. He pointed them out to Hawk. "I'll go take a look. The rest of you stay here, and if trouble comes at you, maybe you can fort up in that deadfall over yonder."

"I can go—"

"No, you stay here and look after the others," Preacher interrupted. "I'll be back when I've got a better idea what we're dealin' with."

Hawk didn't argue. He had questioned his father's decisions many times in the past, but on this occasion he knew Preacher was right. One of them had to stay there, and Hawk didn't really want to leave Caroline. He nodded. "Be careful."

Grinning in the moonlight, Preacher said, "If I'd wanted to live life careful-like, I never would've come out here to the mountains in the first place, and you wouldn't have been born, boy." Dismounting, he handed Horse's reins to Hawk, then said to Dog, "Show me what you found."

The two of them loped off into the shadows.

Preacher had no trouble following the big cur. Dog led him along the river for a while, then veered away from the stream to the west. Since they had been sticking close to the river, Preacher wasn't sure why Dog would regard something away from it as a threat, but he understood when they didn't go far before Dog stopped and growled quietly. Whoever was nearby, they were close enough to have heard the riders moving along the river. Dog knew what he was doing, as usual.

Preacher eased forward, rifle at the ready. He spied the small, orange light of campfire embers ahead of him and made no sound as he crept closer. His keen eyes spotted four shapes stretched out on the ground near what was left of the fire. As far as he could tell, the men who had camped there were all sound asleep and hadn't posted a guard. They had to be pretty confident they wouldn't be in any danger.

They were from somewhere around there, he thought. Maybe a hunting party from that Crow village he and his companions sought.

That thought had just gone through Preacher's mind when something grabbed him from behind and jerked him off his feet. Preacher might have thought he'd been latched on to by a grizzly bear, but he didn't feel any claws digging into his flesh, just an incredibly strong grip. Whatever had hold of him flung him through the darkness as if he were a child's rag doll.

It was just sheer luck that Preacher didn't collide with a tree trunk with bone-breaking impact. His wild flight was completely out of his control.

He landed in some brush, hitting it hard enough that branches snapped. The sharp ends of those broken branches jabbed into him. Briars clawed at his flesh, but he wasn't really injured. He fought his way free of the clinging growth and came up on his feet.

Somewhere nearby, Dog growled and snapped, then let out a yelp. The cur came flying out of the darkness and smashed into Preacher, knocking him down. He had broken Dog's fall, though, and kept him from being seriously hurt. Whoever had tossed Preacher aside had done the same with Dog.

Both of them were still on the ground when heavy footsteps stomped toward them. A tall, thick form loomed over Preacher. He rolled to the side as a huge foot slammed down into the dirt where he had been lying a heartbeat earlier. If that crushing foot had landed as its owner intended, Preacher would have had a bunch of broken ribs.

The monster came after him, trying to trample him into the ground. Preacher scrambled out of the way and made it to hands and knees. From there he launched himself at his attacker and caught the man around the knees. He rammed his shoulder against the man's right thigh and drove hard with his feet.

That would have upended most men, but that one seemed to be more of a man-mountain. He didn't go down. He bent over, grabbed the back of Preacher's buckskin shirt, and hauled him up, then shifted his grip to an arm and a leg. With a grunt of effort, he lifted Preacher above his head and poised him there for a second, ready to hurl him again.

Before the huge attacker could carry through, Dog recovered somewhat, leaped, and hit him in the mid-section, staggering him enough so that Preacher was able to writhe out of his grasp. As Preacher fell, he reached out and grabbed handfuls of long, greasy hair. That helped him catch himself. He lowered his head and smashed the top of it into the man's face.

The head-butt was effective. The man stumbled backward. He was a lot taller and heavier than Preacher, but he wasn't facing just the mountain man. Dog had landed lightly on his paws and dashed in to bite at the man's legs. The man bellowed in pain as sharp teeth tore his buckskin trousers and ripped into his flesh. He flailed around with arms as thick as saplings.

Preacher set his feet and hit the man in the face again, this time with his fists in a swift left-right-left combination. The punches rocked the man's head back, putting him off balance. Preacher clubbed both hands together and swung them at the man's jaw in a sledgehammer blow that landed cleanly. The man's head twisted violently on his neck, and his knees buckled.

Preacher realized too late that he was still too close to his opponent. He sprang back as if he were trying to get out of the way of a falling tree, but it wasn't enough. The man was losing consciousness, but he still had enough anger and willpower to catch hold of Preacher's shirt and jerk him closer.

With stunning force, the man's weight came down on top of Preacher. The mountain man felt like a giant was trying to hammer him into the ground. His ribs groaned, and his breath exploded from his lungs.

Stunned, he was incapable of doing anything except lying there gasping for air.

Using iron will and stamina, he recovered quickly. As his senses returned to him, he tried to push his massive, unconscious adversary off of himself. If he could just roll the monster to the side . . .

But it wouldn't have done any good, he realized as he heard Dog growling. He paused in his efforts and looked up to see four more shapes clustered around him. In the moonlight, he could tell that all wore buckskins and had feathers in their hair. Two had bows drawn back and arrows aimed at him. The other two carried flintlock rifles. The sound of the hammers being cocked told Preacher that they were ready to blow his head off and just needed an excuse to do it.

CHAPTER 22

"Hold on there," Preacher said in Crow, guessing that was the most likely language for the men to speak. The great weight pressing down on him made it difficult to talk. "I'm a friend."

"You fought with Big Thunder," one of them replied in an accusing tone.

"If you mean this fella who's built like a mountain, of course I did. He jumped me, threw me around like a kid's toy, and did his durnedest to kill me. I had to fight him to save my own life." Preacher dragged in a breath. "And if you don't get him off me, he's still liable to suffocate me!"

The two warriors holding the bows lowered them and unnocked the arrows, replacing the shafts in the quivers they carried. Then they reached down, took hold of Big Thunder—a good name for the varmint, Preacher thought—and rolled him aside like a log. Big Thunder's arms flopped to the sides. He was still out cold.

Preacher sat up warily. The two men with rifles still had the weapons pointed at him. Even in the moonlight, he could tell they were tense. Preacher didn't like it when nervous fellas aimed guns at him. "You boys are Crow, ain't you?"

"What if we are?" one of the rifle-wielding warriors demanded.

"I'm a friend to the Crow and always have been. I'm looking for the village of Chief Falling Star. My name is Preacher."

That revelation had an instant effect. All four men murmured among themselves.

Then one said, "Preacher?"

"That's right."

"It is known among our people that Preacher's greatest enemies are the Blackfeet. For this reason, Preacher is our friend."

"Now you're gettin' it," the mountain man said.

"Then why did you and your dog attack Big Thunder?"

Preacher couldn't keep a note of exasperation out of his voice as he said, "I told you. The big fella jumped me. How in the world can somebody that size move so quietlike?"

"Big Thunder is light on his feet," the spokesman for the Crow admitted. "He has taken many enemies by surprise."

"I'll bet they were sorry they let him sneak up on them, too," Preacher muttered. A few feet away, Dog growled, so Preacher added, "Easy, Dog. These fellas are our friends." He turned his attention back to the men surrounding him. "You boys are a hunting party from Falling Star's village, aren't you?"

"That is right. You know Falling Star?"

"I was through these parts a while back." Preacher could tell from the spokesman's voice that he was young, little more than a boy, in fact. If they were all like that, it was possible they didn't remember his visit to the Crow village. "I shot a grizzly that was about to maul Falling Star's son. I don't recall the youngster's name, but he was mighty grateful to me, and so was Falling Star. He said I was an honored guest in his lodge."

The men looked at each other again.

A different one said, "He speaks of Green Eagle."

"Yeah, that was his name," Preacher agreed. "I remember now."

"Green Eagle died two summers ago of a fever."

"I'm mighty sorry to hear that," Preacher said solemnly.

"But the story of how a white man saved his life from a bear is known among our people. I do not believe a white man would know of it . . . unless he was speaking the truth."

"I am," Preacher said. "Take me to Falling Star. He'll remember me."

"We will do this," the first warrior said. "Get up. And keep your dog back."

"You don't have to worry about Dog as long as you're peaceable. He gets upset when he sees somebody tryin' to kill me, though, so you might want to remember that." Preacher climbed to his feet and once again told Dog to stand easy.

One of the warriors went over to Big Thunder, knelt beside him, and began lightly slapping his face. Big Thunder didn't react at first, but after a couple of minutes, a deep rumble that sounded like a distant avalanche came from his throat and his hand shot up and clamped on the other man's face.

"Big Thunder, stop!" one of the other men cried. "That is Kicking Elk!"

Big Thunder grunted and gave the man he held an idle shove. The man landed on his back a few feet away and lay there shaking his head groggily. Big Thunder rolled onto his side, then pushed onto his hands and knees and slowly rose to his feet. From where Preacher stood, it looked like the massive warrior just kept climbing and climbing . . .

Big Thunder was maybe the tallest Indian he had ever seen, Preacher decided. His chest was like a boulder. Actually, his head had a distinctly rock-like shape, too. He looked around, spotted Preacher, snarled, and started toward him with arms outstretched. His fingers flexed as if with the desire to grab Preacher and tear him apart, bit by bit.

"Big Thunder, no!" one of the other men told him. "This man says he is Preacher, the good white friend of our people."

Big Thunder stopped short and stared at Preacher. His jaw was a granite slab, and so was his forehead. "Preacher?"

"That's right, Big Thunder," the mountain man said. "I'm Preacher. Why don't we just call a truce and not let there be any hard feelin's between us?"

"You hurt Big Thunder!"

"I was just tryin' to protect myself."

"Your dog bit Big Thunder!"

"And he was just protectin' me," Preacher explained. "Like you were tryin' to protect your friends. You were standin' guard while they slept, weren't you?"

"It was Big Thunder's turn," a Crow warrior said, somewhat uneasily.

"Look, fellas. I don't hold any grudges for what happened. I just need to get to your village, along with the folks who are travelin' with me, so we can talk to Falling Star. Will you take us?"

"Who travels with you? I see only you."

"There are two white men, trappers like me. My son,

who is half Absaroka." Preacher paused for a second. Getting into Caroline's complicated background wouldn't help matters so he decided it was best to keep things simple. "And a young Crow woman named Butterfly."

"This Crow woman, she is your prisoner?"

"Not hardly," Preacher said emphatically. "In fact, we rescued her from some other white men who wanted to make her their slave, and before that she was a captive of the Blackfoot war chief Angry Sky. We're tryin' to save her from all of them."

That caused more muttering among the Crow warriors. Evidently they recognized Angry Sky's name . . . and they didn't have a very high opinion of him.

One of them confirmed that by saying, "We have heard of this Angry Sky. He is a bad chief, even for a Blackfoot."

"Where are the others you travel with?" another asked Preacher.

"Back downriver a ways. Maybe a mile."

After some low-voiced conferring among them, the spokesman announced, "Two of us will go with you and bring them back here. You are welcome to share our camp, and in the morning you can return to our village with us."

Preacher shook his head. "Waitin' for mornin' ain't a very good idea. I don't know how far behind us Angry Sky and the rest of that bunch is, but I figure they're pretty close, seein' as how a few of 'em ambushed us earlier. If we wait, they're liable to catch up and try to wipe us all out."

"You have brought trouble to our land," another of the young Crow warriors snapped.

"I know, and I'm sorry about that," Preacher told them. "It couldn't be avoided."

"We will all go to fetch the others," said the one who seemed to be the leader. "Then we will return to the village tonight."

A couple of his companions didn't like that decision and weren't shy about expressing their opinion. The leader wouldn't be swayed, though. He told them to break camp, and they grudgingly set about doing so.

"My name is Broken Pine," he told Preacher. "What are the names of your companions?"

Preacher told him, then said, "I appreciate what you're doin', Broken Pine. And I wish there'd been some other way instead of gettin' you and your people dragged into this mess."

The young man's teeth shone briefly in the moonlight as he smiled. "If it means we have a chance to fight the Blackfeet, there is nothing for you to be sorry about, Preacher. Killing Blackfeet is what Crow warriors do."

Accompanied by Broken Pine, Big Thunder, Kicking Elk, and the other two Crow, Preacher didn't have any trouble backtracking the way he and Dog had come. The warriors led their horses, rather than riding, since Preacher was on foot. Big Thunder brought up the rear.

"He will know if anyone follows us," Broken Pine explained to Preacher as they walked side by side at the front of the group with Dog trotting ahead of them. "He has the keenest hearing of any warrior in our village."

"Seems like he's quite a fella," Preacher commented. "I don't recollect ever seein' a bigger Crow . . . or anybody from another tribe, either."

"The Great Spirit blessed him with strength and

skill, it is true, but in some ways Big Thunder is like a child."

Preacher knew what Broken Pine meant. Big Thunder had the mind of a child and probably would never progress beyond that. He had seen such things before, as if nature balanced out an abundance of one thing by taking away from another.

"The woman traveling with you," Broken Pine said. "What village is she from?"

"I don't rightly know," Preacher answered honestly. "She told us that Angry Sky's war party attacked her village and killed most of the warriors, then carried off some women and children as captives, but she didn't say who the chief was or anything like that."

"And she managed to get away from Angry Sky? She must be very brave and resourceful."

"Seems like it," Preacher agreed. "I expect she had some luck on her side, too. But then the luck played out on her, because she ran smack-dab into a bunch of white men who'd come out here to murder honest trappers and steal their furs. A fella name of Jefferson Scarrow is the leader of that group, but I don't know anything else about him except that he wants to get his hands on Butterfly again."

"You took her away from this Scarrow?"

"Yeah." Preacher smiled proudly in the darkness. "Actually, my boy Hawk That Soars sneaked right into their camp and set her free."

"The Absaroka?"

"Yep. Scarrow and the rest of his gang have been after us ever since, and now they've thrown in with Angry Sky."

"Blackfeet and white men working together?" Broken Pine sounded like he had a hard time believing that.

"I know. It's mighty odd, ain't it? But I reckon what it shows is that men who are evil and ruthless enough can form an alliance with each other to get what they want."

"And once they have it, they will try to kill each other," Broken Pine said with a wisdom beyond his years. Preacher had thought the very same thing more than once.

After a moment, the young Crow went on. "This woman Butterfly must be very beautiful if so many men want her and are willing to kill to capture her."

"She's a fine-lookin' gal, that's true enough," Preacher said.

"I am curious. I would like to see her for myself."

Preacher was sure that was true, and the other young men would be interested in Caroline, as well. That had the potential to create some friction between them and Hawk, but any problems like that would have to be worked out later. Survival was more important at the moment, and that meant finding his friends and lighting a shuck for that Crow village upriver.

Preacher knew that Hawk would be wondering what was taking him so long and might be on edge, so when they were close enough he sang out quietly, "Hawk, it's me, and I've brought some new friends with me."

Dog ran on ahead. A moment later, the big cur came bounding back, but he didn't seem happy. He ran in circles and whined to let Preacher know that something was wrong.

"What is it, Dog?" Preacher asked as he and the five Crow warriors came to a stop.

Dog let out a little yip, turned in circles, and dashed off again.

Preacher was acutely aware that Hawk hadn't answered his hail, and neither had anyone else in the party.

Quietly, he said to Broken Pine, "You fellas stay here. I'm gonna have a look around."

"If there is trouble, we should come with you."

"No, I reckon I can handle it, but if I holler, you and the rest o' the boys come a-runnin'."

Leaving them there, Preacher catfooted forward through the trees. He was close enough to the river to hear it flowing over its rocky bed. His keen eyes picked out the three dead trees that had fallen across each other. He had told Hawk that would be a good place to fort up if necessary.

No one moved around the deadfalls. He didn't even see the horses, and it was difficult to miss anything that big, even in the moonlight.

"Hawk!" Preacher called again, louder this time. "Hawk, are you here? Charlie? Aaron?"

He almost called White Buffalo's name but caught himself before he did. It would take some time for his brain to adjust to the fact that the garrulous old-timer was dead.

Preacher stalked up to the deadfalls and looked all around the logs. No one was there. Some of the grass nearby was beaten down, though, and that was a sure sign of feet stomping around heavily, probably during a fight. Several branches on a small bush were broken, too. Something had happened there, sure enough, and although Preacher didn't know what it was, he could be certain of one thing.

Hawk and the others were gone.

CHAPTER 23

Earlier in the night, Angry Sky had moved his warriors on the eastern side of the river to the western bank since he now had a better idea of where his quarry was. He pushed his combined force at such a rapid pace that Jefferson Scarrow thought the horses would be worn out and unable to continue by morning.

But if they caught up, killed Preacher and the others, and recaptured Butterfly, it wouldn't matter what the horses were capable of, Scarrow supposed. He just had to make sure all the Blackfeet were dead shortly after that, too, so he and Plumlee and the others wouldn't have to flee with the girl.

They could rest for a while instead. He would be able to take his time with her, and then he and his men could resume the activities that had brought them out there in the first place, namely stealing furs and getting rich.

Before they had gone far enough to exhaust the horses, and after his scouts warned that they were getting close to the place where they would find who they were after, Angry Sky called a halt. He ordered his men to dismount, then told Scarrow and the others in

English, "We will go on foot from here." The sneer on
the war chief's face was evident in his voice as he
added, "Are you and the others capable of moving quietly, white man?"

"We can be quiet just fine," Plumlee blustered.

Scarrow raised a hand in a signal for him not to get
carried away. "We'll do our very best," he promised
Angry Sky. "I don't believe we'll give away our approach, if that's what you're worried about."

"Be careful that you do not," the Blackfoot said
curtly. "This has gone on too long. I would be done
with it."

"I feel exactly the same way," Scarrow said, and
meant it.

They moved forward through the darkness. Scarrow noticed that several of the Blackfeet fell back a
little, so that the war party was split, some in front of
the white men and some behind. They were surrounded, in other words, and Scarrow was certain
Angry Sky had arranged things that way on purpose.
He wanted his men to be in position to betray the
whites as soon as they had achieved their objective.

Scarrow didn't intend to give the savages that opportunity. He whispered to Plumlee, "Pass the word
to the men. As soon as the men we're after are dead,
they're to open fire on the Blackfeet."

"I like the sound o' that," Plumlee replied, also in a
whisper. He drifted back a few steps and spoke to the
next man in line in a voice too low to be overheard.

They all advanced stealthily upriver until Angry Sky
motioned for them to halt and held some sort of con-
ference with several other Blackfeet.

Scarrow wasn't going to be left out of things, whether
Angry Sky liked it or not. Boldly, he moved closer to
the knot of warriors and asked, "Is something wrong?"

"Quiet!" Angry Sky snapped at him. "I sent the scouts out again, and they have returned with news. Preacher is no longer with the group we seek."

"He's not? Where could he have gone?"

Angry Sky shook his head. "I do not know. But it worries me."

Such caution seemed odd coming from a war chief with Angry Sky's evidently fearsome reputation. Scarrow said, "It seems to me this is a turn of good fortune for us. From what we've heard about him, Preacher is our most formidable enemy. Now we won't have to deal with him in order to get the girl back."

"Every Blackfoot in this land hates and fears Preacher," Angry Sky said. "To be the warrior who kills him would bring great honor. This is something you cannot understand, white man."

Scarrow frowned. "Wait a minute. What are you saying? That you'd rather kill Preacher than take Butterfly back from the ones who stole her?"

"I would do both," Angry Sky declared. "My people will sing songs about Preacher's death for many moons, and I would have them sing of me, as well."

"So what is it you intend to do? Wait for Preacher to come back from wherever he is before you try to recover the girl?"

Scarrow knew he was treading on shaky ground by standing up to Angry Sky. The war chief was accustomed to making all the decisions and being obeyed without question. Scarrow didn't want to be seen as weak in front of his men, though, and he reminded himself that his group actually outnumbered Angry Sky's. If anyone should be the leader, he thought, it was him.

Angry Sky shook his head. "If we wait for Preacher

to return, we must fight all of them. We strike now, while he is gone."

"I like the sound of that."

"But we do not kill the others. We take them prisoner."

"Hold on there," Scarrow said. "Why not wipe them out while we have the chance?"

"Because if we take them alive, then Preacher will have to come to us. One man against a little more than twenty. He will have no chance. Then, once he is dead, we can take our time killing the others."

Scarrow wondered how much of Angry Sky's plan was strategic and how much was sheer bloodlust. He wanted a chance to torture the other men in Preacher's party. Two of them were white, so that made sense. The Blackfoot hatred for white men went back decades. Scarrow had heard that it stemmed from an incident thirty years earlier when the expedition led by Lewis and Clark first penetrated the then-unknown frontier.

But giving in to the savages' bloodthirstiness might not be the best move.

Scarrow said, "Don't you think that Preacher will come after us to save the girl, whether the others are dead or not? It would make matters simpler to go ahead and kill them."

"I have decided," Angry Sky replied in a flat, hard voice that didn't allow for any argument.

Scarrow could tell that if he pressed the issue, it would mean a fight. A fight that couldn't be won without suffering some losses. And once the battle began, the short-lived alliance would be over and the Blackfeet would have to be wiped out.

None of that appealed to him, so even though it went against his better judgment, he said, "All right,

Angry Sky, but it may not be possible to take all of them alive. Some may fight to the death."

"So be it, but we will spare the ones we can . . . for now."

The anticipation in the war chief's voice at the thought of the grisly fate he had in store for any captives made a tiny shiver go through Jefferson Scarrow.

The longer Preacher was gone, the more Hawk worried, although he wouldn't admit that to the others . . . and was reluctant to admit it even to himself.

Logically, he knew that his father could handle any trouble the situation threw at him. Even though he and Preacher hadn't been partners for all that long— hadn't even known of each other's existence until fairly recently—they had shared enough adventures since then that Hawk had complete confidence in Preacher's ability to take care of himself.

His friendship for Charlie and Aaron, though, along with the growing affection he felt for Butterfly, made him concerned. If something *did* happen to Preacher, as unlikely as that was, then it would be up to Hawk to see that the others reached the safe haven of the Crow village. He was sure he could do that . . . but he would feel better about things when Preacher showed up again.

The loss of White Buffalo earlier tonight had already shaken Hawk deeply. The old-timer really had been like a grandfather to him. With White Buffalo gone, Hawk wasn't exactly the last of the Absaroka—there were other bands scattered across the frontier—but at that moment, he felt like it.

As if sensing how troubled he was, Butterfly went over to him. "Sit and talk with me, Hawk That Soars," she suggested, motioning with a graceful hand toward the deadfalls. "Perhaps it will make you feel better."

"I feel fine," he said without hesitation, unwilling to admit any weakness, especially to a woman.

"You must grieve for White Buffalo."

"He died as a warrior would want to die," Hawk said stubbornly. "When there is time, I will sing a song in his honor."

"And I will sing a song of mourning for him," she promised. "But tonight, there is nothing more we can do for him."

The thought of sitting on one of the logs next to Butterfly and talking with her appealed to Hawk, but he still shook his head. "I must keep watch. Our pursuers may catch up to us at any time."

"Aaron and Charlie are both watching for the enemy."

That was true. The two young trappers held their rifles ready and stalked around the outer edges of the open area, alert for trouble. Hawk knew they didn't have the same capabilities he and Preacher did, but he reminded himself that they had stayed in the mountains and continued trapping during the time he and Preacher had gone back down the Missouri River to St. Louis, and they had survived.

But as far as he knew, they hadn't run into any real danger during that period. Not like the danger that currently faced them.

Still, Butterfly had to be frightened. She was just asking him for a few moments of comfort. And he could remain alert while he was sitting with her . . .

"Come," he said. "We will sit."

"Good," Butterfly said as she touched his arm for a second. In the moonlight, he could see the shy smile on her face.

They moved over to the deadfalls and sat down on one of them. After a moment of silence, Butterfly asked, "What will you do once we reach Falling Star's village, Hawk That Soars?"

"Preacher believes you will be safe there. He and I will resume trapping, along with Aaron and Charlie."

"There is no chance that you would . . . stay there, too?"

He couldn't be sure what she was asking, but he knew what his response was, anyway. "I cannot. I must go with Preacher."

"Is trapping beaver that important?"

There was more to it than that—a lot more—but he wasn't sure how much he should tell her. He knew that once freed of the responsibility for Butterfly's safety, Preacher would want to hunt down the men responsible for White Buffalo's death. He would avenge the old warrior. All the white men led by Jefferson Scarrow would die, and so would the members of Angry Sky's war party. Once Preacher set off on the vengeance trail, nothing would stop him or ever slow him down for very long.

Hawk intended to be at his father's side on that quest. He owed it to White Buffalo.

Being a woman, Butterfly would never understand that, Hawk thought. So he said, "I cannot live with the Crow. They are not my people."

"The Crow and the Absaroka are related, and you are the last of your band. They would take you in, Hawk, you know that."

She was right about that, of course, and he also noticed that she had just called him Hawk, as Preacher did, instead of his full name. He found himself liking that.

"They will take you in, Butterfly. They have no such obligation to me."

"Preacher calls me Caroline," she said, changing the subject. "It is a strange name to my ears . . . but it has a pretty sound to it."

"It does," Hawk agreed. "Would you rather that I call you Caroline?"

"Will you make me go to a land of strangers, as Charlie and Aaron believe is the right thing to do?"

"Back east?" Hawk shook his head. "I believe it would be difficult to locate your white family, and even if we could, they would not want you now that you have lived as an Indian."

"You sound bitter."

"I know white men," he said. "I have not seen a great many of them . . . but enough to know what they are like." He looked off into the night. "These plains and valleys and mountains are home for people like you and me, Butterfly. I will not call you Caroline. While that may have been your name once, it is not your name now."

She leaned against him and whispered, "I feel the same way, Hawk That Soars."

He enjoyed the soft, warm pressure of her body. It wasn't enough to make him forget all the bad things that had happened, but it helped. He knew he ought to get up and join Charlie and Aaron in standing guard, but he hated to leave Butterfly . . .

He happened to be looking toward Charlie when the stocky young trapper went, *"Urk!"* and jerked backward toward the trees. In that split second, Hawk realized someone had gotten behind Charlie, looped an arm around his neck, and pulled him violently into the shadows. If Hawk had been a white man, he would have cursed himself in that moment for allowing himself to be distracted by Butterfly's warmth and beauty.

He leaped to his feet and cried, "Aaron, look out!"

It was too late. Two figures sprang at Aaron as if from nowhere and bore him off his feet. Hawk heard the meaty thuds of fists and feet striking flesh.

Butterfly screamed.

Hawk whirled around and saw several men charging at them from a different direction. He flung his rifle to his shoulder and fired. The sight of an attacker flying backward as if slapped down by a giant hand rewarded him.

But then the others were on him. He lashed out with the rifle butt, felt it connect solidly with flesh and bone. Then he dropped the rifle and grabbed his pistols. Before he could pull them free, however, strong, wiry hands clamped on his arms and pinioned them at his side. The struggling knot of men surged back and forth on the grass, stamping heavily on it as they tried to subdue Hawk.

Something slammed against his head and stunned him. Red explosions burst behind his eyes. His brain still worked enough for him to realize he had been struck with a war club or the flat of a tomahawk. Whatever it was, the blow left him only half-conscious and unable to put up as much of a fight as he wanted to. He tried to force his muscles to work, but they stubbornly refused.

He was aware of Butterfly screaming and then shouting in anger. She wouldn't just allow them to take her without resisting, but too many shadowy figures swarmed around her. Around Hawk, too. Someone kicked him in the back of his right knee and made the leg buckle. A weight landed on his back and forced him to the ground. Feet thudded into his ribs in vicious kicks.

Hawk gasped, "Butterfly!" then something hit him in the head again and he passed out.

CHAPTER 24

As soon as Preacher realized Hawk and the others were gone, he knew the Blackfeet and the fur thieves had been there. If it had not been for the signs of a struggle, he might have thought it was possible Hawk had moved the party on purpose, say, in case he'd discovered that pursuit was closing in on them.

The sign told a different story, though. At least he didn't see any dark splotches on the ground where blood had splashed . . . and no sprawled corpses to be seen, either.

Dog whined at his side, and Preacher said, "Yeah, you knew somethin' was wrong, didn't you, old son? You can pick up the scent, though, ain't no doubt about that. Find Hawk!"

At that command, Dog bounded off while Preacher turned back toward the area where he had left Broken Pine and the other young Crow hunters. "Broken Pine!" he called. "Come on in!"

A moment later, the five warriors emerged from the shadows.

Broken Pine looked around curiously and asked, "Your friends are not here?"

"Looks like somebody took 'em," Preacher said. "In these parts, I reckon only one bunch could responsible for that."

"Angry Sky and the Blackfeet," Broken Pine said grimly.

"Yeah, and Scarrow and the rest o' those renegade whites."

"There are no bodies?"

"Not that I've seen so far." Preacher turned toward the river. "But I'm gonna take a better look around, just to be sure."

"We will help," Broken Pine offered. He turned his head and added to his companions, "Be careful and watch for trouble."

With the assistance of the Crow, Preacher thoroughly searched the immediate area. No bodies and still no blood. He found a couple of other places where the grass looked like struggles might have taken place. Whatever had happened, it had been violent but also quick and apparently not fatal.

But after trying so hard to kill all of them except Caroline, why would Angry Sky and Scarrow have left Hawk, Aaron, and Charlie alive? The answer Preacher thought of immediately was that they wanted to use his son and his friends as bait. Angry Sky had been hoping to kill Preacher, too, and the easiest way to do that would be to lure him into a trap.

That was what the war chief believed, anyway, Preacher thought. But it might turn out that idea was wrong . . .

When they had all assembled again, Preacher told the Crow, "My hunch is that Angry Sky carried off the rest of 'em to lure me into comin' after him. Dog will have picked up the trail by now, so he'll be back any minute. It won't be hard to find the varmints I'm lookin' for. You fellas can head on back to your village and let Falling Star know what's goin' on. Tell him I'll be there with the rest of 'em as soon as I can."

Big Thunder surprised the mountain man by saying in his rumbling voice, "Preacher is going after the bad men alone?" Maybe he understood more about what was going on than Broken Pine gave him credit for.

"Well, that's what I figured on doin'."

"Preacher should not go alone."

"Big Thunder is right," Broken Pine said. "We will come with you."

"Now hold on just a minute. This ain't your fight—"

"You were bringing the girl Butterfly to our village knowing the Blackfeet would follow you."

"Yeah, but I didn't have any other choice if I was gonna save her life," Preacher said.

"We would help you save her life."

"I didn't even know you fellas until a little while ago. You ain't part of this trouble."

Kicking Elk said, "I want to see this girl so beautiful many men fight over her."

Mutters of agreement came from the other Crow warriors, except for Big Thunder, who just stood there gazing at Preacher. Maybe because he had whipped the galoot, Big Thunder had sort of latched on to him like a puppy, Preacher realized.

Angry Sky and Scarrow expected him to be alone, he thought. They probably figured that with the size of their combined group, he wouldn't stand a chance against them. If he had a few folks fighting on his side, it might throw all their plans out of kilter. The five Crow wouldn't be enough to even the odds, by any means, but if they went along, they would give him the element of surprise, Preacher decided.

But four could do that just as well as five, so he said,

"All right, I'll go along with it, but you've got to send one man back to the village so Falling Star will know what's goin' on. That's the only way I'll agree with what you're sayin'."

Broken Pine considered that countersuggestion, but only for a moment before he nodded. "Moose Horn, you have the fastest pony. Take him and ride for home."

Moose Horn wanted to argue that he should get to go along and kill some Blackfeet, but Broken Pine overrode his objections and sent him on his way.

About then, Dog came trotting back and sat with his tongue lolling out and an eager expression on his face that Preacher could see in the gray light. The sun would be up before too much longer.

Dog wasn't the only one who showed up. Shaking his head up and down, Horse emerged from the trees. All the other mounts were gone, no doubt taken along with the prisoners, but it didn't surprise Preacher that they hadn't been able to catch Horse.

"Your stallion?" Broken Pine asked as Horse came up and bumped his head against Preacher's shoulder.

"Yeah," the mountain man said. "He's pretty much a one-man horse, although he'll tolerate Hawk takin' care of him. But I'm thinkin' that when they tried to catch him, he broke loose and headed for the tall and uncut."

"So we will all be mounted."

"Yeah, and that's good," Preacher said, "because it won't be much longer until we're burnin' daylight."

The pain Hawk felt as consciousness seeped back into his brain made him aware that he was still alive. When his thoughts became coherent, he was a little surprised to realize that the Blackfeet hadn't killed him out of hand as soon as he was knocked out. For some reason they must have decided to keep him alive.

And *that* didn't bode well at all.

He kept his eyes closed and used his other senses to figure out where he was and what was going on. He didn't want to let on that he had regained consciousness until he had a better idea of the situation.

He felt warmth on his face and felt a steady light through his eyelids, so he knew the sun was up and shining on him. Woodsmoke tickled his nose and brought with it the smell of roasting meat. Even under those circumstances, the aroma caused his stomach to cramp and made him realize he was hungry, as bizarre as that seemed.

Voices sounded nearby. Men were talking in harsh tones. Some of the words were Blackfoot, but snatches of English were mixed in with them.

"—them alive is a bad idea."

"As soon as Preacher—"

"—don't like the looks on those redskins' faces—"

"—away from the girl—"

The girl. They were talking about Butterfly. So she was still alive, which Hawk expected considering how much trouble men had gone to in order to recapture her. But in the chaos of battle, accidents could always happen, and some misfortune could have befallen her. Hawk was greatly relieved to know that evidently it hadn't.

He was lying on the ground, on his right side, he realized as he continued taking stock. Dirt was in his mouth. He'd probably gotten it there when his captors pitched him on the ground. He risked opening the right eye but only to a narrow slit.

The first thing he saw was Aaron Buckley sitting in a dejected posture about five feet away. His knees were drawn up and his head leaned forward, resting on them. Rawhide thongs were lashed around his wrists, binding them.

Beyond Aaron, Hawk could see a man's leg clad in buckskin trousers. From the leg's position, he could tell that the man was sitting on the ground, too. That had to be Charlie, Hawk thought. So his friends were still alive.

Why?

Why hadn't the Blackfeet killed all three of them? The war party had managed to sneak up on them while they were waiting for Preacher. That knowledge rankled, but it didn't do anything to ease Hawk's puzzlement. The Blackfeet could have shot him and Charlie and Aaron from concealment, and they never would have known what happened.

Instead they had taken him and his friends prisoner. Hawk couldn't help but wonder if they intended to torture the three of them to their deaths.

Another possibility existed, Hawk mused. Preacher had been gone when the war party attacked. The Blackfeet might intend to use their captives as bait to lure the mountain man into a trap. Hawk knew how the Blackfeet felt about Preacher. They would do almost anything for a chance to kill their legendary nemesis.

Beyond Aaron and Charlie, a couple of Blackfoot warriors walked past, but no one else came into Hawk's very limited field of view. His curiosity overwhelmed him. He had to know where Butterfly was. He opened both eyes, lifted his head, and looked around.

He saw immediately that they were in a narrow canyon with rocky, almost sheer walls. Patches of grass grew on the canyon floor, and off to Hawk's left were a few scrubby trees. Back to the right, the canyon narrowed down to a small opening. Several Blackfeet stood near there, apparently posted as guards.

The rest of the Blackfeet were scattered around in small groups. So were the bearded, hard-looking white men, except for two who sat with a tall, burly Blackfoot who wore a scowl on his face as he talked to them. Hawk wondered if that was Angry Sky. The name would fit him.

Hawk didn't pay too much attention to that trio because a few feet beyond them, sitting on a rock with her head down and her eyes turned to the ground, was Butterfly. She didn't appear to be injured, as far as he could tell, and she wasn't tied up, but her shoulders slumped and an unmistakable air of defeat and despair hung around her.

Hawk couldn't blame her for feeling that way. Despite everything he and the others had done to try to get her to safety, including White Buffalo making the ultimate sacrifice, she was back in the hands of her worst enemies.

One of the white men talking to the surly Blackfoot noticed that Hawk was awake and nudged his companion with an elbow. He was thick-bodied, with rusty hair and a face that bore a distinct resemblance to a hog. The other man was much leaner, with dark, bushy side whiskers.

That man spoke to the Blackfoot. "Our young friend has regained consciousness."

"No Absaroka is a friend of mine," the man replied in good English. "They are all vermin that should be exterminated from the face of the earth."

Hawk felt the same way about the Blackfeet.

The three men got to their feet and walked toward him. Their path took them past Charlie and Aaron. Hawk could see the young trappers better now. Both had some scrapes and bruises to show that they had put up a fight when they were captured, but they didn't look to be seriously injured.

Hawk couldn't bring himself to believe that that condition would prevail for much longer.

The Blackfoot snapped a command as he and the two white men approached. Several warriors closed in around Hawk. Two of them took hold of his arms and jerked him to his feet. His head still pounded from the blow earlier, and he was unsteady enough that he might have fallen if they hadn't been holding him up.

The Blackfoot and the two fur thieves came to a stop in front of Hawk. He glanced past them and saw that Butterfly had lifted her head and was watching the confrontation with an anxious expression on her face.

"I am Angry Sky," the Blackfoot declared, confirming Hawk's hunch.

Hawk's chin jutted out as he answered with pride in his voice, "I am Hawk That Soars."

Angry Sky's right arm came up and the back of his hand cracked across Hawk's cheek, jolting his head to the side. The pain inside his skull thundered even worse, but he didn't show it as he hung in the cruel grip of the two warriors and snarled defiantly at Angry Sky.

"I care nothing about who you are," the Blackfoot war chief said. "Only that the one called Preacher values your life. Or will he abandon you here to die?"

"Preacher cares nothing for me," Hawk replied in a rasping voice. He didn't want his captors to know of the blood relation between the two of them and hoped that Charlie, Aaron, and Butterfly hadn't said anything about it. "But he will hunt you down anyway. Because killing Blackfeet is what he does best."

Several warriors standing nearby glared at him and moved closer, their hands reaching for knives or tomahawks.

Angry Sky waved them back. "You live only because you will help us kill Preacher."

"I will never—"

"Preacher will come to free you and your friends and the Crow girl, and then we will kill the Ghost Killer, at last. No longer will he prey on our people."

Aaron and Charlie had lifted their heads, too, casting off their dejected poses at least for the moment.

Aaron protested. "Preacher never preyed on anyone. All he's ever done is protect innocent people from evil."

Angry Sky gestured toward Aaron. One of the warriors drew his knife, grabbed Aaron's hair, and jerked his head back. Hawk tensed his muscles, but the shape he was in, he couldn't break free as the warrior brought the blade to Aaron's throat.

He didn't swipe the keen steel across the taut flesh, though, just held it there threateningly.

The white man with the side whiskers said, "It would probably be a good idea if you kept your opinions to yourself, lad. Angry Sky doesn't need *all* of you to serve as bait for Preacher, you know. I daresay, just Butterfly herself would be sufficient, if it came down to that."

Aaron didn't say anything more, but he was pale and motionless while the Blackfoot warrior held the knife at his throat for a moment longer. Then the man moved the blade away, let go of Aaron's hair, and stepped back.

"The next time, blood will be spilled," Angry Sky promised. He nodded to his men and added, "Tie this one and guard them all. Preacher will come soon, and then this canyon will run red with blood."

He might be right about that, Hawk thought as his captors jerked his hands behind his back and wound rawhide thongs around his wrists. But Angry Sky was wrong about just whose blood was going to be spilled.

CHAPTER 25

Dog never wavered from the scent as he led Preacher and the four young Crow warriors back to the east, away from the river and toward a wide basin.

As they rode side by side, Preacher asked Broken Pine, "Do you fellas ever hunt over yonder?"

"Not very often," Broken Pine answered. "More game can be found west of the river. There are few streams or waterholes in the basin, and trees and grass are sparse, so deer and elk and antelope have no good reason to venture in there. Mostly there are snakes and lizards, and we do not hunt them."

"Snakes and lizards is a pretty good description of the varmints we're huntin' today," Preacher muttered. "Except when critters kill, they're just doin' what comes natural to them for their own survival. They don't kill outta pure meanness and greed, like the fellas we're after."

Preacher couldn't be sure how much of a lead their quarry might have, since he didn't know exactly when in the night Hawk and the others had been captured. Because of that, he proceeded cautiously, although it was unlikely Dog would allow them to stumble right into the midst of their enemies.

Around mid-morning, as they entered the area where vegetation was sparse, Preacher spotted horse tracks along the path Dog was following. He reined in and swung down to take a closer look. Unshod, just as he expected, which meant Indian ponies. Jefferson Scarrow's gang of fur thieves hadn't been mounted during Preacher's first encounter with them, but they were now.

"We can follow these tracks," he said. "That means Dog can go on ahead and maybe find out where they're holed up. Hunt, Dog! Find Hawk!"

The big cur whirled and dashed off, soon vanishing in the rugged terrain. Preacher and the Crow warriors took advantage of the opportunity to rest their horses for a few minutes.

"How many men did you say we are following?" Kicking Elk asked.

"Around twenty," Preacher replied. "Maybe a few more than that. Some Blackfoot, some white. And all bad."

"There are many more of them than us," the fourth warrior said. He was a stocky youngster who had been introduced to Preacher as Dark Neck. A deep brown birthmark covered the right side of his neck and extended up to his jaw.

"I still say you fellas don't have to come along," Preacher said. "I sure wouldn't hold it against you if you wanted to head on back to your village."

Dark Neck bristled a little. "That is not what I meant," he declared. "If there are so many enemies, then vanquishing them will bring great glory and honor to our names!"

Big Thunder let out an exultant yip of agreement.

Preacher smiled at them. "I'm proud to have you fellas on my side, that's for sure. Let's mount up and ride."

He had no trouble following the sign left by the Blackfeet and the fur thieves. They weren't going to any trouble to hide their trail, and Preacher knew why that was. They *wanted* him to follow them. Now that Angry Sky had recaptured Caroline, he was getting greedy. He wanted Preacher dead, too.

Preacher had been in that region before, but it had been awhile. Mountain ranges surrounded it on all sides, with only a few gaps. The semiarid basin between the peaks was a two-day ride from one side to the other. Bony ridges and deep canyons broke up stretches of dusty plains. A river ran through there somewhere, one of the rare streams that ran from south to north because of a quirk of geography, but the vegetation that grew along it was a mere ribbon of green in a broad, sweeping vista of browns, tans, and reds. Looking out over the basin from the heights of any of the surrounding mountain ranges, the horizontal streaks of different colors were visible in the places where those ridges reared up. In its own stark way, the basin was beautiful, but that impression didn't last long when a person was actually trying to make his way through it. Then it was just ugly and dangerous.

At that time of year, it was hot, too. By the middle of the day, with the sun high overhead, the temperature was uncomfortable and Preacher was glad for the shade his wide-brimmed brown hat provided. He missed the cooler air of the high country that he could see behind him whenever he turned in the saddle and looked back over his shoulder.

The trail led beside one of those long, streaked ridges. Preacher was thinking about calling another halt when he spotted Dog up ahead, trotting toward them. Preacher knew Dog wouldn't be back if he hadn't been successful in finding Hawk.

Preacher dismounted as Dog came up to them. He dropped to one knee, scratched the big cur's ears, and asked, "Did you find Hawk, old son?"

Dog turned, ran away a few yards, then stopped and looked back at the mountain man.

Preacher grinned. "I knew you wouldn't let me down." He stood up and turned to look at the Crow warriors. "I'll go ahead on foot and scout around some with Dog. You fellas wait here."

"Big Thunder will go with Preacher," the massive young man said. He started to climb down from his horse.

Preacher held up a hand and said, "No, Big Thunder. I'm obliged to you for offering, but that's not a good idea. I'll go by myself this time. You need to stay here with Broken Pine and the others. Don't worry, I'll come back and get you before there's any fightin'. You won't miss out on anything." He looked at the others. "None of you will. You can bet a warbonnet on that."

"All right, Preacher," Broken Pine said with a nod. "But if we hear shooting—"

"You'll know to come a-runnin' and be ready for trouble," Preacher agreed. He motioned for Dog to lead the way.

After they had followed the ridge for about half a mile, a wide canyon opened up on Preacher's left. Dog angled into it.

The canyon serpentined through the rugged landscape, making numerous wide bends. Preacher relied on Dog to make sure no ambushes lurked around any of those blind spots. Smaller canyons branched off here and there, and Preacher figured even smaller canyons intersected them. Some of those canyons would connect up, more than likely, forming a maze where a man could get lost in a big hurry if he didn't pay attention to where he was going—and where he had been.

Preacher's own instincts along those lines were excellent. Once he had traveled a route, he never forgot it. He was confident he could find his way back out, and any time he couldn't, Dog could.

He wasn't sure how far along the canyon they had gone—the way it twisted around, estimating distances was all but impossible—but after a while, Dog stopped, looked back at Preacher, and whined.

"We're gettin' close, are we?" Preacher asked quietly. He moved up alongside the big cur, paused long enough to give one of Dog's ears a scratch, then eased forward. The canyon took another of those bends right up ahead. Preacher took his hat off, leaned forward, and reached a spot where he could see around it.

Right away he spotted the mouth of one of those smaller canyons about a hundred yards away, on the left side of the one he and Dog had been following. That was the only such opening he spied. The main canyon was empty, so Preacher knew it had to be what—or *who*—was in the smaller one that had Dog's hackles up.

He drew back and whispered, "That's where they are, huh? I wonder if there's a back door into there."

In the labyrinth of canyons, that was possible. He looked up at the ridge beside him. It was fairly steep, but it fell back in a series of terracelike ledges that he thought he might be able to climb. The differing horizontal streaks of color followed those ledges.

"Stay," he told Dog. "I'll be back."

He used the thin length of rawhide he carried in his possibles pouch to rig a sling for his rifle and arranged the long-barreled weapon on his back so it would be out of the way. Then he found the likeliest-looking place and started climbing it.

The ridge's sandstone face was rough enough that Preacher had no trouble locating footholds and hand-holds. He reached the lowest ledge and moved along it until he found a good place to continue the ascent. In that back-and-forth fashion he rose higher and higher above the canyon floor.

The sun was bright and hot. Sweat trickled down the mountain man's back. Several times during the climb, he hit a stretch that seemed impassable. Stubbornly, he kept searching and each time found a route that he could handle, so he didn't have to climb all the way down and start over. He wanted to avoid any such delays. While it made sense that Angry Sky would keep the prisoners alive if he intended to use them as bait, truthfully he didn't need *all* of them, and Preacher knew it. As long as there was a chance any of them were still alive, he would continue to try to rescue them.

Unfortunately, Angry Sky was probably well aware of that fact, too.

The interminable climb finally came to an end, and Preacher rolled onto the top of the ridge. It wasn't very wide, fifty feet at most, and on the other side it dropped in the same sort of terracelike ledges. Ahead, another ridge came in from the left and merged to form a plateau. The smaller canyon Preacher had seen cut through there.

Several rock spires jutted up even higher on top of

the ridge. Preacher was about to stand up and catfoot toward the smaller canyon when he caught a glimpse of movement behind one of those spires. He froze where he was, flat on the ridge crest, and waited to see what was going to happen.

A couple of minutes dragged by, then a buckskin-clad warrior stepped out from behind the rock spire far enough for Preacher to see him in profile. The Blackfoot peered along the canyon, which meant he wasn't staring directly at Preacher, but he was looking in the mountain man's general direction.

Preacher was absolutely motionless, not even breathing. He knew that movement caught the eye faster than anything else. That was how he had spotted the Blackfoot sentry, after all. The man had shifted around restlessly and given away his position. Angry Sky wouldn't be happy if he knew about that. The guard's carelessness probably came from him knowing that he was watching for only one man . . . as far as he knew.

Preacher thought he was going to have to risk taking a shallow breath, but the man drifted back behind the rock spire. Instantly, Preacher shifted his pistols, knife, and tomahawk around behind his back and started crawling closer. He had to get a look down into the canyon to see what sort of situation he would be facing when he tried to rescue the prisoners.

That meant he would have to deal with the guard. If there was only one, and if none of the other Blackfeet came to relieve him any time soon, that wouldn't be too much of a problem. Preacher stayed low, ready to freeze in place again if he needed to.

Slowly, foot by foot, Preacher closed in on the rock spire. He aimed for the side of it away from the canyon, thinking an approach from that direction would give him the best chance of surprising the sentry. He was careful not to let any of his weapons scrape on the ground as he crawled.

Finally, he reached the spire. He lay there for a moment and heard the guard moving around a little on the far side of the rock. No voices, though, which he hoped meant the Blackfoot was alone. With great caution, Preacher climbed to his feet, making not a single sound. He shifted his pistols, knife, and tomahawk again so he could reach them easier, pressed his back against the spire, and slid around it.

The guard was facing the other direction, still watching the main canyon. He was probably supposed to give some sort of signal to the rest of the war party in the smaller canyon if he spotted Preacher. Judging by his casual attitude, he had no idea that the man he was supposed to be watching for was within arm's reach of him at that very moment . . . nor that his life would be ending very shortly.

Preacher hesitated and looked down into the smaller canyon. Due to the canyon's narrowness and the ridge's height, he couldn't really see who was down there or what was going on. The faint murmur of voices reached his ears. The combined force of Blackfoot warriors and white renegades was hidden in the canyon, all right. He was certain of that. And the prisoners had to be with them, too.

A faint whisper of steel against leather was the only sound as Preacher slipped his knife out of its sheath. Only a narrow space separated the spire from the drop-off into the smaller canyon, so he knew he would have to be careful and not allow the guard's body or anything else to drop down there. The resulting clatter if that happened would alert Angry Sky and his men and they would know something was wrong.

When Preacher struck, it was almost too fast for the eye to follow. His right hand went around the guard's head and clamped over his mouth and nose so he couldn't even snort. His left drove the knife into the man's back. Long years of experience in such grim work guided the blade between the Blackfoot's ribs. It pierced his heart and made him spasm as death swiftly claimed him. Preacher pulled the dying man back against him and pressed both of them tight against the spire until he was sure life had fled from his enemy.

Then Preacher dragged the man back around the spire to where there was more room and lowered the corpse to the ground. He took the man's knife and tomahawk. He never knew when extra weapons might come in handy.

While he'd been crawling toward the spire, he had studied both rims of the canyon and hadn't spotted any more sentries so he was free from the threat of discovery. He moved along the rimrock above the smaller canyon, still being careful not to dislodge any rocks that might fall and warn those below that someone was moving around up there.

He was looking for that back door he had thought about earlier and after searching for a quarter of a mile, he found it. The canyon narrowed down and petered out. The ledges had ended even sooner, so the walls were practically sheer. But more of those rock spires rose like rotted teeth in ravaged gums, and a man with a rope could wrap it around one of them, climb down into the canyon, and get behind Angry Sky, Jefferson Scarrow, and the rest of that blood-thirsty bunch.

The trick would be freeing the prisoners and getting them out the same way with arrows and rifle balls flying around them.

Preacher knew that would be impossible. But he had the glimmering of an idea . . .

CHAPTER 26

Broken Pine and the other young Crow warriors were waiting where Preacher had left them when he and Dog rejoined them. They were sitting against the base of the ridge, maybe not quite as alert as they should have been under the circumstances, but Big Thunder had been watching for Preacher.

He sprang to his feet as soon as the mountain man came into view. A grin split the massive warrior's face. "Preacher is back," he announced.

The other three warriors scrambled up, as well.

Broken Pine asked, "Did you find them?"

Preacher nodded. "They're in a small side canyon about a mile from here. Looks like there's only one good way in, and we wouldn't have a chance if we attacked it head-on."

"What else can we do?"

Dark Neck declared, "I will not ride away when there are Blackfeet to be slain."

"Neither will I," Kicking Elk added.

"Nobody's ridin' away," Preacher said. "You three fellas are gonna try to fight your way in as soon as it gets good and dark."

Broken Pine frowned at him. "I thought you just said such an attack would stand no chance."

"Well . . . you're gonna make 'em *think* you're tryin' to fight your way in, anyway."

Understanding appeared on Broken Pine's face. "You want us to keep them occupied while you do something else."

"Yep. Big Thunder, can you climb?"

An even more childlike grin appeared in the face that seemed to be made out of stone slabs and lumps. "Big Thunder is the best tree climber there is!"

Preacher smiled at his enthusiasm. "There ain't any trees around here for you to climb, Big Thunder, but how are you at climbin' rocks?"

"Big Thunder can climb anything!"

Preacher nodded at that confident declaration. "You'll get a chance to try. And I know from firsthand experience that you're mighty strong. I need you to climb to the top of the ridge and haul some folks up on a rope."

Big Thunder turned to the sandstone wall and started looking for a good place to climb.

"No, not right here and now," Preacher went on. "I'll take you to the place and tell you what to do, but not just yet. All right?"

"Big Thunder will do whatever Preacher says. Preacher is the only man who ever defeated Big Thunder. He is a great man."

"I'm glad you think so, instead of wantin' to wallop me some more."

"We will fight again someday. Big Thunder likes to fight!"

"We'll see about that," Preacher promised vaguely. He never wanted to tangle with the towering galoot again, but Big Thunder didn't have to know that.

With Big Thunder mollified for the moment, Preacher explained his plan to Broken Pine, Kicking Elk, and Dark Neck.

He began by describing exactly where the small canyon was, then said, "You fellas will head down there when it gets closer to night. Big Thunder and I will climb up on the ridge and head for a place where I can get down into the canyon by usin' the rope I've got on Horse's saddle."

"Big Thunder will hold the rope!"

"No, not just then. I'll tie it around a rock that's stickin' up in a good place for it."

Big Thunder looked disappointed, so Preacher went on. "But you'll have plenty to do a little while after that."

"Big Thunder will go down in the canyon with Preacher and kill Blackfeet?" The giant warrior's thick fingers flexed in anticipation. Preacher didn't know if Big Thunder was thinking about strangling Blackfeet . . . or just tearing them apart with his bare hands.

"I need you to stay on top of the ridge. Then, your friends here will attack the canyon and keep all the varmints in there busy for a spell while I free the prisoners and take them to where the rope's hangin' down. That's when you haul 'em up and outta there."

Big Thunder frowned, evidently deep in thought as he considered everything Preacher had said, but finally he nodded in understanding.

"Big Thunder can do that."

"I never doubted it. That's why I came up with the idea in the first place." Preacher turned back to the other Crow. "Take Horse with you and keep him close. Ride to where you can throw some shots into the mouth of the canyon where they're holed up. Gallop around, fire some arrows in there, yip a lot like there's a whole war party of you. Don't stay out in the open too long at a time, though. I don't want anything to happen to you fellas."

"When do we do this?" Broken Pine asked.

Preacher thought about that question for a couple of seconds before answering. He didn't want to give any sort of signal from atop the ridge, because Angry Sky might be canny enough to notice it and realize that someone was up there.

"Wait until this much of the moon is above the horizon," he said, holding up his hand so there was about an inch of space between his thumb and forefinger. "I'll start down into the canyon as soon as the moon touches the horizon. Durin' the time it takes to rise that much more, I can get down there, figure out what to do, maybe take care of a guard or two, and start freein' the prisoners."

"How long do we continue the attack?"

"If you can keep the varmints busy for fifteen minutes or so, that'll give me time to get Butterfly loose and out of the canyon, and probably Aaron and Charlie, too. Hawk and me will take our chances if we have to. We're used to it." Preacher paused. "But if Angry Sky and the rest of that bunch come boilin' outta there and start after you, you fellas light out as fast you can. Don't wait for nobody or nothin', and don't look back."

None of them seemed happy about that, but Broken Pine said, "If we all get away, where will we meet?"

Preacher had to think about that, too. "We'll follow the top of that ridge as far as we can. Angry Sky can't get to us very easily as long as we're up there. Remember the place close to the western edge of the basin where all those rocks were in a circle?"

Broken Pine nodded. "The Devil's Eye?"

"That's what your people call it?"

"No, some white trappers who came through several summers ago gave it that name." Broken Pine blew out a disdainful little breath. "The Crow people are not that fanciful."

"Well, just so we all know where we're headed. We'll meet you there as soon as we can. But if the pursuit's close behind you and you can't stop there, don't worry about it. Just head on back to your village. Not even a mad dog like Angry Sky would attack it." Preacher looked around at the four young men. "Everybody clear on what we're doin'?"

They nodded and muttered agreement.

"Maybe we ought to hunt some shade and rest a mite, then," Preacher said. "It's liable to be a busy night."

During the rest of the morning, Hawk could sense the anger and frustration growing among his captors, red and white alike. Angry Sky had expected Preacher to already have shown up, but there had been no warning from the guards posted at the canyon mouth or the one on top of the ridge. They would have let the others know right away if they saw any sign of the mountain man.

Around midday, Jefferson Scarrow drifted over to the prisoners. "It's beginning to look as if your friend Preacher is going to leave you to your fate, gentlemen."

"He won't do that," Charlie said. "He rescued me once before, remember? That didn't turn out so well for you. And it's going to be worse this time, mark my words."

"Worse for whom?" Scarrow asked. "And I wouldn't

advise you to talk like that around Angry Sky. He might take offense."

"What would happen if he did?" Aaron asked. "He'd kill us? He's planning to do that anyway, and in the most painful way possible, unless I miss my guess."

Charlie paled. "Don't talk like that. We're going to be all right."

Scarrow smiled. "Hope springs eternal. But I'd be sure to make peace with my Maker, if I were you fellows."

Hawk spoke up. "What will happen to Butterfly?"

"You're more worried about the fair maiden than your own lives, I take it? How chivalrous." For a second, naked lust appeared on Scarrow's face. He controlled the reaction quickly and went on. "Don't concern yourselves. I'll see to it that she's not mistreated."

"How can you do that?" Hawk wanted to know. "She is Angry Sky's woman now, not yours."

Scarrow's jaw tightened. "Angry Sky *believes* she's going to belong to him, but he's wrong. I'm not going to allow such a rare gem to go through life as the slave of a savage."

"So you're going to make her *your* slave, instead," Aaron said. "That doesn't really seem any better."

"I'll treat her decently," Scarrow snapped. "She won't spend the rest of her life producing squalling red brats for that beast."

Hawk wished Angry Sky could have heard those words. He knew the Blackfoot war chief understood English. If Angry Sky was aware of what Scarrow planned, it might lead to a falling-out between the two groups before either of them intended. And such a clash could only reduce the odds against Preacher.

However, Angry Sky was a good fifty yards away, at the base of a narrow, zigzagging trail that led to the rimrock where a sentry was posted. He spoke to a warrior with him, and then the man began to climb. Hawk knew he had to be going up there to relieve the other guard.

After his last curt comment, Scarrow turned on his heel and stalked away. Charlie watched him go and said quietly, "Sooner or later, he and Angry Sky are going to be at each other's throats."

"Not soon enough to help us, though," Aaron said. "We'll all be dead before they reach that point."

Charlie turned his head to look at Hawk. "You don't believe Preacher has abandoned us, do you? He'd never do that! Would he?"

"He would not," Hawk said.

Butterfly still sat on a rock on the other side of the campfire, which by now had burned down to ashes and a few embers. Her head was lowered again. She seemed as depressed and defeated as Aaron. Hawk wished she would look up, so he could meet her eyes and try to convey to her somehow that everything was going to be all right. No matter what the odds, no matter how desperate the situation, he had absolute faith in Preacher. The mountain man would find some way to rescue them and defeat their enemies.

Butterfly looked up just then, all right, but only because everyone else in the canyon did as well. A strident, surprised shout came floating down from the ridge. Harsh words followed, and Angry Sky shouted back up at the man he had just sent up the trail. Hawk understood enough of the Blackfoot tongue to realize they were talking about someone being dead.

The guard who had been posted up there earlier to watch for Preacher? Who else could it be?

Hawk felt a little thrill go through him when he heard Angry Sky's furious exclamation that included the Blackfoot words for "Ghost Killer." Preacher had been there, all right. No doubt about it.

"What's going on?" Charlie asked.

"The warrior Angry Sky sent up to the top of the ridge to take over for the other guard has found a dead man," Hawk explained. "It must be the first guard. Preacher has been up there."

Both young trappers stared at him.

Aaron said, "If Preacher was that close, why didn't he do something to help us?"

"Because it was too dangerous just then," Hawk said. "Dangerous for us, not for him. He was looking to see how things are here. He knew he could not attempt to free us just then without getting all of us killed."

"That makes sense, I guess," Charlie said. "But he's coming back for us, isn't he?"

"Never doubt that," Hawk said.

Angry Sky gestured and barked orders, and two more members of his war party started climbing to the top of the ridge. Hawk supposed they were going to retrieve the dead man's body.

With that done, Angry Sky whirled and strode toward the prisoners. Scarrow and Plumlee followed him.

Charlie looked like he wanted to crawl into a hole somewhere and just disappear. Aaron's expression remained dull and barely interested in what was going on around him. Hawk's face was impassive, showing neither defiance nor apprehension.

Across the way, Butterfly watched, wide-eyed and terrified.

Angry Sky came to a stop in front of the three

young men and said in English, "The Ghost Killer has been here."

"I know," Hawk said calmly. "I heard you speak of him."

"One of my warriors is dead!"

"Those who are Preacher's enemies usually wind up that way."

Angry Sky's lips curled in a snarl. "Did you know he was there?"

"The Ghost Killer comes and goes as he pleases, and no one knows unless he wishes it to be so."

"It will not help you any for me to lose one man."

"One *more* man," Hawk said. "How many has Preacher already killed? How many more *will* he kill before this is over?" Most of the Blackfeet and the white renegades were looking at him, so he raised his voice and went on. "None of you will leave this canyon alive unless you release us and flee now! And even that may not be enough to save you from the vengeance of the Ghost Killer!"

He didn't actually expect that to accomplish anything, but it felt good to voice the dire threat.

A second later, he regretted it to the depth of his being.

Angry Sky barked another order and two of his men leaped forward to grab Aaron's arms and jerk him to his feet.

"The dying begins now," Angry Sky said.

CHAPTER 27

Charlie's hands were tied in front of him. Even at his best he wasn't what anyone would call graceful, but at that moment he was able to leap up and shout, "No! You can't do that!"

The much more athletic Hawk stood even though his hands were tied behind his back, an acknowledgment that his captors considered him a greater threat. He took a step forward before Hogarth Plumlee smashed a fist into his face and knocked him back. Tied as he was, Hawk couldn't maintain his balance and went down hard.

A few feet away, one of the Blackfeet brought a war club down across the back of Charlie's shoulders and knocked him face forward onto the ground.

"Stop it!" Aaron cried, but the words weren't directed at the Blackfoot or Plumlee. "Charlie, Hawk, stop! There's nothing you can do to help me! Don't throw your lives away!"

Hawk tried to struggle up again anyway, despite that plea, but Plumlee sank a brutal kick into his side that rolled him over.

Butterfly leaped up, crying "Hawk!" and tried to rush

toward him, but Scarrow got in her way and grabbed her by the arms.

"Stay back, my dear," he told her in English, even though she couldn't understand it. He echoed Aaron's words as he went on. "There's nothing you can do for any of them."

Angry Sky glanced toward the two of them, and from the fire that flashed for a second in his dark eyes, he didn't like seeing Scarrow holding Butterfly. Neither did Hawk, who saw the war chief's reaction. But Angry Sky was too full of rage over the fact that Preacher had been so close, had killed one of his men, and had disappeared without his presence even being known. Angry Sky had to let that fury out first, before he did anything about Scarrow.

The war chief held out his hand and one of his men placed a tomahawk in it as Aaron was hauled over to stand in front of him. Aaron wasn't putting up a fight. Despair had totally engulfed him. He stared dully at Angry Sky.

"You die now, white man," Angry Sky rasped.

"No!" Charlie cried. "Aaron, get away from there!"

Hawk had managed to lift his head so he could see what was happening, although part of him wished that he hadn't. Aaron finally turned his head and looked back. "Good-bye, Charlie. You were always a good friend. I hope you make it out of—"

Before he could finish the sentence, Angry Sky smashed the tomahawk into his head.

From where he was, Hawk heard the crunch of bone, saw the way Aaron's eyes went wide with shock and pain. Knowing he was probably about to die and having it happen were two different things. Blood welled from the horrible wound on the side of his head as Angry Sky jerked the tomahawk back.

Then Angry Sky struck again. The two men holding Aaron had a difficult time keeping him upright as Angry Sky slammed the tomahawk into the young trapper's head three more times, turning it into a gruesome, shattered mess that no longer looked human. Blood and brain matter flew from the shattered skull and splattered across Angry Sky's chest and face, which was twisted in a grotesque rictus of hate.

Hawk knew that Aaron was dead, had died instantly from that first blow. He no longer felt the savage mutilation, but that was scant comfort for the others in the face of such a brutal display. All the renegades in Scarrow's bunch looked on in stunned silence, including Plumlee. Even some of the other Blackfeet looked a little shocked by what they were witnessing.

Butterfly had turned her head away from the grisly spectacle and pressed her face against Jefferson Scarrow's face as sobs shook her entire body.

He patted her lightly on the back as he said quietly, "There, there, my dear. It'll be over soon."

It had to be over. There was nothing left for Angry Sky to do to Aaron Buckley unless he wanted to keep hacking with the tomahawk and chop the young man's body into pieces. Hawk thought he might actually do that, but then Angry Sky abruptly lowered the tomahawk and stepped back. His blood-splattered chest heaved with the depth of his emotion. Insane hatred still contorted his face.

He tossed the gore-smeared tomahawk aside, flung out his left arm, and pointed toward the canyon mouth. The two warriors lowered Aaron's body to the ground, then picked it up by the arms and legs and carried it toward the opening. Angry Sky called orders after them. They took Aaron's body out into the main canyon and placed it on the ground again, with the broken remains of the young man's shattered head turned toward the direction they had come from.

The way Preacher likely would come from, Hawk thought. Angry Sky wanted the corpse to be the first sight that greeted the mountain man's eyes.

Angry Sky swung back to Hawk and Charlie. "Preacher should come soon, or there will be more dead white men for the buzzards to feast on."

"But we don't have any way of making Preacher come here sooner," Charlie said.

"Then pray to whatever spirits you pray to, white man . . . because your death will not be so easy."

Broken Pine and the other warriors dozed in the shade of an overhanging rock during the afternoon. Preacher could have slept, too, knowing that Dog and Horse would alert him if anything threatening came near, but even though he rested with his back against the rock, he didn't sleep. He was worried about what might have happened when Angry Sky discovered that his guard atop the ridge had been killed. If there had been some other way to find out what he needed to know, Preacher would have taken it.

Hawk, Caroline, Charlie, and Aaron were all in deadly danger as long as they were in the hands of those men. Sometimes at moments like this, Preacher felt a bone-deep weariness at the fact that people he cared about kept winding up in such peril. He hadn't known any of those four all that long—Caroline only a few days, Hawk, Aaron, and Charlie less than two years—but they were important to him anyway. He wanted to get all of them out of this mess safely.

Not that he blamed himself for any of it. They had all gone into it willingly, with their eyes wide open.

Caroline was the exception, of course. She hadn't had any control over anything that had happened.

Still, Preacher was tired of trouble following him around. He wondered what it would be like to live a peaceful life, surrounded by friends and family, without rotten bastards trying to kill him all the time.

He had an overpowering suspicion that he would never find out . . . and if White Buffalo's dying prophecy was right, Preacher had long, long years of hell-raising and blood-spilling still in front of him.

Late in the day, he woke the others, who looked a little sheepish about sleeping the afternoon away. "All right, fellas. We'd best get ready. The time to head out will be here before you know it."

He took the coiled rope from the pack of gear strapped to Horse's saddle, then he patted the rangy gray stallion on the shoulder and stroked his nose. "You're gonna have to go with Broken Pine. Wish I could take you with me, hoss, but there just ain't no way you can go the places where I got to go."

He dropped to a knee beside Dog and repeated the heartfelt farewell. "Stay with Broken Pine and them other boys. Fight if you have to, but keep yourself safe." He looked into the big cur's brown eyes. "Danged if I don't think ol' White Buffalo was right. You savvy ever' word I'm sayin', don't you?"

Dog whined and licked Preacher's cheek. Preacher hugged the thick neck for a second, then stood up and nodded to Big Thunder.

"You ready, son?"

"Big Thunder is ready to go with Preacher!"

Preacher put the coil of rope over his left arm so it hung from his shoulder, then took up Horse's reins to lead the stallion. As the sun lowered, the group proceeded along the ridge to the spot where the smaller canyon was visible right around the bend.

Preacher had a hunch that the Blackfeet had discovered the dead guard. Another man, maybe two, would be posted on top of the ridge behind that rock spire, keeping watch on the main canyon. Despite that, he motioned for the others to stay back, took off his hat, and risked a glance around the bend. He wanted to know if anything had changed since he'd been there.

Something had changed, all right. And the sight of it was like a giant fist slamming into Preacher's gut.

A body lay in the main canyon, not far from the entrance to the smaller one. Preacher recognized it by its contours as Aaron Buckley. He had no doubt that Aaron was dead. Although the sunlight no longer penetrated directly into the canyon that late in the day, he could see the bloody ruin that had been Aaron's head. It looked like somebody had taken a tomahawk to it and wielded the weapon with great savagery and fury.

Angry Sky. Preacher had no doubt about that, either.

First White Buffalo had died, and now Aaron. Rage boiled up inside Preacher. Rage the likes of which he had experienced before in his life, but only on rare occasions. He had been to the so-called Colter's Hell in the Yellowstone country to the west, with its bubbling, molten pits that sometimes erupted in towers of scalding water. The rage felt like that inside him, white-hot and with the pressure building until it simply had to explode . . .

Not yet, he told himself as he drew in a deep, ragged breath. Aaron was dead, but Hawk, Caroline, and Charlie might still be alive. More than likely they were, or Angry Sky would have had their bodies pitched out into the open, as well, to taunt Preacher about his failure to save them.

The young Crow warriors saw the emotion on his face when he drew back from the bend and gave him apprehensive looks.

Broken Pine asked, "What is wrong, Preacher?"

"One of my friends is dead. A young fella named Aaron, not much older than you boys. His body's layin' out in the main canyon, in front of the entrance to the one where they're holed up. I'm bettin' Angry Sky killed him and had him dumped there." A bitter, sour taste spread under Preacher's tongue as he added, "As a message to me."

"This man is evil," Broken Pine declared solemnly. "Of course, we knew that . . . because he is Blackfoot."

"I reckon he's one of the worst I've run across from any tribe," Preacher said. Again he took a deep breath, and felt his rage subside—for the moment. "But our plan stays the same. It's still the best chance we've got of freein' the other prisoners. Are all you fellas ready?"

Nods from the four young men. They no longer seemed quite so eager to go into battle, but they still looked plenty determined.

Preacher checked the sun. It had sunk partially behind the mountains to the west. Dusk had begun to settle down over the basin. By the time he and Big Thunder completed the climb that was ahead of them, full night would have fallen but the moon wouldn't rise for a while longer. That would give them enough time to get into position.

"Come on," he said to Big Thunder. "We'd best get started while we've still got a little light to see by."

At first he pointed out handholds and footholds to his massive companion, but he soon realized that Big Thunder didn't really need the help. He was a good climber, just as he had claimed. With his long reach and great strength, probably an even better climber than Preacher.

Shadows gathered quickly once the sun was down. Preacher and Big Thunder had to slow their pace and rely more on touch than sight as they searched for their next grips. But their progress up the ridge was steady, and stars were just beginning to appear in the deep-blue-shading-to-black sky above them as they rolled over the rim onto level ground.

"Stay down," Preacher whispered to Big Thunder. "The guards may be watchin' up here now. The fella who was on duty earlier wasn't expectin' anybody to make that climb, but they know now that somebody did."

The Blackfeet knew that *he* was the one who had scaled the ridge and killed that sentry, Preacher thought. He was sure they had been talking about Ghost Killer among themselves. That was all right. It never hurt anything for an enemy to be a mite spooked. Made them more likely to be careless now and then.

When the night had grown darker, Preacher figured it was safe for him and Big Thunder to make their move. They wouldn't be silhouetted as they dashed along the ridge toward the far end of the small canyon.

"Just move as quiet as you can," he told Big Thunder as he rose to his feet.

The giant warrior did likewise. Big Thunder was surprisingly light on his feet as he followed the mountain man.

Within minutes they arrived at their destination. Preacher took the coiled rope off his shoulder and started to loop it around the rock spire he had chosen to anchor it.

Big Thunder stuck out a paw and said in a quiet rumble, "Big Thunder can tie rope. Big Thunder is good at tying knots."

Everything he had claimed so far had turned out to be true, so Preacher handed him the rope. While Big Thunder was tending to that chore, Preacher stepped to the rim and looked along the narrow canyon. He saw a campfire burning at the other end, a quarter of a mile away. A few dark figures moved around it, coming between him and the flames. Preacher searched for the other captives but couldn't see them from where he was.

That was all right, he told himself. He would be seeing them soon enough, when he freed them.

"The rope is ready," Big Thunder said behind him.

Preacher turned and stepped over to the spire, which was about four feet in diameter and maybe twice that tall. He took the rope when Big Thunder held it out to him and leaned back against it, testing the strength of both the spire and the knot. It was absolutely secure, he decided, just as Big Thunder had promised.

"Here's how we'll work this," Preacher said. "You hold on to the rope while I climb down into the canyon. When I reach the bottom, I'll tug on it a couple of times to let you know I got there all right. Then you just hang on to the rope and wait. When you feel me tug on it twice again, that's when you start haulin' up whoever's on the other end. I'll try to send the girl up first, if I can. You won't have any trouble with her, because she don't weigh much. Charlie will come next, but he's bigger."

"Big Thunder can pull him up."

"I know you can. Then, if there's time, me and Hawk will come up. If I don't make it out of the canyon but Hawk does, he's in charge. You understand, Big Thunder?"

The massive warrior nodded.

"And if neither one of us make it," Preacher went on, "you take Charlie and the girl and follow this ridge as far as it goes, got that? You know where that place is, the one Broken Pine and I talked about? The Devil's Eye?"

"Big Thunder knows. Big Thunder can find it."

"Then we're all set," Preacher said with a grin as he clapped a hand on Big Thunder's upper arm.

"Big Thunder wishes he was going down to kill Blackfeet, too."

"Let's just get those prisoners out of there, and then . . . well, I got a feelin' you might still get a chance to do that, Big Thunder."

CHAPTER 28

Aaron's horrific death at the hands of Angry Sky left the other three prisoners numb with shock and grief. For Hawk, however, that feeling didn't last long before pure fury replaced it. Somehow, Aaron's death would be avenged. Hawk didn't know exactly how that would come about just yet, but he swore to himself that Angry Sky would pay.

And not just the war chief. Hawk blamed the other Blackfeet, and the white renegades, as well. Jefferson Scarrow, Hog Plumlee, and the other fur thieves had played a significant part in the deaths of Aaron Buckley and White Buffalo, too. Everyone in the combined group deserved to be wiped out, as far as Hawk was concerned.

Given his current state of helplessness, most people would consider his current thoughts nothing more than bravado. But Hawk knew better. Justice would triumph, and those evil men would get what was coming to them.

Preacher was still out there somewhere. It was only a matter of time . . .

Time that passed slowly during the afternoon. Hawk

and Charlie both managed to struggle into sitting positions and scoot up against the canyon wall. Scarrow led Butterfly back to the slab of rock near the campfire and sat her down on it again. The rest of the men drifted back into whatever activities they had been doing to pass the time before the body of the dead sentry was discovered.

Angry Sky paced like a caged animal, too full of pent-up hatred to remain still. From time to time he glared over at Hawk and Charlie, and Hawk could tell that he wanted to go ahead and slaughter them, too.

It might have been his imagination, but Hawk thought he could hear the thousands of flies that were already buzzing around Aaron's corpse and realized those flies might be feasting on him or Charlie, or both of them, before the day was over.

The hours dragged past until the sun began to sink in the western sky. The oppressive heat eased a little.

Charlie said in a strained voice, "Preacher's not coming back, is he? If he was, he would have been here by now."

"I never expected him to make his move during the day," Hawk replied. "Night is when the Ghost Killer moves."

"All that Ghost Killer talk may unnerve the Blackfeet, but it doesn't change the fact that he'd be outnumbered about twenty to one. He'd have to be insane to think that he can do anything to help us. He must have realized that." A shudder went through Charlie. "We're going to end up like poor Aaron—"

"No," Hawk said flatly. "I know that will not happen. We may not live through the night, but Preacher will not abandon us."

Charlie just shook his head glumly. A few minutes

later, Hawk heard soft sobs coming from him as his shoulders shook. Charlie's nerve had broken. Hawk couldn't blame his friend for that, but his own resolve was still steely.

In the narrow canyon, night fell quickly once the sun was down. One of the Blackfeet stirred up the campfire and rekindled it. Despite the heat of the day, it usually got cool at night in those parts.

In the flickering light from the fire, Jefferson Scarrow went to the rock where Butterfly was sitting and sat down beside her. He spoke to her quietly enough that Hawk couldn't hear what he was saying. Butterfly kept her head down and didn't give any sign that she heard Scarrow's words, even though she had to, with him right beside her.

Hawk wasn't the only one who noticed the one-sided conversation. Angry Sky stalked over, planted himself in front of the rock, and said sharply to Scarrow, "What are you doing, white man?"

Scarrow looked up and in a cool voice replied, "Simply reassuring the young lady that everything is going to be all right."

"I say what happens here, not you!"

"I was under the impression that we're equals of a sort. After all, our forces number approximately the same." A confident smile tugged at Scarrow's mouth. "In fact, I believe I have a few *more* men under my command than you do, Angry Sky."

Hawk wondered if Scarrow was trying to force a confrontation between his men and the Blackfeet. The renegade leader could have decided that Preacher wasn't going to make a move against them after all, despite the guard's death. Scarrow was wrong, if that was what he thought, but he might not know that. He

could think the time had come for the showdown with
Angry Sky, and nothing would provoke that faster
than paying more attention to Butterfly than the war
chief liked.

The scene on the other side of the campfire had
broken through Charlie's gloom and caught his attention. He sniffled and then whispered to Hawk, "What's
going on? Are they about to fight?"

"I do not know," Hawk replied, "but that may be
true."

"I hope Scarrow and his men win. If they do, they'll
just shoot us in the head, I'll bet, instead of torturing
us to death like those savages would."

"Perhaps neither of those things will happen."

"I wish I could hope so, but—"

Charlie stopped short as Angry Sky reached to his
waist and pulled out a sheathed knife. Scarrow came
to his feet, his hand moving toward the butt of a pistol
stuck behind his belt. Like a thunderstorm about to
break, an air of wild, impending violence hung over
the canyon.

Preacher was ready when the first rounded sliver of
moon appeared over the eastern horizon. He took
hold of the rope, wrapped it one turn around his
waist, and told Big Thunder, "Wait for those tugs, like
I told you."

"Big Thunder will be ready."

Preacher backed up to the rim, felt underneath
him with a foot, got it planted, and then let his weight
carry him out into the open air above the drop into
the canyon. He pushed off, swung back in as he
dropped several feet, and let the powerful muscles in

his legs absorb the impact as the soles of both boots struck the canyon wall. He pushed off again, out, back, and down, playing out the rope as he did so. It was a quick way to make such a descent. He had learned it several years earlier from a Prussian trapper who'd climbed up and down mountains all over Europe before coming to America.

Even so, it took Preacher several minutes to reach the bottom of the canyon because he was careful and didn't get in a hurry. A fall would be disastrous. It would bust a leg, at the very least, and doom all his plans, not to mention the prisoners.

Relief went through him when he had solid ground under his feet again. He unwound the rope from his waist, stepped back, and gave it two sharp tugs. An answering tug came from Big Thunder. Preacher released the rope and let it hang there as he turned toward the camp at the canyon's other end.

The shadows were thick and the orange light from the fire didn't reach near that far, so Preacher wasn't worried about being spotted as he moved stealthily. Angry Sky really should have posted some guards at that end, too, but his arrogance must have prevented him from doing so. That was a break for Preacher, although he was confident he could have dealt with that problem if he'd needed to.

As he moved closer, he finally spotted the captives and mentally heaved a sigh of relief when he saw that Hawk, Charlie, and Butterfly were all still alive and apparently unharmed. Hawk and Charlie were tied up, sitting with their backs against the canyon wall. Butterfly was over by the fire with Jefferson Scarrow perched beside her on a bench-like slab of rock. As Preacher watched, Angry Sky went over and started talking to them. Evidently it wasn't a friendly conversation, because Angry Sky pulled a knife and Scarrow stood up and reached for a pistol.

Before things had a chance to get any more interesting between the two of them, shots rang out. Preacher heard whooping and pounding hoofbeats and the Blackfeet at the canyon mouth started shooting out into the main canyon.

Broken Pine, Kicking Elk, and Dark Neck had just showed up right on time.

Preacher broke into a run. Even at that faster pace, his feet made almost no sound on the hard ground as he hurried toward the camp. In the firelight, he saw not only Angry Sky but also Scarrow, Plumlee, and most of the other Blackfeet and fur thieves running toward the canyon mouth to meet the attack. Only a couple of warriors hung back, probably at Angry Sky's command, to keep an eye on the captives.

Butterfly stood up from the rock and started to run around the fire toward Hawk and Charlie. One of the pair moved to block her path. She tried to dart around him, but he grabbed her arm and jerked her to a stop. The other warrior watched what they were doing, and in doing so he turned his back toward Hawk and Charlie.

Preacher wasn't a bit surprised when Hawk seized the opportunity. The young Absaroka got his feet under him, surged upright, and drove forward, lowering his shoulder to ram it into the back of the guard watching the struggle between Butterfly and the other man. The unexpected impact knocked the startled warrior off his feet.

Charlie, whose hands were tied in front of him rather than behind his back like Hawk's, had gotten to his feet, too, and charged forward. As Hawk rolled aside, Charlie dropped onto the fallen warrior's back with both knees. He grabbed the man's long hair, jerked his head up, and slammed it down against the stony ground as hard as he could. In a seeming frenzy, Charlie kept smashing the Blackfoot's face into the ground.

Realizing what was going on, the warrior holding Butterfly let go of her and whirled toward Charlie and Hawk. He yanked an arrow from his quiver, and drew back his bow to launch the shaft aimed at Charlie.

Preacher had already pulled his tomahawk from his belt. Running full speed, he whipped his arm back and forward and threw the tomahawk. It whirled blindingly across the intervening space and struck perfectly, the head burying itself in the center of the warrior's forehead. He was able to loose the arrow, but it flew high as he fell over backward with blood and brains oozing out around the tomahawk.

Hawk got to his knees and exclaimed, "Preacher!"

The mountain man raced up to them. The diversionary attack was still going on, but Preacher didn't figure it would be long before somebody looked back in his direction and saw what was going on. He pulled his knife out and bent down behind Hawk, who knew what he needed to do and raised his bound wrists away from his body to give his father room to cut him free.

While doing that, Preacher said, "Charlie, grab Butterfly and head for the back end of the canyon. There's a rope hanging there waiting for you."

"We can't climb out before they discover what's happening!" Charlie gasped.

"Just wrap the rope snug around Butterfly under her arms and make sure she's got a good hold of it,"

Preacher said. "Then tug on the rope a couple of times. There's a friend up on the rimrock who'll haul her outta here. Once she's safe, you can go up."

"What about you and Hawk?" Charlie asked.

Hawk's wrists came free as the last of the rawhide strands parted under the keen blade of Preacher's knife. "We will make sure you have the chance to escape."

"Go!" Preacher barked.

Charlie took hold of Butterfly's arm and tugged her along with him as he broke into a run toward the far end of the canyon.

"Are you all right?" Preacher asked Hawk as he helped his son to his feet.

"Yes, and so are Butterfly and Charlie. But Aaron—"

"I know. I saw. One more score to settle with that bunch. But not here and now."

Hawk argued, "If we attack them from behind, while they are not expecting it—"

"They'll still kill us," Preacher said. "There are too many of 'em. But they'll come after us, and then we'll fight 'em at a time and place of *our* choosin'."

Hawk looked like he still didn't care for the idea, but he didn't protest again. He just stripped the dead guards of their quivers of arrows and picked up the fallen bow. Preacher wrenched his tomahawk free of the cleaved skull and glanced at the other Blackfoot. Charlie had busted the varmint's head to pieces by slamming it against the ground.

Side by side, Preacher and Hawk began backing away from the campfire.

They were still at the edge of the circle of light it cast when shouts of alarm went up from the combined force of Blackfeet and white renegades who had taken cover behind the rocks at the canyon mouth to return the fire from outside. The escape had been discovered, and Preacher had a hunch that Angry Sky was smart enough to realize everything else had been a diversion.

At least half the bunch ran toward them, several firing arrows as they came. The shafts fluttered around Preacher and Hawk as they turned and broke into a run.

Preacher's eyes adjusted quickly once they were away from the firelight, and the moon was high enough to be casting silvery illumination over the ridge. He spotted a bulky shape about halfway up the canyon wall. Charlie was trying to climb and help himself get to the top, but Preacher figured Big Thunder was doing most of the lifting.

The fact that Charlie was on the rope meant that Butterfly was safely atop the ridge. Preacher felt some relief at that. Things were going to be mighty close for him and Hawk, though. But he had known there was a good chance it would turn out that way.

"Keep an eye on Charlie," he told Hawk as they stopped at the bottom of the wall and turned to face the killers hurrying toward them. "As soon as he gets to the top, Big Thunder will toss the rope back down. You get up it as quick as you can."

"We will go together," Hawk said.

Preacher shook his head. "Nope. You don't know Big Thunder, but he's mighty, well, big. But not big and strong enough to haul both of us outta here. You can scramble up in a hurry, though, and then cover me while I come after you."

"Preacher, no—"

"I know you ain't ever been very good at doin' what

your ol' pa tells you to, but this time you ain't got any choice." Preacher glanced up over his shoulder and saw Charlie disappear over the rim. A few seconds later, the rope came tumbling back down. "Damn it, boy, go!"

Hawk still hesitated, but only for a heartbeat. Then he grabbed the rope, leaped up, planted his feet against the wall, and started climbing as fast as he could, grunting from the effort as the muscles in his arms and shoulders and back worked smoothly.

Preacher turned, pulled both pistols from his belt and cocked them, then grinned as he waited for the onslaught to wash over him.

CHAPTER 29

The men in the forefront of the charge were Blackfoot warriors, but Preacher didn't see Angry Sky among them. Some of the others had raced out ahead of the war chief. Nor did he see Scarrow or Plumlee.

But all of them were the enemy, so as soon as they were in range, he raised the pistols and pulled the triggers.

The weapons boomed and bucked in his hands as the heavy powder charges sent the double-shotted balls scything into the attackers' front ranks. Two men went down and another stumbled badly from an obvious hit. Preacher rammed the empty pistols behind his belt again and reached for his knife and tomahawk.

Before he could draw those out, something clattered beside him. He glanced down and saw a bow and a quiver of arrows lying there on the ground that must have been thrown from the top of the stone wall.

The rope tumbled down beside him as well. Hawk shouted from the rimrock, "Tie it around your chest!"

Preacher understood instantly. He grabbed the rope, wound it around his chest, and tied it in place with a fast knot, ducking an arrow that flew near his head. Then he snatched up the bow and quiver and yelled, "Go!"

The rope tightened around his chest as he was jerked off his feet and started rising.

More arrows whipped around him. A shot blasted and the ball hummed past him to send dirt and rock chips flying as it slammed into the canyon wall. Shooting up at an angle was difficult, but the men trying to kill Preacher were still coming pretty close.

He needed to discourage them and managed to get the quiver slung over his shoulder and pulled out an arrow. Nocking it, drawing the bow, and firing were all awkward because the movements made him sway at the end of the rope while his friends on the rimrock hauled him up. Preacher managed to send several arrows zipping into the crowd of Blackfeet and fur thieves, though. Shouts of pain and surprise rewarded his efforts.

As fast as he was rising, he knew that Hawk, Charlie, and Big Thunder all had to be pulling on the rope. Maybe even Caroline. It didn't take long for Preacher to reach the top. The arrows fired up at him began to fall short, but the rifle balls still came too close for comfort, so he was glad when Big Thunder's huge hands suddenly took hold of him and swung him onto solid ground again.

"Everybody all right?" Preacher asked.

"Yes," Hawk said.

"Let's get outta here, then. There's a trail up here, close to the other end of the canyon, and some o' those varmints may be on their way up it already!"

Preacher was untying the rope around his chest as he spoke, and Big Thunder unfastened the knot at the other end, where it was wrapped around the spire. Preacher tossed all the rope to Big Thunder and told him to hang on to it. Then he picked up his rifle from where he had left it lying on the ground before his descent into the canyon. He led the way along the ridge with Hawk and Caroline right behind him, Charlie next in line, and Big Thunder in the rear.

They moved fast in the moonlight. The footing was a little tricky because of the shadows, but they couldn't afford to take the time to be careful and had to trust to luck. They had gone a few hundred yards, Preacher judged, before he heard shouts rising behind them and knew the pursuit had reached the crest.

"Keep goin'," he called to Hawk and Caroline as he moved aside to let them pass. "I'll slow the bastards down!"

For once Hawk didn't argue. Preacher knew his son wanted to keep the young woman safe above all else. He didn't blame Hawk a bit for that. He would have been surprised—and a little disappointed—if Hawk *didn't* feel that way.

Charlie stumbled past him as well, but Big Thunder stopped and asked, "Is Preacher going to fight the Blackfeet now?"

"I'm just gonna take a few potshots at 'em. Nothin' you can help me with, Big Thunder."

"Big Thunder can shoot an arrow a long way!"

Preacher patted the stock of his rifle and said, "Not as far as this little darlin' can throw a ball. So you go on and keep the others safe for me, all right?"

Big Thunder was clearly reluctant, but he nodded and lumbered on after Hawk, Caroline, and Charlie.

Preacher lifted the rifle to his shoulder and squinted over the barrel. The pursuers were still at least two hundred yards away and trying to aim at distant flickers of movement in the moonlight was useless.

He just squeezed the trigger and fired a round in

their general direction, then reloaded as quickly as possible and squeezed off another. Spurts of orange muzzle flame winked an answer at him. He reloaded, then turned and ran after the others.

It was going to be a long chase. Preacher knew that if it had been just Hawk, Big Thunder, and himself trying to get away, they could keep running all night. But Caroline and Charlie wouldn't be able to maintain that pace. They would have to stop and rest, probably sooner rather than later. That would give the pursuit enough time to cut into their lead and maybe even catch up.

"Preacher!" That was Big Thunder's rumbling voice.

The mountain man spotted the massive warrior standing near the rimrock and waving toward him. Preacher angled in that direction.

"Hawk found a good way down," Big Thunder went on when Preacher joined him. He pointed at a narrow crack that appeared to lead into a tiny side canyon.

Preacher remembered how those little passages formed a maze. This one might lead out and provide a way for them to give the slip to the Blackfeet and the fur thieves. Or it might be a dead end where they would be trapped and slaughtered. Preacher figured the odds were about even on those two options.

But shoot, life was a gamble to start with, wasn't it? And they still had enough of a lead that if they disappeared, Angry Sky, Scarrow, and the others couldn't be sure where they had gone.

Preacher said, "Let's go, Big Thunder," and plunged into the steep, talus-covered trail that led down through the crack. His feet tried to slide out from under him, but he managed to keep his balance as he descended into pitch darkness.

* * *

Jefferson Scarrow caught hold of Hogarth Plumlee's arm and stopped him. Ahead of the two white men, four Blackfeet continued the chase, yelling incoherently.

Plumlee said, "Why'd you stop me, Jeff? That bastard Preacher's gettin' away!"

"For now," Scarrow replied. "But I really don't think blind pursuit in the darkness is a good idea. From everything we've seen of him so far, Preacher is exactly the sort who would decide to wait and plan an ambush. If there's a trap waiting somewhere up ahead, we'll let our redskinned friends be the ones to waltz right into it."

"Those heathens are no friends of mine. I'll kill a man who gets in my way and never lose a lick o' sleep over it, but what Angry Sky did to that kid . . ." Plumlee finished with an eloquently disgusted shake of his head.

"Let's get back to camp," Scarrow said. "Angry Sky has lost four more men. He's down to eight now, and half of them are up here on this ridge chasing Preacher, so he may be getting desperate. I don't trust him. He may decide he has to go ahead and eliminate some of *our* men."

"You and him were about to go to fightin' over that gal, before all hell broke loose," Plumlee pointed out. "I'm startin' to think this might be a good time for us to cut our losses, Jeff. Just let Preacher and the others go." He held up a hand to forestall Scarrow's objection. "I know, it'd stick in your craw to do that. Mine, too. But you and me and the rest o' the boys could sorta just drift away and head back to where we cached them furs. We can still be rich."

"And let Preacher get away with stealing what's mine not once but twice?" Scarrow shook his head. "I can't do that, Hog. I'm sorry."

Plumlee couldn't hold in his frustration. "But she's just a gal!" he exploded. "She ain't worth nowhere near as much as them pelts are. I don't care how pretty she is, or if she's red or white. If we keep chasin' after her, we're all gonna wind up dead!"

"If that's the way you feel, then perhaps *you* should withdraw," Scarrow suggested coldly. "And any of the others who agree with you can go back, too. But I'm going to have that girl again, and more important, I'm going to watch Preacher die with my own eyes."

Plumlee hesitated by saying, "Well . . . well . . . hell! You've been doin' the thinkin' for both of us ever since I threw in with you, Jeff, and I ain't ever been sorry about that so far. You ain't steered us wrong yet." He sighed. "So maybe you're right about this, too. I ain't gonna run out on you, no matter what. That's for damn sure."

Scarrow clapped a hand on his burly friend's shoulder. "I'm glad to hear that."

As they started back along the ridge toward the trail that would take them down into the canyon, Scarrow went on.

"Those men who launched the attack a short time ago have to be working with Preacher. Where he found such allies, I have no idea, but the timing of everything makes it clear the attack was a diversion so Preacher could free the prisoners. They were on horseback, so we can follow them as soon as it's light enough to see. They're bound to rendezvous with Preacher and the others. We'll find them that way."

"What about the Blackfeet?"

"That's up to Angry Sky. However, I have a feeling that our days of working together may be coming to an end."

"Best thing might be just to walk in and shoot the son of a bitch."

"Simple, but direct and effective," Scarrow said. "Unfortunately, if he *is* willing to cooperate, he and his men give us even more of a numerical advantage. I suppose we shouldn't squander that if there's a chance to salvage it."

"So you ain't gonna kill him?"

"Not right away. I'd still like for Preacher to die first, just to be certain. But it's really up to Angry Sky. He can die now," Scarrow said, "or he can die later."

Preacher reached the bottom of the treacherous path and found Hawk, Caroline, and Charlie waiting for him and Big Thunder. The side canyon in which they found themselves was so narrow it amounted to little more than a fissure in the earth. The amount of light that penetrated into its depths was so small that Preacher could barely make out the others.

Even so, his instincts were good enough that he had a pretty good idea which direction they should go. "We'll head this way," he said, pointing to the right. "That ought to take us toward the western edge of the basin, and that's where Broken Pine and the others will be waitin' for us."

"Who are these warriors you speak of?" Hawk asked as the group set out again. Caroline and Charlie were both still breathing a little hard, but at least they'd gotten a chance to rest for a few minutes and in the narrow canyon they had to move at a slower pace instead of a flat-out run.

Preacher explained how he had run into the Crow hunting party from Falling Star's village. "And it's a good thing I did, too," he added. "I don't think we could've pulled off that escape without Big Thunder's help, not to mention the distraction Broken Pine and his pards gave us."

"The Crow are good people," Hawk said. "I have always known it is so. Thank you for your help, Big Thunder."

"When do we fight the Blackfeet?" Big Thunder asked.

"Might be sooner than you think," Preacher said, although in reality he hoped their enemies would never be able to track them in that labyrinth of small, twisting canyons.

Their route forked frequently, with Preacher choosing the paths he thought were more likely to lead them out. He called a halt from time to time to give the others a chance to rest, but perhaps just as important, to listen closely for any sounds of their pursuers closing in. Although the way the maze muffled and distorted sounds, the varmints could be very close by and not sound like it, he thought. But he didn't hear anything, so his hopes kept rising.

He warned himself not to get too confident of their getaway. Trouble seemed to have a way of finding him, no matter what he did.

In a situation such as that, time didn't mean much. Hours passed and seemed more like days or months, especially to the exhausted Caroline and Charlie. They kept going valiantly, though, and tried not to slow the others down. Finally, in the gray light of dawn, they stumbled around a bend and found semiarid plains opening in front of them and in the distance the mountains.

Preacher could see, perhaps five miles away, the line of green that marked the course of the river on which Falling Star's village was located.

"Take a minute to catch your breath," he told the others.

"Thank God we're out of there," Charlie said as he sank wearily onto the ground. "I had visions of wandering around in there forever and never finding our way out."

Hawk said, "Preacher knew where he was going the whole time."

"Is that true, Preacher?" Charlie asked.

The mountain man smiled. "Let's say it is." He was glad to be out of the canyons as well and to have their real destination in sight.

But the fact of the matter was that their situation had just gotten more dangerous. They would be traveling out in the open, and if Angry Sky and Scarrow had any sense, they would have abandoned the search back in the canyons in favor of riding out there to look for the fugitives. Riders on horseback could cast back and forth and cover a lot of ground.

And if they were spotted, Preacher and his companions couldn't outrun the pursuit on foot.

While the others were resting, he stood and stared toward the mountains, studying the terrain and trying to figure out where that rock formation called the Devil's Eye was. He had seen it the day before and marked it in his mind in relation to other landmarks, and now he had to locate those peaks and figure out the best route to reach the rendezvous.

When he had a pretty good idea of the direction they needed to go, he turned to the others and told them, "Hate to say it, but I reckon we'd best get movin' again."

Charlie suppressed a groan but climbed to his feet. Hawk and Caroline were sitting on the ground, too. Hawk got up and took Caroline's hand to help her. Big Thunder had stood close to Preacher the whole time, as tireless as a tree.

As Preacher led the way out and the others fell in behind him, Charlie said, "I'm sorry we have to leave Aaron's body behind. He . . . he should have had a decent burial. If I ever make it back to Virginia, I don't know what I'll tell his family."

"Tell them he died with his friends close by and that he was laid to rest in a beautiful spot," Hawk said.

"You mean I should lie?"

"Sometimes the truth serves no purpose but pain. And if a lie serves to ease unnecessary pain, that is the more noble path."

"Maybe you're right," Charlie said. "I'll think about it. I guess first we need to get out of here alive. If we don't, there won't be anybody to tell what happened to us, truth or lies."

The boy was right about that, Preacher thought.

Five miles never seemed so long as it did that early morning. Their steps seemed to bring them no closer to their destination. It hung there in front of them, forever out of reach.

But as the sun rose, its golden rays spreading across the landscape, Preacher's keen eyes spied the ragged cluster of rocks ahead of them. Viewed from higher on the slopes beyond them, those boulders were arranged in the rough semblance of an eye, with a huge, rounded rock in the middle representing the pupil. Nobody had placed them that way. From what Preacher understood of such things from talking to natural scientists he had met in the past, the boulders probably had been spewed from some volcano eruption millions of years in the past and landed that way by accident. Or maybe God had dropped them there while He was walking around putting the earth together. Preacher figured either explanation made sense, and the only thing he was really worried about was whether Broken Pine, Kicking Elk, and Dark Neck would be there waiting for them with the horses.

"That's them," he said as he pointed out the boulders to his companions. "That's where we're headed. Looks like it's only about half a mile more."

"Preacher . . ." Hawk said in a warning tone.

Preacher looked around. Dust rose behind them, enough that Preacher knew it had to come from horses' hooves.

"Is it them?" Charlie asked with panic edging into his voice.

"Can't be anybody else," Preacher said, "but we don't know if they've spotted us yet. Come on. Time to hustle again!"

They ran for their lives.

CHAPTER 30

When Jefferson Scarrow and Hog Plumlee got back to the camp the night before, they had found a definite air of tension hanging over the canyon. The fire had been built up, probably so the two sides could keep a better eye on each other. Angry Sky, with a bloodstained bandage wrapped around his left thigh where a pistol ball had creased him during the fracas, was on one side of the canyon with his remaining warriors, while the rest of Scarrow's men were on the other side. They all eyed each other warily.

"Did you find Preacher and the prisoners?" Angry Sky demanded as soon as Scarrow and Plumlee walked into the circle of firelight.

Scarrow shook his head. "The rest of your men are still chasing them, but I doubt if they're going to have any luck. And those people aren't exactly prisoners any more, are they? They got away from us, there's no denying that."

"Preacher stole them!"

"Well, yes, we're in agreement on that," Scarrow said. "Preacher is to blame for all our troubles. He's killed your men, he's killed my men, he's frustrated us at every turn. He's either the most damnably *lucky* man I've ever seen . . . or perhaps he actually deserves the reputation he has."

Angry Sky clenched a fist in front of him and rasped, "It is time for Preacher to die!"

"We have to find him first. I'd suggest following the men who staged that attack on our camp to distract us while he freed the prisoners. It's highly likely they plan to meet up later."

Angry Sky looked like he wanted to argue just on general principles, but what Scarrow said made sense and the war chief knew it. After glaring for a moment longer, he jerked his head in a nod and said, "We know which way they went when they fled. We will pick up their trail as soon as it is light enough to see."

"My thinking exactly," Scarrow said. All they had to do was to keep from killing each other before the night was over. That might be a challenge, but he believed he was up to it. He desired Preacher's death more than Angry Sky's.

But he would get around to killing the Blackfoot, too, he promised himself.

Far into the night, the Blackfeet who had continued chasing Preacher and the others dragged back into camp, their efforts having turned out as unsuccessful as Scarrow expected. Angry Sky berated them for failing, which accomplished nothing, of course. Scarrow had harbored some hope that the men would get lost and not make it back to camp by the time he and the others rode out. That would have put Angry Sky at even more of a disadvantage. But the savages were still outnumbered, and all of them might come in handy once Preacher was cornered and it was time to wipe out the mountain man and his allies once and for all, so Scarrow supposed he could live with the turn of events.

The tension in the camp didn't ease until the eastern sky began to turn gray with dawn's approach. Then everyone had plenty to keep them busy as they got ready to leave.

The party still numbered twenty-two strong as they rode out—eight Blackfoot warriors and fourteen white renegades. Scarrow wasn't sure how many men they would be facing. During the brief fight at the canyon mouth the night before, he had never been able to tell how many attackers were out there in the dark. Ultimately he had decided there hadn't been more than a handful. Preacher would have them on his side, provided he was able to rendezvous with them first, plus the young Indian called Hawk and the almost useless Charlie. Less than ten men total, almost certainly, which meant they would be outnumbered more than two to one.

He and his companions would succeed, Scarrow told himself. Preacher *had* been lucky so far, but now his luck was going to change.

The Blackfeet were expert trackers, Scarrow had to give them credit for that. One of the savages found the tracks they were looking for almost right away and led them back along the main canyon. They paused to examine all the branches to make sure their quarry hadn't veered off, but it soon became obvious the men they were following had wanted to get out of that wasteland as quickly as possible. Scarrow couldn't blame them for that. It had seemed like a good place to trap Preacher, but other than that, the basin was just ugly and inhospitable.

The part about trapping Preacher hadn't worked out all that well, either, Scarrow mused.

"You really reckon we're gonna find 'em, Jeff?" Plumlee asked after a while.

The sun was up and peeking over the mountain range to the east.

"Seems to me like they could hide out back there where we were for a long time."

"And live on what?" Scarrow asked. "According to Angry Sky, there's very little game to be found in this region, and not much water, either. No, they'll head for the mountains. They're on foot, remember. They have to meet up with their friends if they're going to have any chance to get away. Just keep your eyes peeled, Hog."

As it turned out, Angry Sky was the one to spot their quarry first. "There!" the war chief roared a short time later as he leveled an arm and pointed toward the mountains in the west.

"I don't see a blamed thing!" Plumlee said.

"Nor do I," Scarrow said, "but our friend thinks he does, anyway, and there he goes."

Angry Sky raced ahead, leaning forward over his pony's neck. Scarrow booted his pony into a run and called back over his shoulder to Plumlee and his other men, "Come on! I'm not going to let the Blackfeet catch up first! *Preacher is mine!*"

Preacher glanced over his shoulder and saw what he expected to see. The dust cloud appeared to be drawing closer and moving faster. The pursuers had spotted them.

The others were all running as fast as they could.

Charlie's face was red, and his chest heaved mightily. Preacher hoped the young trapper's heart would hold out. Caroline looked almost as exhausted, but Hawk was right beside her, his hand clamped around her arm, supporting her and helping her run.

Big Thunder loped along. He looked over at Preacher and called, "We fight Blackfeet now!"

"Soon!" Preacher promised. He tried to figure distances.

He and his companions had been closer to the Devil's Eye than the pursuers were to them when the chase started, but those swift little Indian ponies could run more than twice as fast as people on foot. They couldn't make it to the rocks in time, Preacher thought bleakly.

As he glanced toward the ring of boulders again, he saw movement there. A man on horseback erupted from the formation and galloped toward them, leading four riderless mounts, including Horse. At that distance, Preacher couldn't tell which young Crow warrior was taking this desperate chance, but he was grateful, whoever it was.

He heard rifles booming behind them, although he didn't think they were in range yet. Let the varmints waste their powder and shot.

With Preacher and his companions dashing toward the rocks and the warrior bringing the horses out to meet them, the gap closed quickly. Broken Pine was the one running the risk, Preacher saw as they came together. The youngster hauled his pony to a halt and the other horses stopped, too.

"Get mounted!" Preacher called. "Fast!"

Hawk leaped onto a pony and pulled Caroline up behind him. Charlie was more awkward, but he managed to scramble onto one of the ponies, too.

Big Thunder said to Preacher, "We stay and fight!"

"No, get goin', dadblast it!" the mountain man ordered.

At that moment, a rifle ball struck his hat and sent it flying off his head. Angered, Preacher turned, brought his own rifle to his shoulder, and pressed the trigger. The pursuers were only a little more than a hundred yards away, so Preacher was able to see it when a Blackfoot warrior flung his arms out and toppled backward off his lunging pony.

Preacher vaulted onto Horse's back and waved his empty rifle in a taunting gesture, then wheeled the big stallion and pounded after the others.

Puffs of powder smoke came from the Devil's Eye as Kicking Elk and Dark Neck fired toward the Blackfeet and the fur thieves. Preacher didn't figure that would slow down the pursuit much, if any, but they might get lucky and plug another one or two of the varmints.

A moment later, he saw that they were going to make it, then instantly berated himself for thinking such a thing and jinxing them. However, the usual stroke of bad luck didn't come crashing down. None of the ponies tripped and fell, nobody got hit by a wild, blindly fired rifle shot, and they all raced through a gap between two boulders, into the shelter of the rock formation.

Not that the Devil's Eye was impregnable, by any means. The defenders had cover, but they were very much outnumbered. If Scarrow, Angry Sky, and the other men pushed their attack and were willing to take some losses, they might very well overrun the position. If they made it inside the rock formation, anything could happen.

Preacher swung down from Horse, pausing only to feel a second of relief when he saw that Dog was with the Crow warriors and apparently unharmed. Then he called, "Make your shots count, boys! There's more o' them than there is of us!"

Hawk jumped down from his pony and helped Caroline dismount. As soon as she sank exhaustedly to the ground with her back against one of the boulders, he turned to Preacher and said, "Give me one of your pistols."

"I was thinkin' the same thing." Preacher handed a pistol to Hawk and held out the other one to Charlie, who had managed to dismount without falling down from weariness. "Be sure you got a good target before you take the shot."

Charlie swallowed hard and nodded as he took the weapon.

The four Crow kept up a steady fire at the attackers, but it wasn't easy to hit a man on a fast-moving horse. Preacher swiftly reloaded his rifle and aimed at the charging riders, hoping to draw a bead on Angry Sky or Scarrow. He couldn't pick out either of them in the dust and the crowd, so he went ahead and squeezed off the shot. A warrior fell from his galloping pony, but Preacher didn't think it was Angry Sky.

Two or three more ponies were riderless. The shots fired by Broken Pine, Kicking Elk, Dark Neck, and Big Thunder were having an effect. But the charge continued, prompting Charlie to cry out, "Why don't they stop?"

"Because they want this over with as much as we do," Preacher said. "Comes a time when you can't put off the showdown any longer.

And that time was now.

CHAPTER 31

Preacher reloaded and fired again. One of the fur thieves fell forward over his pony's neck, slid off, and got tangled in the animal's flashing legs. The pony stumbled and went down in a welter of flailing limbs. Two Blackfoot warriors jumped their ponies over the fallen one without slowing down.

With no time to reload again, Preacher reversed his rifle, gripped it by the barrel, and swung it like a club as one of the attackers raced through a gap in the ring of boulders. The blow swept a white renegade off his mount. He landed hard enough on his back to stun him, and before he could recover, Preacher slammed the rifle butt into the middle of his face and shattered his skull.

More riders reached the Devil's Eye and crowded through the gaps. Pistols blasted as the deadly work took place at close range. Charlie swung around, holding the pistol Preacher had given him in both hands, and fired as a Blackfoot warrior lunged at him with a tomahawk. The lead ball smashed into the warrior's chest and drove him off his feet.

An instant later, a renegade stabbed Charlie in the

left shoulder with a hunting knife. Charlie slumped back against the boulder behind him and slashed at the man's head with the empty pistol. The barrel raked across the man's face and opened a cut, but he snarled, yanked the blade free from Charlie's shoulder, and raised it for a killing stroke.

Before that blow could fall, Big Thunder grabbed the man's head from behind with both hands and wrenched so hard that he tore it right off the man's shoulders. Big Thunder flung the head aside and grabbed the dead man's body before it could fall. With a roar, he raised the corpse above his head and flung it at a knot of men trying to close in around Hawk and Caroline. The flying body bowled a couple of them off their feet.

Hawk fired his pistol at close range into another man, then grappled with yet another. Caroline screamed as a Blackfoot grabbed her, but her hand fell on a knife someone had dropped and brought it up into the man's neck, driving it deep. Blood poured out around it.

In the wild melee that filled the inside of the Devil's Eye, Preacher struck right and left with his knife and tomahawk, hewing down enemies like stalks of bloody corn. Dog was in the thick of the battle, as well, ripping and slashing with his teeth. Crimson smeared his muzzle as he harked back to his primitive wolf ancestors.

Big Thunder had just broken a man's arm like a twig when Hogarth Plumlee tackled him from behind. The big Crow towered over Plumlee, but the thickset renegade was the only one in his bunch who might come close to matching Big Thunder's strength. Just bringing Big Thunder down was an amazing feat, but Plumlee accomplished it. He scrambled onto Big

Thunder's back, clamped his arms around the young man's neck, and bore down viciously with a choke hold.

Big Thunder kicked into a roll. His weight came over on top of Plumlee, weakening the renegade's hold. Big Thunder grasped Plumlee's arms and tore them free. They rolled over and over in the dust, under the feet of fighting men, wrestling doggedly as each tried for a death grip.

Suddenly, Big Thunder got his arms where he wanted them and closed them around Plumlee's neck. The muscles in his arms and shoulders stood out so much as he heaved that they looked like they were about to rip through his buckskin shirt. His grunt of effort and the sharp crack of Plumlee's neck breaking sounded together. Plumlee's body slumped in death.

A few feet away, Jefferson Scarrow thrust a pistol at Hawk's face and fired at almost point-blank range. Hawk jerked his head aside just in time. The ball ripped past his right ear, drawing a drop of blood from the lobe. Burning powder stung Hawk's cheek. Rock splinters from where the ball struck the boulder behind him peppered the back of his neck. The pistol's thundering report deafened him.

But he didn't have to hear in order to lunge forward and tackle Scarrow. They went down and battled desperately hand to hand right in front of Caroline. She had pulled the knife from the throat of the man she'd killed and leaned forward clutching the weapon's handle as she waited for an opening to stab Scarrow. As close as he was to Hawk, she couldn't risk it yet.

Scarrow wound up on top with his hands locked around Hawk's throat. Hawk slammed his fists into the man's ears but failed to loosen his grip. Despite his lean build, Scarrow was strong and dug his thumbs into Hawk's throat, seeking to crush his windpipe.

Caroline leaned in and rammed the knife into his side.

It wasn't a killing blow, but it was enough to make Scarrow scream and let go. Hawk threw him off, then lunged after him, grabbed the knife, and ripped the blade across Scarrow's belly. Scarrow shrieked again as blood came out over Hawk's hand in a hot gush. Hawk yanked the knife out and slammed it once, twice, three times into Scarrow's chest as hard as he could. Scarrow spasmed with each strike. His head tipped far back, the cords standing out in his neck as his face contorted in an agonized rictus.

His features froze that way as death claimed him. Hawk lay on top of the corpse, breathing hard from exertion and emotion. He left the blade buried in Scarrow's chest as he pushed himself up and turned to draw Caroline into his blood-drenched arms.

Elsewhere in the Devil's Eye, Preacher's instincts warned him and made him duck as something swept at his head from behind. The tomahawk swung by Angry Sky barely missed him. Preacher twisted around and slashed at the Blackfoot war chief with his tomahawk. Angry Sky jerked back to avoid the blow by a fraction of an inch. Then he bored in on Preacher, hacking with the tomahawk and slashing with his knife, and if his wounded leg hampered him any, Preacher couldn't tell it. He had his hands full parrying the deadly blows and trying to strike back with his own knife and tomahawk.

The two men, two of the best pure fighters on the frontier, put on a blinding display of speed and skill then. Tomahawk handles thudded together. Knife blades clashed with the clarion ring of steel. Preacher and Angry Sky puffed and panted with effort. Preacher felt the icy bite of Angry Sky's blade, followed by a hot rush of blood. He saw crimson fly as his own steel ripped Blackfoot flesh. During what seemed like an infinitely long moment but was really just a matter of a few heartbeats, neither man was ever more than a hair's breadth away from death.

Then Preacher took a hard smash to the side of the head from Angry Sky's tomahawk and felt his brain spin wildly. Knowing he had only a shaved fraction of time to respond, he darted forward, taking advantage of how the blow Angry Sky had landed had turned the war chief slightly. Preacher's knife flickered out like a striking snake. The blade went into Angry Sky's left side, slid through his ribs, and penetrated all the way to the war chief's black heart. Angry Sky's dark eyes widened immensely as he felt it pierce his core. He collapsed against Preacher as his dying breath rattled in his throat.

Preacher moved aside and let the corpse fall face-down.

Then he looked around and realized that the battle was over. The Devil's Eye was sure as hell bloodshot, he thought as he saw the bodies littering the ground. Hawk, Caroline, and Charlie were all on their feet, although Charlie was wounded. Big Thunder and Broken Pine had survived as well. Kicking Elk and Dark Neck were both down, crumpled in death, their buckskins soaked with blood from their wounds. A pang of grief at their passing went through Preacher. He hadn't known them long, but he respected them as fine warriors and men. Without their help, it was entirely possible he and the others never would have survived to reach that grim point.

"It was a good fight," Big Thunder rumbled, "but Big Thunder is sad that his friends are gone."

"So am I, Big Thunder," Preacher said.

Hawk said, "Someone comes."

Preacher turned and saw a large group of men on ponies riding hard toward them from the direction of the river.

"It is Falling Star and the men from our village," Broken Pine said. "Moose Horn has brought them, but they are too late to help us."

"They will help us mourn," Big Thunder said.

Preacher could only nod solemnly.

Wounds both physical and emotional healed over the next few weeks in the Crow village. Kicking Elk and Dark Neck were grieved for and laid to rest with the proper ceremony. Several young women seemed to adopt Charlie and made sure that he was nursed back to health. Preacher's iron constitution ensured that he shook off all the effects of battle in short order.

Hawk and Caroline, or Butterfly as he still called her and Preacher sometimes thought of her, spent nearly all their time together. Although she had been born white, all the people of Falling Star's village seemed to regard her as one of their own. Preacher knew she would be welcome to stay there from now on. She would have a home again.

What Preacher didn't know . . . was what Hawk was going to do.

The day came when Dog looked toward the mountains and whined. Horse threw his head up and down restlessly when Preacher patted him on the shoulder that fine morning.

"I know," the mountain man said quietly. "I'm feelin' it, too."

He found Hawk and Caroline beside the river, and when they turned to greet him, Preacher saw understanding dawn in his son's eyes.

Hawk said, "It is time, Preacher?"

"For me it is," Preacher answered without hesitation. "What about you?"

Hawk drew in a deep breath and said, "The time has come for me, as well." He reached over and took Butterfly's hand. "The time to tell you that I am staying here."

The decision came as no surprise, but Preacher felt a little surge of disappointment anyway. At the same time, that emotion was mixed with happiness and, yes, a little relief. Hawk could stay, live a good life, raise a fine family with Butterfly, far away from all the hell raising and blood spilling that inevitably would be his lot if he remained with Preacher. In other words, the sort of destiny that any father worth his salt would wish for his child.

Preacher put out his hand. "I wish you both the best of luck."

Hawk clasped his hand, and Preacher pulled him into a hard, back-slapping embrace. Then he hugged Butterfly and kissed her on the cheek. "Make sure this boy behaves himself," he told her in the Crow tongue.

"I will," she promised with a smile. "We will be very happy together."

Preacher looked at them and added, "If you ever find yourself needin' my help—"

"You will know, and you will come in our hour of need," Hawk said.

"Bet a hat on it," Preacher said.

A little later, he hunted up Charlie and said, "I'll be

ridin' out after a while. Figure I'll try to find those furs Scarrow and his bunch stole, and even if I don't, there's the pile we cached and plenty more beaver out there. Are you comin' along with me?"

Charlie looked around. Several yards away, a few plump, pretty Crow girls watched him and giggled among themselves as his gaze turned toward them.

"I think maybe I'd better go with you," Charlie said, "or else there's liable to be trouble here sooner or later. And I'm, uh, really not looking to spend the rest of my life in this village. In fact"—he drew in a breath—"I think I'm going home."

"Back to Virginia?"

"Yes. No offense, Preacher, but I've had my fill of the frontier life. I'll stay with you the rest of this season, but when we take furs downriver to St. Louis, that's where we'll part ways."

"Fair enough," the mountain man allowed.

"I'll need to tell Aaron's family what happened, too. Some of it, anyway. I think Hawk was right, though, about a lie sometimes being the nobler path."

"You do what you think best, son. It'll take us a few days to get back to where we left our gear, so we'd best be gettin' ready to ride."

Before they could leave, Big Thunder hurried up. "Preacher, you and Big Thunder never fought again. You promised Big Thunder another good fight."

"Well, shoot, I figure on comin' back to see you one of these days, Big Thunder, and I thought that'd be somethin' for us to look forward to."

A huge smile lit up the massive warrior's rocky face. "You will not forget?"

"I could never forget Big Thunder," Preacher said, meaning every word of it.

"Big Thunder could come with you . . . ?"

Preacher shook his head and lowered his voice. "I'm obliged to you for the offer, but I'd kind of like it if you'd stay here and sort of keep an eye on Hawk for me. The boy can take care of himself, but sometimes he might need a hand."

"Big Thunder will do this." An eager nod accompanied the reply.

Preacher slapped him on the arm and said, "Thanks, Big Thunder."

It was better that Big Thunder not come with him, Preacher thought as he and Charlie rode away from the village. To tell the truth, he was glad Charlie had decided to go back to Virginia, too. The way trouble followed him, Preacher figured he ought to travel alone for a while, so that innocent folks wouldn't find themselves in danger quite so often. Maybe one of these days he would meet some fella who was every bit as much of a hell-roarin' varmint as he was himself . . .

But until then, Preacher would ride the wilderness trails with Dog and Horse, and be content.

*Keep reading for a special preivew of
the first book in a New Series!*

THE BLACK HILLS
by William W. Johnstone
with J.A. Johnstone

*Meet Hunter Buchanon, a towering mountain of a man,
who learned how to track prey in Georgia, kill in
the Civil War, and prospect in the Black Hills of Dakota.
Now he's trying to live a peaceful gun-free life—
but fate has other plans for him . . .*

A MAN AND HIS COYOTE
When Hunter Buchanon rescued a wounded coyote
pup—and named him Bobby Lee—he had no idea
the cute little varmint would grow up to be such a
loyal companion. Coyotes aren't known to be man's
best friend. Most of them are as fierce and wild as
the Black Hills they roam. But Bobby Lee is
different. When Hunter is ambushed on the road,
Bobby Lee leaps to his defense. And when the
attacker tries to shoot Bobby Lee, Hunter returns
the favor by hitting the man with a rock. By the
time the smoke clears, the coyote-loving
ex-Confederate is covered in blood—and the
other guy's got a knife in his chest. Now Hunter
has to explain it all to the local sheriff.
Which is going to be tough. Because the man
he just killed is the sheriff's deputy . . .

Coming soon, whereever Pinnacle books are sold.

CHAPTER 1

As the supply wagon rocked and clattered along the old army road west of Tigerville, Dakota Territory, Hunter Buchanon heard the light thumps of four padded feet and looked into the buttes to his left to see a coyote leap from a trough between two bluffs and onto the chalky slope above the trail.

The brush wolf lifted its long, pointed nose and launched a chortling, yammering wail toward the brassy afternoon sky, causing Hunter to set his jaws against the tooth-gnashing din.

Hunter drew back on the reins of the stout Missouri mule in the traces. As the wagon lurched to a grinding halt, he frowned up at the nettled coyote.

"What is it, Bobby Lee?"

As if in reply, the beast turned to Hunter and mewled, yipped, and lifted each front foot in turn, fidgeting his distress. Hunter had adopted the coyote two years ago, when he'd found it injured up in the hills above his family's horse ranch just west of where Hunter was now.

The pup had survived an attack by some raptor—an owl or a hawk, likely—but just barely. The pup, while only a few weeks old, had appeared to be on its own. Hunter had suspected its mother—possibly the rest of its family, as well—had been shot by ranchers.

He had taken the pup home and nursed it back to health, feeding it bits of rabbit and squirrel meat and dribbling goat's milk into its mouth from a sponge, and here it still was after two years, close by its savior's side, though Hunter had assured the friendly but wily beast it was free to venture back into the wild, its true home, whenever it pleased.

Hunter wished he'd learned the coyote's language over their months together, but while they communicated after a fashion, there was much that was mysterious about Bobby Lee. However, the apprehensive cast to the coyote's gaze could not be mistaken. Trouble was afoot.

As if to validate Hunter's suspicion, something made the air shiver.

A veteran of the War Between the States on the Confederate side of that bloody conflagration, Hunter Buchanon was all too familiar with the spine-shriveling, mind-numbing sound of a deadheading bullet. The slug kicked up dirt and gravel just inches from the troubled coyote, which squealed and ran.

An eyeblink later, the rifle's ripping report sounded from a butte over the trail to Hunter's right.

The ex-Confederate cursed and hurled himself off the wagon seat—all two-hundred-plus pounds and six-feet-four inches of the twenty-six-year-old man. He rolled fleetly off a shoulder and hurled himself into the brush along the trail just as the mule, braying wildly, took off running straight up the trail, dragging the wagon along behind it. Dust from the buckboard's churning wheels swept over Hunter, offering him fleeting cover.

He scrambled out of the brush and scampered straight up the bluff Bobby Lee had been perched on.

More bullets chewed into the bluff around his hammering boots, the rifle cracking angrily behind him. Breathing hard, Hunter lunged quickly, cursing under his breath. Though a big man, he was nearly as fleet-footed as he'd been when as a young Rebel soldier he'd run hog-wild behind Union lines, assassinating federal officers with a bowie knife or his Whitworth rifled musket with a Davidson scope, and blowing up supply lines—quick and wily as a Georgia mountain panther.

He'd been in his early teens back then, still wet behind the ears, but he'd become a backwoods warrior legend of sorts—as revered and idolized by his fellow Confederates as he was feared and hated by the Bluebellies.

Those days were over now. And while he might have still been fleet enough to scamper up the butte ahead of the bushwhacker's bullets, and scramble behind a tombstone-size boulder as another bullet smashed into it with a screeching whine, he had no gun on his hip to reach for. Even if the mule, old Titus, hadn't lit out with the wagon, there was no rifle or shotgun in it. The only knife he had on him was a folding barlow knife. He could feel the solid lump of the jackknife now in the right pocket of his buckskin trousers.

The barlow felt supremely small and inadequate as another bullet screeched in from the butte on the opposite side of the trail, and smacked the face of the boulder.

The rifle's hammering wail echoed shrilly.

"Law, law!" Hunter muttered. "That fella's really out to trim my wick!"

He jerked his head down as yet another bullet came

screeching in and smashed the face of the boulder with another hammering crash.

"Hey, you with the rifle!" Hunter shouted. "Why don't you put the long gun down so we can talk this out like grown-ups?"

The shooter replied by hurling another bullet against Hunter's rock.

Hunter cursed to himself, then shouted, "Is that a definite no or a maybe?"

Again, the shooter replied in the only language he cared to communicate in.

"All right, then," Hunter said under his breath. "Have it your way!"

He waited for another bullet to smash against his covering rock, then heaved himself to his feet and dashed straight up the butte. He covered the fifteen feet in three long strides, crouched forward, keeping his head down, trying to make himself as small as possible.

He hurled himself up and over the butte's crest as a slug tore hotly along his right side, tracing the natural furrow between two ribs.

Hunter hit the butte's opposite slope and rolled halfway to the bottom. When he finally broke his fall, he winced against the burn in his side and lifted his left arm to see the tear in his linsey-woolsey tunic.

He jerked up the garment, exposing his washboard belly and slab-like chest as well as the thin line of blood the bullet had drawn across his side, about halfway between his shoulder and waist. Not a wound, just a graze hardly deep enough to bleed, but it ached like six bee stings.

"Son of Satan!" Hunter exclaimed. "What in the hell is this fella's problem?"

Was he after the mule? The wagon? Possibly the ale

Hunter was hauling to town to sell in several Tigerville saloons? His father, Angus Buchanon, was a brewmaster, using old Buchanon family recipes his own father had carried over from Scotland to concoct a dark, creamy ale that was much favored by the miners, prospectors, and cowhands in and around this neck of the Black Hills.

Something told Hunter the shooter wasn't after any of those things. Just a sense he had. The man seemed so damn determined to kill him that maybe that was *all* he wanted.

Time to find out.

He knew a rare but vexing regret that he wasn't armed. He knew he should keep at least a six-shooter in the wagon. This was wild country, after all. Populated by men nearly as dangerous as the wildcats and grizzlies that stalked these pine-clad hills, elk parks, and beaver meadows east of the Rockies.

But he'd had his fill of guns and knives . . . of killing . . . during the war. Just looking at a pistol or a rifle or even a skinning knife conjured bloody memories. After Appomattox, he'd sworn that he would never again raise a gun or a knife against another human being. Not carrying a weapon when he wasn't hunting was his way of trimming his chances of having to break that promise to himself.

So far, he'd made good on that promise.

So far . . .

Reacting more than thinking about the situation, a trait that had held him in good stead during the war, Hunter heaved himself to his feet and took long, lunging, sliding strides to the bottom of the butte, loosing small landslides in his wake.

He followed a crease between buttes back to the west.

When he figured he'd run a good fifty yards, he made a hard left turn between another pair of low buttes.

This route took him back to the trail, which he crossed at a sharp curve shaded by cottonwoods. Pushing through low cottonwood branches, he hightailed it into another crease between the chalky bluffs on the shooter's side of the trail.

He climbed the shoulder of another low butte and paused in the shade of a lightning-topped pine.

On one knee, taking slow deep breaths, his broad, muscular chest rising and falling deeply, his mind worked calmly. The shock and fear he'd known when he'd heard the rifle's first crack had dwindled. The old natural instincts and battle-tested abilities moved to the forefront of his warrior's mind.

He had no weapons. No traditional weapons, that was. But he had an enemy who apparently wanted him dead. His own mind recoiled at the notion of killing, but there was no point in denying the fact that whoever was out to kill him needed to be rendered unable to do so.

Hunter picked out a rock that fit easily into the palm of his right hand. Working the rock around in his hand like a lump of clay, he scanned the high crest of a bluff just ahead and above him on his right. That was the highest point of ground anywhere around. It likely gave a clear view of the old army trail. It was probably from that high point that the bushwhacker had hurled his lead.

Hunter tossed the rock up and caught it, steeling his resolve, then moved quickly down the slope. He was trying to work around behind the ambusher when he spied movement out the corner of his left eye.

Stopping, crouching, he swung his head around to see a man—a man-shaped shadow, rather—walk out from the butte's far end, directly below the high, stony, pine-peppered ridge from which the bushwhacker had probably fired at Hunter. The man, carrying a rifle in both hands across his chest, dropped down below a hump of grassy ground and disappeared from Hunter's view.

Hunter sprang forward, running across the face of the steep bluff, about ten yards up from the bottom. There was a slight ridge at the end of the bluff, and Hunter stayed behind it, running almost silently on the balls of his worn, mule-eared boots into which the tops of his buckskin trousers were tucked.

He gained the base of the slight ridge, slowly climbed.

Near the top, he got down on one knee, swept a lock of his long, thick blond hair back from his eyes, and cast his blue-eyed gaze into the hollow below. His belly tightened; his heart quickened.

The man was there. A big, bearded man with a battered brown hat. He was hunkered down behind a low, flat-topped boulder, a grimy red bandanna ruffling in the slight breeze. He cradled a Winchester repeating rifle in his thick arms tufted with thick, black curls. The stout limbs strained the sleeves of his red-and-black-checked shirt beneath a worn deerskin vest.

Hunter couldn't see his face. The man's head was turned slightly away. He was looking in the direction of the trail, searching for his quarry. There was a wary set to his head and shoulders.

The man knew whom he'd been shooting at. He was aware he'd made a grave mistake by not sending those first shots home. He knew that a Buchanon would not tuck his tail and run. At least, not run *away*. Armed or unarmed, having sworn off killing or not, a Buchanon would run *toward* trouble.

If one of Hunter's brothers—the younger Tye or the older Shep, or even their one-armed father, old Angus—were in Hunter's position now, this man would already be dead. None of them subscribed to Hunter's pacifism. Of course, neither Tye nor Shep had fought in the war. Old Angus had fought in the Georgia state militia, and he'd lost an arm for his trouble. Still, the old mossy horn wouldn't give up his rifle until they rolled him into his cold, black grave.

Hunter rose a little higher on his knees. He raised his right arm, adjusting the rock in his fingers, preparing for the throw. His gut tightened again, and he drew his head down sharply. The man had turned toward him.

Had he heard him? Smelled him? *Sensed* he was here?

Hunter lifted his head again slowly, until his eyes cleared the top of his covering ridge. The man's face was turned slightly toward Hunter, looking off toward Hunter's left. Hunter still couldn't get a good look at him. The man's hat brim shaded his face. If Hunter jerked his head and shoulders up to throw the rock, the man would see him and likely shoot before Hunter could make the toss.

Damn.

The familiar patter of four padded feet sounded.

The man turned his head sharply back to his right, away from Hunter.

Bobby Lee leaped onto a low boulder down the slope below the shooter. The coyote lifted its long, pointed snout and sent a screeching din rising toward the brassy summer sky.

"Why, you mangy bag o' fleas!" the bushwhacker raked out through gritted teeth.

He raised the Winchester to his shoulder, aiming toward the yammering coyote.

Hunter raised his head and shoulders above the ridge, drew his arm back, and thrust it forward, throwing the rock as hard as he could.

CHAPTER 2

Hunter's aim was true, as it should be after all his years of killing squirrels, gophers, rabbits, and sometimes even turkeys with everything from rocks to spare bullets. A Buchanon was nothing if not thrifty.

The rock thumped sharply off his stalker's head.

The man yowled and fell forward, cursing and rolling down the grassy slope toward where Bobby Lee danced in zany, manic circles atop his boulder. Hunter leaped to his feet and ran. He jumped the boulder behind which his stalker had been crouching, and continued down toward where the man was still rolling, flattening grass and plowing through a chokecherry thicket.

The man rolled out the other side of the thicket and came to rest at the slope's bottom, about ten feet from where Bobby Lee stood atop the boulder, glaring down at the bushwhacker, baring his fangs and growling. The man had lost both his hat and his rifle during his fall, but now as he pushed onto his hands and knees, shaking his head, his thick, curly hair flying, he slid his right hand back for the Colt .44 still holstered on his right thigh.

From behind the man, Hunter grabbed the gun, ripping free the keeper thong from over the hammer and jerking the weapon from its holster.

"Hey!" the man said, turning his head to peer behind him.

Hunter recognized that broad, bearded face and the cow-stupid, glaring eyes reflecting the afternoon sunlight. Also reflecting the sun was the five-pointed badge pinned to the man's brush-scarred vest.

"Chaney?" Hunter said, tossing the man's gun away. "What in blazes—?"

But then Deputy Sheriff Luke Chaney was suddenly on his feet, moving fast for a big man with a considerable paunch and broad, fleshy hips. Dust and dead grass coating him, he wheeled to face the taller ex-Confederate. From somewhere he'd produced a Green River knife; he clenched its hide-wrapped handle tightly in his right hand as he stood, crouching, a menacing grin curling his thick, wet lips inside his dusty, curly, dark-brown beard.

The Green River's steel blade glinted in the afternoon sunshine.

"Come on, Buchanon," Chaney said, lunging toward Hunter. "They say you Reb devils got some fight in you—even if you don't wear a gun!"

He slashed the Green River knife from right to left and would have laid open Hunter's belly if Hunter hadn't leaped back. The Green River's razor-edged blade had come within an inch or even less of doing just that. The knowledge caused a burn of rage to rise up from the base of the ex-Confederate's back, spreading across his shoulders and blazing in his clean-shaven cheeks.

Hunter faced his opponent, crouching, arms spread, ready to parry Chaney's next assault. "What the hell's this about, Chaney? What's your beef with me?"

Chaney curled his mouth in a sneering grin, then lunged, slashing with the knife. Overconfidence was the man's Achilles' heel. He'd just retreated from another attempt at eviscerating Hunter when Hunter sprang forward, kicking upward with his left boot, the toe of which smashed against the underside of Chaney's right hand.

There was the dull snap of breaking bone.

Taken by surprise, Chaney gave a hard, indignant grunt. The knife flew out of his hand, arcing sharply up, flashing in the sunlight before landing not far from where Bobby Lee now sat on the boulder, watching the fight with a devilish glint in his long, yellow eyes, a low whine of apprehension issuing from deep in his chest.

Chaney grabbed his wrist and bellowed, "Damn you, Reb devil—you broke my wrist!"

He stood there, knees buckling, crouched over his injured hand, as Hunter walked wide around him and scooped the knife up out of the tawny grass. He brushed off the knife and started to turn, saying, "Now suppose you tell me what—"

He stopped when he saw Chaney coming toward him like a bull out of a chute, head down, eyes glinting malevolently, a sinister smile tugging at his mouth corners. Hunter stepped to one side. Chaney plowed into Hunter's right chest and shoulder, gave a yelp, and stumbled away.

Bobby Lee lifted his head and sent a warbling cry careening skyward.

Dazed by Chaney's assault, Hunter swung around toward where Chaney stood six feet away, his back to Hunter. The deputy sheriff was leaning forward as though he were looking for something on the ground. Hunter looked at his own right hand.

He was no longer holding the knife. His hand was slick and bright with fresh blood.

Chaney turned to face Hunter. The Green River was sticking out of Chaney's belly, the handle angled down. Doubtless, the knifepoint was embedded in the deputy's heart. Reacting instinctively when Chaney had bulled toward him, the old warrior instincts coming alive in him, Hunter had dropped the knife handle slightly, angling the blade up toward his assailant's heart.

He'd killed countless Union soldiers that way. Only, he'd done so consciously. He'd killed Luke Chaney without thinking.

Hunter's heart thudded as Chaney stared at him in wide-eyed horror.

The deputy had both his big, bloody hands wrapped around the knife handle protruding from his belly. He took one stumbling step backward, wincing slightly as he tried to pull out the knife. He opened his mouth as though to speak, but no words made it past his lips.

Chaney's eyes rolled up in their sockets. His chin lifted and he tumbled straight back to the ground with a heavy thud and a breathy chuff as the air was punched from his lungs. He lay still.

Yipping softly, Bobby Lee dropped down off of the boulder, ran over to Chaney, and hiked a back leg, sending a yellow stream dribbling onto the dead deputy's forehead.

Hunter stared in shock at the dead man.

He raised his bloody hands, stared at them. A million images of bloody death flashed through his mind all at once. The screams and wails of the wounded and dying, the concussion of hammering Napoleon cannons and howitzers, the crackle of musket fire.

Hunter felt as though he'd been kicked in the head. His legs buckled. He dropped to his knees. Sagging back onto his butt, he stared at his blood-washed hands.

He was still sitting there maybe ten, fifteen minutes later, staring at his hands. Bobby Lee lay beside him, calmly chewing burrs out of his mottled gray-brown coat. Suddenly, the coyote lifted his head and sniffed, twitching his ears. Then Hunter heard them too—hoof thuds rising in the distance.

Bobby Lee mewled softly, staring off toward Hunter's right.

Hunter felt inert, unable to react though warning bells tolled in his head.

The hoof thuds continued to grow louder until the rider appeared, swinging through a crease between the buttes. She turned her head toward Hunter and Bobby Lee, and drew back on the reins of her fine buckskin stallion. Sunlight glinted off the long, dark-red curls cascading like amber honey down from her man's felt hat to spill across her shoulders.

Annabelle Ludlow batted her heels against the buckskin's flanks, and the gelding galloped forward until the girl drew back on the reins again and sat for a moment, staring down in horror at Luke Chaney lying dead in the tawny grass. She was nineteen years old—a rare beauty with emerald eyes in a fine, smooth, heart-shaped face lightly tanned by the sun. She wore a calico blouse and tight, badly faded and frayed denim jeans, the cuffs of which were pulled down over her men's small-size western riding boots, which she wore without spurs.

The boots were as worn and scuffed as any cow-puncher's.

A green-eyed, rustic beauty was Annabelle Ludlow, with long slender legs and womanly curves. A rich girl to boot, being the daughter of one of the wealthiest men in the Hills. By looking at her you'd think she was the daughter of a small shotgun rancher whose wife sold eggs to help make ends meet. Annabelle didn't believe in flaunting her riches, and that was only one of the many things Hunter Buchanon loved about her.

"I was airing Ivan out nearby," she said after nearly a minute had passed. She'd named her horse Ivanhoe, after the hero of a book she loved. "I heard the shots. What happened?"

It was as if she'd whispered the query from a long ways away. Hunter had barely heard her.

As he sat there on his butt in the grass, in his mind he was a thousand miles east and more than ten years back in time, and he was pulling his bowie knife out of the wool-clad belly of a young Union picket. It was late—one or two in the morning—and he'd been sent to blow up several supply wagons along the Tennessee River, using the Union's own Ketchum grenades. Those wagons were heavily guarded, and the young man he'd just killed had been one of those guards.

There'd been a clear half-moon, and the milky light of the moon shone in the young soldier's eyes as Hunter, his hand closed over the private's mouth to muffle any scream, jerked him over backward from behind. He pulled the bloody knife out of the young man's belly and found himself staring into a pair of impossibly young, anguished, and terrified eyes gazing back at him in silent pleading.

The soldier was tall and willowy. He had the body of a sixteen- or seventeen-year-old. But the face, speckled with red pimples, and the wide-open eyes were that of a boy a good bit younger. Hunter dragged him almost silently back into the woods along the river, the water lapping behind him. The soldier's body seemed impossibly light. He did not struggle with his killer.

He was bleeding out and dying fast.

Hunter lay him down on the spongy ground and slid his hand away from the young man's mouth.

"Oh God," the boy had wheezed, drawing air into his lungs. "Oh God . . . I'm . . . I'm dyin'—ain't I?" It seemed a genuine question that the boy answered himself. "I'm dyin'!"

Hunter stared down at him. He'd killed so many almost without thinking about it. That's what you had to do as a soldier. You had to numb yourself against killing. You killed for the greater good. You killed for the freedom of the Confederacy, to stamp out the uppity Yankee aggressors. But as much as he wanted to ignore the innocent eyes staring up at him this moonlit night along the Tennessee, he found his mind recoiling in horror and revulsion at the fear he'd inflicted, the life he'd just taken.

The boy had whispered so softly that Hunter could barely hear him.

"Ma an' Pa . . . never gonna . . . see 'em again. My lovely May!" The boy's eyes filled with tears. "We was gonna be married as soon as I went home!"

Hunter felt as though it were his own heart that had been pierced with the knife he kept honed to a razor's edge. He looked at the blood glistening low on the young soldier's blue-clad belly, wishing that he could take back what he'd just done, return this horrified soldier's life to him. Return Ma and Pa to him, and the girl, May, whom he loved and intended to marry.

Horror and sorrow exploded inside of Hunter. He dropped the bloody knife, grabbed the young man by his collar, and drew his head up to his own. "I'm sorry!" he sobbed. "I'm sorry!"

The young man stared back at him, twin half-moons floating in his eyes as though on the surface of a night-dark lake. The soldier opened his mouth as though to speak, but he couldn't get any words out.

Pain twisted his face. His lower jaw fell slack. His eyes rolled back until all Hunter could see were their whites.

The soldier's raspy breaths fell silent, and his chest grew still. Hunter released him and he fell, lifeless as a sack of grain, to the ground.

"I'm sorry," the Confederate heard himself mutter.

But then it wasn't the young Union soldier lying before him in the light of the Tennessee moon. It was Luke Chaney lying sprawled in the tawny grass of the Black Hills, blood glistening brightly in the light of the afternoon sun.

Annabelle knelt beside Hunter, her hand on his thigh, gazing into his eyes with concern. "Hunter? Hunter, can you hear me? Hunter!"

CHAPTER 3

Hunter slid his gaze slowly toward his girl. He'd been only vaguely aware of Annabelle's presence, but now as that moonlit night of so long ago mercifully dwindled into the past, he was aware of her worried green gaze on him.

He placed his hand over hers, atop his right thigh. He found modest comfort in the warmth of her flesh. "I'm all right."

"Where were you?"

Hunter shook his head and winced against the throbbing in his temples. He leaned forward, pressed his fists against his head as though to knead away the pain that normally came at night, on the heels of his frequent nightmares.

"You were back with that boy you killed," Annabelle said, placing a comforting hand on his shoulder. "With the young Union soldier."

Hunter pressed his hands to his temples once more, then lifted his head and cast his gaze toward where Chaney lay in the grass. Bobby Lee lay ten feet from the body, in a scrap of shade offered by a cedar branch.

He was staring at Hunter and mewling deep in his throat with concern.

"What happened?" Annabelle asked again.

"I was on my way to town with Angus's beer. Sidewinder ambushed me." Hunter turned to her, grabbed her arms, and squeezed. "I swear, Annabelle. I didn't mean to kill him. I kicked the knife out of his hand. I walked over to pick it up. As I turned, he ran into me. I must've—"

"Shhh, shhh." Annabelle wrapped her arms around him, hugging him. "It's all right. He gave you no choice. I heard the shooting from the next ridge north. He was out for blood, obviously."

Annabelle pulled away from Hunter and gazed guiltily into his eyes. "This is my fault."

He frowned. "What're you talking about?"

"I caught him following me again the other day. I was driving a wagonload of supplies up to the men manning my father's line cabin on Beaver Ridge. When I topped a hill I saw Luke following me from about a quarter-mile back. I pulled the wagon off the trail and waited. When he rode up, I threatened him with my Winchester.

"I swear, Hunter, I was so mad to find that vermin dogging my heels again, after I had refused his marriage proposal in no uncertain terms, that I almost shot him right then and there! I told him once and for all to leave me alone, or I'd shoot him. And . . ." She dropped her eyes demurely. "And I made the mistake of telling him that when I married, you'd be the one . . ."

Hunter smiled and placed a hand on her cheek. "Well . . . I kinda like the sound of that myself."

"I do too." Annabelle kissed his hand. "But I'm

afraid that might be the reason he ambushed you here today. Why you had to kill him."

"Well, whatever the reason," Hunter said, turning to Chaney once more, "he's dead."

"I'll ride over to the mine and tell my father. He'll know what to do."

Luke Chaney's father, Max Chaney, was a business partner of Annabelle's father, Graham Ludlow. Chaney had wanted his thuggish son to marry Annabelle, and had tried to arrange it with Graham Ludlow. Ludlow wouldn't hear of it. It might have stressed his and Chaney's business partnership, but Ludlow had set his sights on higher fruit than the ungainly, foulmouthed, and whore-mongering Luke Chaney.

The man Ludlow wanted for his future son-in-law was the somewhat prissy but well-bred and well-heeled son of an eastern railroad magnate currently working to build a railroad that would connect the Black Hills with Sydney, Nebraska. The young man's name was Kenneth Earnshaw, and he'd graduated the previous fall from none other than Harvard University.

"No," Hunter said, grabbing Annabelle's arm before she could walk back to her horse. "No, I'll take care of it. Chaney's Stillwell's deputy. I'm going to take him on into Tigerville and tell Stillwell what happened."

"That's crazy, Hunter!"

"Telling what happened out here ain't crazy. It's the only thing to do."

"Stillwell will sic his other cutthroat deputies on you! He'll kill you!"

Some called Frank Stillwell a lawman-for-hire. In other words, he was a gun-for-hire who sometimes wore a badge. A couple of years ago, Tigerville and the hills around it had been a hotbed of bloody violence. This was right after General George Armstrong

Custer had opened the Hills to gold-seekers in 1874, despite the Hills still belonging to the Sioux Indians, as per the Laramie Treaty of 1868.

Men and mules and horses and placer mining equipment poured up the Missouri River from Kansas and Missouri by riverboat and mule- and ox-train, and the great Black Hills Gold Rush exploded.

Naturally, crime also exploded, in the forms of claim-jumping and bloody murder as well as the stealing of gold being hauled by ore wagons, called "Treasure Coaches," southwest to Cheyenne, Wyoming, and the nearest railroad. Tigerville was on the Cheyenne-Custer-Deadwood Stage Line, and the coaches negotiating that formidable country were often preyed upon by road agents.

For those bloody reasons, the commissioners of Pennington County, chief among them Annabelle's father, Graham Ludlow, brought in Stillwell and the small gang of hardtails who rode with him, also calling themselves "lawmen." Max Chaney got Luke a job as another of Stillwell's deputies, and the big, gun-savvy, boorish Luke fit right in. Bona fide crime dwindled while the death rate went up. It was still said in these parts that you couldn't ride any of the roads spoking out of Tigerville and into the surrounding hills without coming upon Stillwell's low-hanging "tree fruit" in the form of hanged men.

Men hanged without benefit of trial.

Many of those men had once fought for the Confederacy. It seemed that most of the "tree fruit" Stillwell "grew" hailed from the South, which wasn't one bit fishy at all, given Stillwell's history of being second-in-command of one of the worst Union prisoner-of-war camps during the Civil War and having a widely known and much-talked-about hatred for the warriors of the old South.

"He won't kill me, Anna," Hunter said, sounding more confident than he felt. "Not even Stillwell or his tough nuts will kill an unarmed man. Not in town in broad daylight, anyways." He glanced at Chaney again, and flared an angry nostril.

"At least fetch your pa and your brothers. You need someone to back you in town, Hunter."

He shook his head stubbornly. "Pa an' Shep an' Tye would only come armed. It'd look like we were spoiling for a fight. Knowin' Pa an' Shep like I do—they'd likely start one. A fight is what I'm trying to avoid."

Anna glowered up at him, said softly, "Just bury him out here." She glanced at the dead man. "Toss him into a ravine and kick some dirt on him. It's better than what he deserves."

Hunter placed two fingers on her chin and gently turned her head toward his. Her green eyes glistened in the sunlight. "You know that's not how I do things, Anna."

"Oh, I know it's not. And that's why I love you. But I don't want you to die, Hunter. I love you and want to spend the rest of my life with you, you big Southern scalawag!" She rose up onto the toes of her boots, wrapped her arms around his neck, and kissed him passionately. Hunter returned the kiss, basking in the comfort of the girl in his arms.

Finally, he eased her away from him.

"Can I borrow Ivan to fetch my wagon?"

"You know you can."

"Obliged." Hunter walked over and grabbed the buckskin's reins. He swung up into the saddle and galloped off in the direction from which Anna had come.

He found the wagon not far up the trail. The mule,

Titus, was too lazy to have run far. Angus's beer kegs were still secure in the box, stacked against the front panel and tied down with heavy ropes.

Hunter stepped off the buckskin's back and into the wagon. He tied Ivan to the tailgate and climbed over the beer kegs into the driver's box. A few minutes later he swung back into the buttes south of the trail and saw Annabelle sitting on the ground not far from Chaney's slack figure.

Bobby Lee lay close beside her, his head on her thigh. She stroked the coyote affectionately. The coyote gave his tail intermittent, satisfied thumps against the ground and blinked his long yellow eyes slowly, luxuriously.

Hunter gave a wry snort. His coyote friend appeared to be appropriating the affections of his gal. It seemed sometimes that most all the males in the county were in love with Annabelle Ludlow. Hunter couldn't blame them. She was a rare, striking beauty, and a girl of heart and substance. If he got his way—and he was determined to—he was going to marry the girl, and he and she were going to raise a whole passel of young'uns right here in the Black Hills, on a wild horse ranch of their own.

If he had his way, and the girl's father didn't get his . . .

Trouble was likely afoot in that regard, but Hunter didn't want to think about Graham Ludlow at the moment. Right now he had his hands full with Sheriff Frank Stillwell.

Annabelle was no hothouse flower. Despite Hunter's protestations, she helped him haul Luke Chaney over to the wagon and dump him into the box. Most girls would have been stricken with the vapors over such a task. Annabelle merely scowled down at the dead man, her disdain for him plain in the set of her fine jaws, then brushed her hands on her jeans when they were done with the job.

"Don't worry about me now," Hunter told her, taking her once more in his arms. "I'll be fine."

"At least take my Winchester." Anna glanced at the carbine she always carried in her saddle scabbard.

"No. Going in armed will only be asking for trouble. Like I said, don't worry, now."

Annabelle sighed in defeat. "I am going to worry about you," she said with crisp defiance, gazing up at him, her green eyes as clear as a mountain lake, a wry humor crinkling their corners. "When you're finished, you meet me at our usual place so I can make sure you're still of one piece."

"And if I'm not?"

Annabelle pursed her lips angrily and reached up to snap her index finger against the underside of his hat brim. "Everything better be in its rightful place. I'll be checking!"

Hunter chuckled. He kissed her once more and climbed into the wagon. Bobby Lee was already mounted on the seat to his right.

Hunter turned the wagon around, pinched his hat brim to his girl standing gazing up at him admonishingly, fists on her hips. He rattled on past her, threaded the crease between the buttes, and swung onto the main trail.

A half hour later, a nettling apprehension raked chill fingers across the back of the ex-Confederate's neck as the town of Tigerville appeared before him, sprawling across a low dip of tawny ground surrounded by the narrow spikes of pine-clad knolls that sloped from higher ridges toward the town. The hillocks and natural dikes seemed to be pointing out Tigerville to weary travelers who, having journeyed this far off the beaten path, had lost hope of finding any hint of civilization at all out here in this vast, rugged, pine-bearded and gold-spotted country east of the Rockies.

Tigerville, named after the now-defunct Bengal Mine, was far from the howling hub of boisterous humanity that was Deadwood, fifty miles north. But Tigerville was no slouch in that regard, either. Now as Hunter rattled and clomped down the town's main street, he was surrounded by the din of player pianos, three-piece bands, and laughing women disporting their wares from boardwalks and the second-floor galleries of sporting parlors, of which Tigerville had several of note.

Men of all sizes, shapes, and colors, including blacks and blanket Indians, crisscrossed the street still muddy from an earlier rain, some with frothy ale mugs in their fists and/or painted ladies on their arms. There were miners, prospectors, cowpunchers, market hunters, railroad surveyors, soldiers from the local cavalry out-post, as well as cardsharps, run-of-the-mill rowdies, grubline-riding tough nuts, and confidence men.

The buildings were mostly wood-frame and false-fronted business establishments with more than a few of Tigerville's original crude log cabins and tent shacks remaining to give testament to its humble roots.

The King Solomon's Mine, owned by Graham Ludlow and Max Chaney, sat on the high ridge to the east of town, like the castle ruins of some van-quished lord overlooking the humble dwellings of his unwashed subjects. Gray tailings stretched down the mountain below the mine, around which was a beehive of activity including men at work with picks and shovels, handcars rolling in and out of the mine portals, thundering ore drays traversing trails switch-backing up and down the mountain's face, as well as the constant, reverberating hammering of the stamping mill in its giant timber frame at the base of the ridge, behind the barrack-like, wood-frame mine office.

Hunter turned his attention to the street before him. The office of the county sheriff was on the east side, roughly two-thirds of the way through the half-mile length of Custer Avenue. Hunter angled Titus toward the jailhouse, and felt another cold-fingered massage of apprehension.

Sheriff Frank Stillwell was tipped back in a hide-bottom chair on the front porch, his five-pointed star glistening on his brown wool vest. His high-topped black boots were crossed on the rail before him. As Hunter turned the mule up to the hitching rack fronting the sheriff's long, unpainted, wood-frame office, Still-well's mud-black eyes turned to regard him with customary malignancy.

Connect with Us

Visit us online at
KensingtonBooks.com
to read more from your favorite authors, see books
by series, view reading group guides, and more.

for sneak peeks, chances to win books and prize packs,
and to share your thoughts with other readers.

facebook.com/kensingtonpublishing
twitter.com/kensingtonbooks

Tell us what you think!

To share your thoughts, submit a review,
or sign up for our eNewsletters, please visit:
KensingtonBooks.com/TellUs.